Linc

Heart of Resistance

Sarah Tate

Ragged Bears Publishing

For
Aksinia and Miranda

RAGGED BEARS
Published by Ragged Bears Publishing Ltd.
Unit 14A, Bennetts Field Industrial Estate,
Southgate Road,
Wincanton,
Somerset BA9 9DT, UK

First published 2010
1 3 5 7 9 10 8 6 4 2

A CIP catalogue record for this book is available from the British
Library

ISBN 978 1 85714 427 7

Printed in Poland

Contents

Acknowledgements   vii

Chapter 1 The Home Front   11
Chapter 2 After the Bomb   36
Chapter 3 On the Run   60
Chapter 4 Alone   80
Chapter 5 Thief!   101
Chapter 6 David   118
Chapter 7 The Gift   138
Chapter 8 The Maquis   150
Chapter 9 Into Free France   173
Chapter 10 The Wolf   195
Chapter 11 The Shepherds   217
Chapter 12 Prisoner   233
Chapter 13 South through the Snow   257
Chapter 14 Home   276
Chapter 15 Saint Sylvester's Day   302

Acknowledgements

The publishers gratefully acknowledge permission to reproduce copyright material.

Walter de la Mare: From Complete Poems. Reprinted by permission of The Literary Trustees of Walter de la Mare and The Society of Authors as their representative.

Every effort has been made to trace copyright holders but if any omissions have been made please let us know and acknowledgement will be made in the next edition.

'We can do no great things,
only small things with great love'

Mother Theresa

Chapter 1

The Home Front

Here lies a most beautiful lady
Light of step and heart was she
I think she was the most beautiful lady
That ever was in the West Country.
            An Epitaph *Walter de la Mare*

Silently they slipped among the shadows of the ruined buildings. Five boys, quieter than secrets, a girl, her face white and still. It was dusk and there was a rose-coloured sunset which cast long, dark shapes across the piles of rubble and left corners amongst the isolated walls, blacker than the deepest night.

Agnes crouched in one of these. She hardly dared to breathe for fear someone should hear her and yet she was sure that the beating of her heart was audible, so loud did it seem to her. From nowhere, at once, a hand grasped her shoulder. She jumped, stifling her scream. She had heard nothing. How had he got there?

She smothered a giggle then, her hand over her mouth. It was the small red-haired boy who had recently joined the gang. He put a finger to his lips, gesturing her to silence, then crouched beside her. The setting sun, just beyond their dark corner, illuminated the details of what had once been a house, someone's home. Bricks, chunks of plaster, wood from a door or window frame, a piece of cloth which may have been a curtain or some clothing; further off, a broken armchair, crushed and upside down amidst the dust.

Harry lumbered past them, clambering and slipping over the rubble, about as silent as a herd of rhinoceroses. Agnes and the red-haired boy hissed at him to be quiet, beckoning him into their dark corner. But it was too late, Tom was not far behind him,

'Got you!' he exclaimed triumphantly, spotting the three of them at once. Philip, the last member of the gang, trailed behind him.

'We've been looking for you for ages,' he complained. 'He found me almost straight away.'

'Thanks, Harry,' Tom grinned at him, 'I knew you'd lead me to the others eventually. It was a bit like following a man with a loud hailer, shouting "Here I am. I'm going this way".'

'I'm sorry,' Harry grinned sheepishly at Agnes, 'I'm just not dainty on my feet. As my uncle always says I'd be useless as a spy, but all right in the Tank Regiment.'

'It doesn't matter,' Agnes smiled at him. 'It's time to go home anyway. My grandmother will be having kittens.'

'Yeah, I'll really cop it too,' said the red-haired boy. 'I'm off. See you.'

The children dispersed, the boys heading north up the dark streets, Agnes turning south along streets where the houses got steadily bigger and grander till she reached home, her grandmother's house. It was a large, white, four storied house, set back a little from the road and with steps leading up to a pillared porch outside the front door. Agnes slipped around the side of the building, through the door into the walled garden and opened the kitchen door at the back as quietly as she could.

Bright light in the kitchen greeted her, dazzling her momentarily after the twilight outside.

'Shut that door quickly, child.' Dilly rose from the kitchen table where she had been sitting, waiting for her. Dilly was their housekeeper. Originally from Jamaica, she was dependably cheerful on most occasions, but tonight she looked cross and stood up with her hands on her large hips. 'And just where you think you been? ' she asked, her tone indignant. 'You in hot water, young lady. Your grandmother goin' to give you a hidin'. She wasted all her time, lookin' for you. Now she's gone to the Red Cross.'

'Why? What time is it?' Agnes asked, still blinking as she looked at the kitchen clock.

'Half past seven. That's the time. And she tell you be back here by half past five.'

The phone rang in the hall. Dilly went out to pick it up.

'Yes, she is,' Agnes heard her say, in her high voice. 'Yes, she just come in now. I tell her, yes. Yes, don't you worry,' she repeated. 'I'll make sure she go to bed now.'

But Eleanor wouldn't be angry Agnes knew. Not really, just worried. She'd been in trouble before for playing with the boys.

'Darling, I know it's been hard for you since all your friends left London,' Eleanor had said on that earlier occasion, 'you can still go down and join them, you know. The school will have you and Wales would be lovely.'

Agnes' school had moved from London to a big, old house in Wales when the war started and all the girls had become boarders. Agnes refused to go. She did not want to leave her grandmother.

'I don't want to, Eleanor. It's not that I'm lonely anyway. I like the boys I play with here. They're nice, different to the children in my school. I know they're a bit rough sometimes, but they're nice to me; they just treat me as one of the gang.'

'I have no objection to you playing with the boys, darling. But can't you bring them here?' Agnes thought for a moment. How out of place the boys would seem in her grandmother's elegant drawing room, or the beautiful garden with the swing on the apple tree and the neatly tended rows of vegetables (new since the war) now taking up half the garden.

What Eleanor had said was that playing in the ruins of bombed houses was forbidden. Only a few weeks before, they had been caught by a police constable, who had accompanied her home, his hand on her shoulder, admonishing her all the way about how a little girl like her from a nice home ought to know better. He had rung the front door bell and stood there with her under the pillared porch, telling her grandmother much the same thing.

'It's one thing for all those ruffians to be breaking the law,' he had said, 'half of them don't know any better. Their dads aren't home to take a strap to them and their mothers is wore out, but not a girl like this, from a nice family, as I've been telling her.'

'Thank you, Constable,' Eleanor had replied graciously, holding the door open to let Agnes in. 'I'm most grateful to you for bringing her home and I'll make sure it doesn't happen again.'

To Agnes' embarrassment, an army officer now emerged from the drawing room with a glass of whisky in his hand, having overheard the conversation. It was George Meredith, Agnes' godfather.

'Don't you worry, Constable,' he put in, 'we'll take care of her. Put a good pair of handcuffs on her and chain her to the wall of the cellar and she won't give you any more trouble.'

The constable looked suspiciously at George, as if he wasn't sure that he was being taken seriously, but eying his uniform, he nodded in approval and when

Eleanor again thanked him so earnestly and with such a serious expression, he managed a quick smile, touched his helmet and turned to go.

The door once closed, George Meredith guffawed with laughter. 'That's my goddaughter. Not yet twelve years old and it takes the strong arm of the law to get her to come home and have lunch with her godfather!'

Agnes smiled sheepishly at him. It was true, she had forgotten he was coming to lunch and it was a few years since she'd seen him. He was an old friend of her mother's, both her parents, of course, after they were married, and special to her for that reason alone.

'I can remember him pushing me really high on the swing when I was little,' she had told Eleanor when she asked Agnes how well she remembered George. 'You got cross with him and told him to stop, because you thought I was frightened and about to come flying off the swing, but I was screaming with excitement really.'

Eleanor smiled, 'I gather he's a little more responsible these days. At least, I hope so. He's in charge of a major part of the army communications network.'

George had grown more serious, but still teased Agnes, often in French, testing her. He spoke good French, as did Eleanor who had made sure that Agnes could speak French as she was growing up, just as her father would have done. Over lunch, George spoke confidentially to Eleanor about France, despite Agnes being there at the table with them.

Eleanor had asked if there was any further talk of a German invasion on the south coast of England.

'Not for the moment,' George answered, 'and meanwhile, the Resistance movement in France is gathering strength apace, although how much difference they can really make in the long term remains to be seen. Still, it keeps the Germans on their mettle.'

'What's the resistance movement?' Agnes interrupted.

'Hush, darling,' said her grandmother, but George answered her question.

'There are large numbers of people in France, working secretly against the German army which has occupied the whole of the northern half of their country, as you know. They work in all kinds of different ways – they blow up railway lines and bridges to make it harder for the Germans to get about. They rescue and hide people who are wanted by the Germans and they are helping a great many of our chaps to escape – getting them back to England instead of allowing them to be caught by the Germans and shot, or locked up in a POW camp for the rest of the war. Even have to get some of their own chaps out sometimes. There's a growing band of French here in London, in de Gaulle's camp. No, to answer your question,' he continued, turning back to Eleanor, 'our defences on the south coast are generally pretty sound and I think our boys down there would pick up on any signs of mass movement or unusual activity on the French coast. There's plenty of spying going on, on both sides no doubt.'

'So there is some traffic across the channel presumably?' Eleanor asked.

'Oh yes, plenty of small boats coming and going, carrying people both ways, and the defence turns a blind eye to them, or at least observes what's going on with a certain tolerance; communications are working overtime anyway, to ensure that some free passage is maintained.'

Eleanor was aware that Agnes was listening attentively. News of France was interesting and it was now nearly three years since France had been invaded by Germany. She had heard the name of General de Gaulle, an important French man, on the side of the Free French and not the Vichy government, who was now in England and made weekly broadcasts to France in the hope of encouraging people to keep fighting. She had also heard it said that there were people in France who were doing very well from co-operating with the German army, but she found it hard to imagine what it must be like for the vast majority of French people to live under their occupation.

'Darling, you know you mustn't repeat anything George says, don't you? Just in case it is important.'

'Yes, I know,' Agnes replied, ' "loose tongues cost lives".'

'Precisely,' agreed George, and smiled at her.

But it was a few weeks since George's visit. Agnes lay awake in bed. Having turned out her light, she pulled back the blackout curtains so that the moonlight could shine in. She felt ashamed that she had caused her grandmother yet more worry and disobeyed her so blatantly. She knew that playing in the ruins was dangerous and she had broken her promise not to do it any more, since her 'arrest'. But it was fun. The war had changed things for children. Adults were too busy to watch them all the time and most fathers were away, fighting for their country, or otherwise wrapped up in the war effort.

Bombed out houses may have been dangerous, but besides hide and seek, they were a great place to build camps, or a source of 'finds' (usually pieces of shell and other military detritus). The gang sometimes grew bigger, then smaller again. Children came and went and people didn't ask questions. Some were orphans living with overstretched relations, some had run away from places in the country where they'd been sent as evacuees, till their parents grew tired of sending them back though they still had little time for them. The boys were a rough lot, but there was no real harm in them. Agnes was usually the only girl, but she had learned to swear and stand up to the best of them. They respected her. She was daring 'for a girl' and better than all of them at moving furtively and almost invisibly from one ruined wall to another. She was small and though slightly built, she was wiry and strong, looking more French than English with her long dark hair and pale olive skin, for all that her mother had been fair and English, 'an English rose', she'd heard people say when they spoke of her mother. At eleven years old, she had lost the round cheeks of the much chubbier five year old who appeared in the last photograph taken with her parents, before they left for Africa.

Besides, she enjoyed playing with the boys for the respect they showed her. She had her own sense of right and wrong and although she wasn't averse to breaking into a can of beans found in a bombed out house, or taking a puff on a stolen cigarette, she was not going to be party to the raiding of a chest of drawers found one day, intact under a pile of rubble. The boys had pulled it out and opening the drawers found old photographs, bundles of letters, diaries and baby clothes carefully wrapped in tissue paper and boxes.

'Chuck it out on the ground,' suggested one boy, 'there might be some money in one of the drawers.'

Agnes rounded on him, 'Leave those things alone. You've got no right to go through someone's personal things.'

'But,' the boy argued, 'this house was bombed ages ago. If they ain't been back by now, they're probably dead.'

'How do you know that?' Agnes retorted angrily. 'How do you know the Dad's not away at war and when he comes back he'll go looking for all that stuff. Maybe it's all he's got left of his family. Or maybe the children were evacuated, but they'll come back for it. You just don't know. Imagine if it was your family's stuff. Leave it alone.'

'All right, there's no need to get shirty,' the boy backed off, defensive, but embarrassed, nonetheless. He hastily pressed things back down into the drawers till he could close them again. He was bigger than Agnes by several inches, but she had shamed him.

Tonight she'd stayed out too late, though and worried her grandmother, which wasn't fair. Eleanor had enough to concern her. In addition to the work she did in the Home Office, she had voluntary work with the Red Cross. Tonight, she was on duty driving an ambulance. Agnes had a standing joke with her about ambulance driving. It stemmed from Eleanor's habit of taking 'short cuts' whenever they were driving out in the countryside. Almost invariably they became hopelessly lost. Before the war, they had divided their time between the house in London and a large house in Kent, which had now been handed over to the Army for a rest home for wounded officers. Sometimes, they had taken the train to Kent for the weekend, but often Eleanor had driven them down herself.

'Don't take any short cuts,' Agnes joked whenever her grandmother was on ambulance driving duty. The fact that at night time there were no street lamps during the black out and many signposts had been removed, could only make matters worse.

The reality was that being on ambulance duty meant that Eleanor would have to wait till late at night in the ambulance station in case of a call out. There had been far less need for Red Cross ambulances of late. It was

1942 and the bombing raids over London had all but ceased a year ago, although there were still plenty of false alarms as planes flew over London heading north and the occasional stray bomb was still dropped over the city.

Dilly usually stayed overnight when Eleanor was on duty, though sometimes Agnes had gone home with her. This was a treat. Dilly, or Diligence, to give her her full name, lived in a terraced cottage in the East end of London, a few bus rides away. Nothing could have been more different from her grandmother's spacious and elegant Georgian house in Kensington. Dilly's cottage was packed with a wild assortment of ornate furniture and was a riot of bright colours. It was a mystery to Agnes how Dilly and her husband and their three big sons had ever managed to live together in that tiny house. Besides, there were always delicious, sweet and spicy things to eat when Dilly was cooking. Even now, in wartime, there were strange and tasty vegetables grown on the allotments by Dilly's Jamaican friends and honey from the bees they kept, to sweeten things while sugar was in short supply.

She had known Diligence all her life. In fact, Dilly had also helped to raise Agnes' mother. Agnes had invented the nickname 'Dilly', however. 'Diligence' posed rather a mouthful in her early years. Eleanor had explained that 'Diligence' meant hard work and application.

'In West Indian families, girls were often given the name of a positive and desirable quality,' she told Agnes, 'such as "Charity" or "Faith" for example. Qualities they would like their children to have I suppose.'

'So,' Agnes mused, 'you might have called me "Wittiness" or "Cleverness" or something like that.'

'No, not exactly, darling. They tend to be rather more worthy, moral qualities I suppose,' Eleanor replied, laughing.

Dilly was good at telling stories; tales of her Jamaican childhood wove a colourful thread into the grey London days of wartime. Agnes' favourite was the one about the baby elephants, the children of elephants used on a banana plantation near Dilly's home.

'They come stealin' bananas they could reach off the trees every night, till pretty soon, Master hired men to guard them trees an' shoo off the babies. They elephants didn't stop long though. They tiptoe real quiet up to the trees while the guards were sleepin' and ate up the bananas. So next, ole Master he ties big wood bells around those elephants' necks to wake up the sleepin' guards and you know what?'

'No, then what happened Dilly?' asked Agnes, despite having heard the story several times.

'Them sneaky elephants, they learn pretty quick. They plug up the bells with soft mud, pushin' it in with they trunks so those bells don't ring no more.'

When Agnes was little, she would clap her hands and laugh at this story, and others and ask for them to be told over again, calling Dilly to order if she left out any details.

Eleanor's stories were different. Most evenings when she was at home she and Agnes read together, then before her grandmother left her to go downstairs, Agnes would ask her about her day at work in the Home Office; what news there was of the war and of friends of Eleanor's or friends of her parents who still stayed in touch.

In Kent, before the war, the house had been full at weekends with friends of her grandmother's, friends of her parents (even after they had gone to Africa) and their children as well. Agnes remembered those times quite well and Eleanor would tell her news she had heard of any of their friends and their children, who were all dispersed and busy and whom they seldom saw now.

In London too, there were often guests staying. Eleanor kept open house for friends who were home on leave and needed a room in London. She also entertained as often as was possible. Usually, Agnes was allowed to stay up and sit with the adults in the drawing room while they had a drink before dinner, but sometimes, there were important people from the Home Office, or well known politicians, and on those occasions Agnes was banished to the kitchen and then straight to bed. On other evenings when Eleanor was going out to dinner, she would always come to say goodnight before she left. Agnes had a kind of competition with herself to keep Eleanor with her, sitting on the edge of her bed, for as long as she could. Eleanor knew this of course and made sure she allowed the extra time, after dressing, before she had to go out. She was always wonderfully elegant; she wore cream silk blouses and pencil slim skirts with high heels and always silk stockings, despite the difficulty of getting them in war time. A simple, but beautiful sapphire and diamond brooch pinned the blouse at her neck or she wore a string of large creamy pearls.

'Have you ever thought about getting married again, Eleanor?' she asked her once, admiring her grandmother's beauty.

'Whatever made you think of that, darling? No, I couldn't replace Henry anyway. He was the love of my life. You're all I need now for family, darling, and besides, look how many wonderful friends I have.'

If she had more time, Agnes would try to steer the conversation to the subject of her parents. These were the stories she liked best and, as with Dilly's stories, she had heard them all before and wanted them retold without any details missing.

'Tell me again about how Mummy and Daddy met,' she might say.

'They met, as you know, darling, when Mummy was a medical student and Daddy was a handsome young French doctor, newly qualified and here in London to study tropical diseases in one of the big hospitals. He was intending to go to Africa and needed to find out about the diseases he would have to deal with there.'

'And why did he stay in London instead … then, anyway?'

'Because he met Mummy of course and she needed to finish her medical degree. And then they got married.'

'Tell me how they met, again.'

'Oh, you know how they met, darling. Your godfather introduced them at a party. He said to your father, "Come and meet the most beautiful girl in London," and that was that! Love at first sight for both of them, or *coup de foudre* as the French say.'

'Which means lightning strike, doesn't it? And then what happened?'

'Well, they got married and then they had you, of course.'

'But then they went to Africa,' Agnes said more quietly.

'Yes, but not straight away,' Eleanor continued, also more quietly. This part was more difficult and she spoke more slowly as if choosing her words carefully to get the story clear. 'They had several blissfully happy years in London, here in this house, with you as a baby and both working as doctors. Then Daddy's friends in Africa pleaded with him to come and help set up a hospital. It was going to be a very important hospital, looking after very many people in an area where there were no doctors before and Mummy, I think, felt a little guilty that she had prevented him from going to Africa before, so she agreed to go with

26

him just for two years while you were little enough not to mind so much.'

'Why didn't they take me?'

'It would have been much too dangerous, darling. There was a great deal of illness where they were going and so many African children were dying of those diseases. Besides it was going to be very hard work.' She paused, then continued, 'It was a very hard decision for them to make you know, to leave you, or for Mummy to go. But in the end I told them they should both go. They were still so very much in love with each other and you were happy here in your home, with Dilly and I. They were working such long hours in London anyway that sometimes we didn't see them for days. All that would have changed after they came back.'

'Why didn't they come back? Before the war started I mean?' Agnes' tone was sad, but not accusatory. This was the part she found hard to understand.

'I think the task of setting up the hospital and finding enough doctors was very much more difficult than either of them imagined. From their letters it seems that every time they were getting ready to leave, there was another crisis; an epidemic of illness or hunger which meant that literally hundreds of people were depending on them. And then the war started and suddenly it was much harder for them to find a way to get home.'

'And then they both got on the boat which was torpedoed,' Agnes finished bluntly.

'Yes,' Eleanor's voice faltered for the first time. She put her slim hand over Agnes', lying on the bedcover, lowering her gaze for a moment. Then looking up, she asked suddenly, 'You do remember Mummy and Daddy quite well, don't you, darling?

'Yes. No. Well, some things, at least,' Agnes thought. She could remember her parents playing with her in the sunshine of the walled garden, but she could not see their faces, which seemed, in her memory, to be in shadow. She thought she remembered her father's big hands as they threw her up and caught her again when she was very small. The sun shone behind his head, casting his face into laughing shadow. Sometimes she caught the trace of a perfume on someone else, or the sound of a laugh that made her think of her mother. She remembered their faces from the wedding photograph which stood on the drawing room piano in a silver frame. But perhaps it was just the photograph she remembered, not the way their faces really were, when they laughed, or smiled, or talked. These were details which seemed to have become hazy like a dream remembered upon waking and then quickly lost.

Mostly, with Eleanor though, they talked about what they would do when the war was over. How they would open up the house in Kent and have all their friends to stay again, and Agnes would get to know all the children who she had lost touch with. And then they would go on holiday to France, to visit her French grandparents. And Eleanor would take her to

Paris when everything had been sorted out and life had settled again.

Agnes slept fitfully that night and when she woke the house seemed especially quiet. It was Saturday. Agnes had not been at school for two years now. At first, Eleanor had hired a series of tutors who had come and gone when they found more urgent things to do and now Eleanor set her work every day which she carried out at the kitchen table in the mornings, under Dilly's supervision, but weekdays had become much less distinct from weekends. Still, Saturday meant that there would be no schoolwork today and her grandmother would be home and free to spend the day with her. She tapped on Eleanor's door and opened it softly, but Eleanor was awake, sitting up in bed with a cup of tea beside her and the morning's letters which she was reading through. Looking up, she smiled at Agnes, and patted the bed beside her.

'Good morning, darling. Did you sleep well? Come and snuggle in here for a moment. We've got to have a little chat, I think.'

Agnes' heart sank.

'I'm so sorry, Eleanor. I had no idea it was so late when I came back last night. We were having such fun, I just forgot the time.'

'I know darling, but the problem doesn't just lie with playing with the boys, does it?'

'What do you mean?'

'Agnes, darling, I'm not giving you the best possible life by keeping you here at the moment, am I? You have no school to go to; all your friends have left London and I am so busy between the Home Office and the Red Cross, that I am not able to spend the time with you that I would like. You would be so much happier in Wales with your school friends, darling. I could come down and visit you sometimes at weekends and we could spend the school holidays together ...'

Agnes was very quiet. She was aware that her heart was beating faster and thoughts rushed through her mind in a jumbled disorder.

'But I can't, Granny,' (she rarely called Eleanor 'Granny') 'I can't leave here. This is my home. I can't leave you. I don't want to.' She burst into tears.

This was unlike Agnes. Eleanor thought of her always as a child with much strength of character, wise beyond her years sometimes, though with a healthy dash of mischief and fun about her, but rarely upset beyond reason. She put her arms around her and held her close as Agnes' sobs slowly subsided.

'Well, let's think about it, darling. Believe me, I would not find it any easier for us to be apart than you would. Perhaps even a great deal harder.'

Dilly had stayed overnight. Eleanor had a dinner party planned that night and Dilly was here to help. Besides, she was lonely in her little house with her husband and grown up sons all away in the forces and was happy to stay over. Agnes was on the swing in the garden which hung from an old apple tree. It was her best thinking spot. She had spent hours, it seemed, just swinging gently back and forth, or turning the seat with her feet on the ground, round and round, twisting together the two strands of the rope above her till they were tight, then leaning back with her feet outstretched looking up at the kaleidoscope of leaf patterns in the apple tree turning round and round in the dappled sunlight, while the rope untwisted. She had been here, on the swing, when her grandmother brought her the news that the ship her parents were travelling on from Africa had been lost, torpedoed by a German warship, with no survivors.

It was three years ago now. Agnes remembered that her life hadn't changed. She had just moved from a time when she knew her parents were going to come back, to knowing that they never would. And even that seemed hard to grasp as a reality, at times. In an odd way, she felt, she missed them more now, than she had then, as their absence stretched away into the future. A year or so after the ship had been sunk, a letter had come for her father from Africa. She had picked it up off the mat and given it to Eleanor.

'What does it say?' she asked, as Eleanor read it. 'Who is it from?'

'It's from an African doctor that your father worked with. It's strange, he must not have heard about the sinking of the ship.' Eleanor looked puzzled. She folded the letter up and did not offer it to Agnes to read. Usually she shared everything with Agnes that had to do with her parents. A few days later, when Agnes asked again about the letter, Eleanor told her that she had posted it on to her father's parents in France, with an accompanying note.

'I thought they should have it really. It said such nice things about your father.' She said no more about it and again, Agnes thought it strange that Eleanor had not shared it with her.

Agnes did not remember her French grandparents. She had met them when she was very young, taken to see them by her proud parents. They lived in the south, in Provence and had a big house with a vineyard. Grandpère too, had been a doctor, but he had never left his native Provence. She and Eleanor had been going to visit them. But then the war started and the plans had had to be cancelled.

It was a beautiful day, for early April. The walled garden caught and held the warmth of the sun. The plum trees esplanaded along the old red brick of the walls were in blossom, as was the apple tree. Agnes wandered back towards the kitchen. She still felt sad and listless, tired from her restless night. She could hear her grandmother and Dilly talking and she paused outside the door.

'Let the child be, Miss Eleanor,' Dilly was saying. 'She's done enough losin' for one short life. She not goin' to be no happier for being far away from you and this house. It's her home, Miss Eleanor, it's all she knows.'

Eleanor sighed, 'You're right Diligence, and it would break my heart to send her away. I just don't feel I'm doing the best for her with the way things are.'

'Don't you fret, Miss Eleanor. Ain't nothin' wrong with that chile'. Got a sensible head on her shoulders and she devoted to you, you know. Just needs a bit more discipline maybe. Keep her away from them rough boys. An' I can stay here more if you like. Got no men folk to go home to right now'

Eleanor listened to Dilly, who had been her housekeeper for almost all the years since she had arrived in England from Jamaica, and next to herself, was the most important living person in Agnes' life. It was a reprieve. There was no more talk of sending her to Wales, but she was forbidden to play with the boys again, for the time being.

'And I shall have to be a little more rigorous about your school work, darling,' Eleanor told her.

The school work programme was somewhat erratic and was based on anything that Eleanor thought might be interesting, or any other topic suggested by visitors to the house. It was thus that a few weeks later, Eleanor had set a somewhat longer than usual project to find out about 'Shakespeare's Life and Times.' Agnes was not best pleased. She knew little enough about Shakespeare it was true, except that he wrote famous plays several hundred years ago, in difficult sounding language, but

33

the research meant hours in the library of the house and a visit to the local reference library as well and the sun had been shining for several days. She wanted to be out in the garden. She had barely started though and it was lunch time. She would have to go on tomorrow. This afternoon she was going home with Dilly. Eleanor was on Red Cross duty that night and Dilly was anxious, naturally, not to miss an evening with her eldest son who was home on leave for a few days.

Agnes could remember, earlier in the war, staying with Dilly when a bombing raid came over. The raids had started over London in September of 1940, now more than a year and a half ago. The East end of London had been worst hit in the first, most devastating raid and borne the brunt of the attacks which had continued for most of the following year. Agnes remembered the hurried, fumbling rush as the sirens went, to get from the house to the Underground station at the end of the road, wrapped up in dressing gown and slippers. After that, Eleanor had bought a Morrison shelter for Dilly to keep in a shed in the tiny garden, since there was no room for an Anderson shelter like the one that had been dug at the end of their garden in Kensington. Once or twice, Dilly and Agnes had crammed themselves into it when the sirens went, giggling with a mixture of fear and amusement at their plight.

But now, three years into the war, things had been quieter for some time. The street in which Dilly lived had been spared from any direct hit, although many surrounding it had been totally or partially destroyed. There were few families who had not lost friends and relations in the nine months of almost continuous bombing. There was still the odd false alarm, but Eleanor felt it was safe enough for Agnes to be there again now.

It would be fun she knew. They would pass by the allotments on the way home and pick up some vegetables and chat with other members of the West Indian community who would be working there. There might be a cup of tea from a kettle, brewed up on a primus stove in one of the allotment huts. Not real tea, which was rationed and in short supply, but a tea made out of herbs and sweetened with honey. Then they would go home and eat roasted vegetables with perhaps some chicken and delicious honey and spice cake and Agnes would eventually fall asleep, warm and full, to the melodious rhythm of voices as Dilly and her son chatted downstairs in the little house, late into the evening.

Chapter 2

After the Bomb

They are all gone into the world of light!
And I alone sit ling'ring here;
Friends Departed *Henry Vaughan*

It had all been just as she had hoped and she had slept soundly all through the night, but today was cloudy and, as she and Dilly made their way back to Kensington on a succession of buses, Agnes knew there would be no getting out of finishing her project.

'As a matter of fact,' Eleanor had reminded her as she was leaving the day before, 'tomorrow is a very appropriate moment to complete a project on Shakespeare. It is the 23rd April, which was his birthday, and the date that he died, oddly enough.'

'Well, that was jolly bad luck to die on his birthday,' Agnes had replied.

As she and Dilly got off the bus and started walking up from the bus stop, Agnes was not relishing the idea of spending the next few hours at the library table.

'Happy Birthday, Mr Shakespeare,' she muttered.

'What's that, darlin'?' Dilly asked, then she seemed to stop, mid-question. Agnes had her hand looped under Dilly's arm and she was speaking as they turned the corner which brought them into view of the street where they lived. At that moment, Agnes was suddenly aware that Dilly's grip had tightened and her arm stiffened. She looked up. There were people at the end of the street and as they approached, she could see a tape across the road, allowing no vehicles or people down into the street. A warden was talking earnestly to the group standing quietly around him. Dilly pushed her way through the crowd, still holding Agnes.

'What happened?'

The people fell back, letting her pass, several of them recognised both Dilly and Agnes. The warden's face fell as he saw them both. He stood aside as Dilly, letting go of Agnes, approached the tape and looked down the street.

'I'm sorry, Missus,' the warden said.'It was a direct hit. Stray bomb. There've been raids on towns up north all night – Cathedral towns. Reckon it was a straggler dumping his last load before heading back to Germany. Bleedin' Jerry!'

The words meant nothing to Agnes but she had an overwhelming sense that her world had been suddenly shattered. Her ears were buzzing as she pushed through the small crowd. The street behind the warden curved slightly and she had a clear view of the tall, white houses which stood well spaced from each other. Her home was only a few yards away, or at least, the place where her home had been. The front of the house had disappeared. On either side, her neighbours' houses stood, almost unmarked, but between them, all that was left of her own and Eleanor's home was a back wall open to the elements like the inside of a doll's house. A few pictures still hung on the suddenly blackened wallpapered walls and smoke charred curtains clung to the frames of the shattered windows, drab with their soaking from the firemen's hose. Beneath them lay an enormous heap of rubble and rafters. The street in front of the house was littered with roof slates, bricks and shattered glass.A long snake of thick hosepipe lay coiled along the street and over the rubble from the nearest hydrant and water continued to ebb from it down the street.

Agnes felt her throat seize up into a viciously aching lump and her eyes glazed with unwept tears, but it was Dilly who asked the question which she could not find words for.

'Miss Eleanor. She was on duty – Red Cross drivin' las' night. Where she now?'

'I'm sorry, missus. I don't know what to say.' The warden lowered his voice, trying to turn his face away from Agnes' upturned gaze.

'It happened early this morning. She was home. They got her out, but there was nothing they could do. I'm sorry, love.' Then after a pause, time to allow

Diligence to take this in, 'What are you going to do with the little girl? Has she got any other relations?'

'Yes,' Dilly replied in a quick, high voice. 'Don't you worry about her. I'll take care of her. She got other family she can go to.'

Agnes suddenly pulled her hand from Dilly's loosened grip and ducked under the barrier tape.

'Hey,' cried the warden, 'You can't go in there. It's dangerous.'

But Agnes ran up the street towards the huge pile of rubble. Great choking sobs shook her as she stood in front of what had been her house, containing everyone and everything that had ever been her family. There was nothing she could readily identify of all the things that make up a home. The furniture had disappeared beneath the great heap of twisted metal, charred wood and tons of bricks. Door frames and window frames were contorted and broken as if made of matchsticks, but looking up, to the second floor, she recognised the fireplace of her grandmother's bedroom, standing on a ledge which was all that remained of the room. A carriage clock still stood on the mantelpiece.

'Hey,' the warden had caught up and was standing behind her. He placed a hand on her shoulder. 'I'm sorry, Miss. You can't stay here. It's dangerous. That wall could go at any moment.'

Dilly was close behind him. 'Jus' give us two minute, please,' she pleaded.

Agnes had pulled away and was already picking

her way across the outer edges of the shattered stones lying jumbled across the road. She stooped and picked up an object. It was a small silver frame containing a photograph of her mother before she got married. It too, had stood on the mantelpiece of Eleanor's bedroom. The glass was shattered, but the black and white photograph was unharmed.

'Must've got blown out in the blast,' said the warden quietly. 'Look, if we find anything else, we'll send it on to you. You'd best get away from here now.'

Dilly put an arm tightly around Agnes' shoulder and led her away. Neither of them spoke as they retraced their steps, taking the bus back to East London. Tears rolled silently down Dilly's big cheeks. Agnes felt numb; there were no tears to come. Not then.

Hours later, Agnes put the question which had been running through her mind all day as she lay curled up in an old armchair by the fire in Dilly's tiny kitchen. It took only a few words to someone on the way down the street for the news to spread quickly and Dilly's neighbours came and went all day, exchanged quiet words with Dilly, who was weeping, patted Agnes on the head and frequently muttered quiet questions to Dilly that they thought she couldn't hear.

'Poor scrap, what's going to become of her? Who can she go to now?'

Dilly's son, Albert, went out in the early afternoon, having also patted her on the arm and slipped some butterscotch sweets into her hand. Her voice was shaky, but she asked it anyway.

'Dilly, what did you mean when you told the warden I had people to go to. Where can I go?'

Dilly looked at her for a long moment before she replied. She knew there was no use in trying to offer Agnes false comfort and besides, she had never been dishonest with any child in the false belief that she might thereby spare the child's feelings.

'Far as I know, darlin'. The only livin' relations you got now is your French grandma and pa. But you're not goin' to France while the war is still ragin', darlin'. You'll jus' have to stay here with me till all that's done and finished with.'

'Oh, Dilly, I want to stay here with you forever. I don't even remember my French grandparents.' She stuck out her jaw and lowered her brows with the determined look she had when she believed passionately in the rightness of something. A look which Dilly normally laughed at. But she didn't laugh now.

'Darlin', you gonna stay here as long as you like. All the same, I'll be lettin' your grandparents know as soon as I can. Least, after the war, you can go visit them. They bound to want you and love you too, Agnes, their own flesh and blood and your father was their only child. Don't forget you're all they've got left too …' she trailed off, not wanting to distress Agnes yet further, with thoughts of her dead father and mother. What a mountain of grief and loss this child had had to bear in so short a life. But she was strong, resilient, reflected Dilly. All she needed was a settled, loving home for a while. God grant that she would have that here with her for the rest of the war at least. She held out her arms to Agnes who stood and stretched her arms around Dilly's not insubstantial stomach, leaning her head against a comfortingly cushiony bosom.

'I know you don't remember your gran'parents in France honey,' Dilly went on after a pause, 'but that don't mean they isn't family or don't love you. Miss Eleanor, she always told me she was going to take you down there to visit them in France after the war. That's why she made you speak French with her all the time. So you could grow up speakin' two languages and could speak to your grandparents over there too.'

A fresh wave of tears flowed steadily down Agnes' cheeks, 'I don't want to go away from you Dilly,' she sobbed, 'I just want to stay here.'

'Don't you fret, darlin'. You're not goin' anywhere for now. You know I'll take care of you jus' so long as I can.' She continued to cuddle Agnes, patting her on the back. 'Why you're like the little girl I never had. Just three lumping great boys, I had. Only trouble is,' she rambled on, 'you is the wrong colour for bein' my girl!' Dilly shook gently with laughter at this and Agnes couldn't help but grin through her tears.

It was quite natural that Agnes had no memory of her French grandmère and grandpère, since she had not seen them since she was a baby. In truth, she knew remarkably little about them, except that they lived near to a southern town called Carpentras. She remembered this because when she was little she had thought it was called 'Carpenters', and she knew that their surname was the same as her own, of course. She had often tried to imagine the rambling farmhouse they lived in which she had been told about. She had told the boys she played with that they were a Count and Countess who lived in a chateau, but as the war went on she had kept quiet about being French. There had been a boy who taunted her.

'The French is all cowards, ain't they? They catapulted to the Germans, they have. My dad said.'

'They what?' said another.

'They given in, ain't they?' the first boy continued, 'France is all run by Germans now.'

'No they ain't,' protested Agnes, falling into the vernacular that she used when she was out with the gang. 'Well, some might have, but there's lots that haven't given in. There's a general who's leading them. He's here in England and organising people in France to fight the Germans.'

The first boy sniffed, unconvinced. 'My dad says they gave in too easy. Should have fought the Germans much harder.'

There were so many uncertainties. For the moment, Dilly was all she had for family and she knew that she was safe. Feeling quite suddenly exhausted, she curled deeper into the armchair and fell asleep.

When she next woke it was dark and she was in Dilly's big bed. Downstairs she could hear Dilly and Albert talking. Their voices were low, but their words floated up through the thin floor enough for Agnes to hear the gist of what they were saying.

'It could be years before anyone can get into France, Ma, and how do you know they'll still be alive?'

'Well, course I don't know that,' Dilly's high, sing-song voice carried despite its softness, 'I don't rightly know anything – except one thing, I won't let Agnes be taken away to no strangers. I love that child as if she were my own and her grandmother, well, she was much more than just someone I worked for. A true lady and a real friend to us she was.Not everyone in England been willin' to treat Jamaicans as fair as she did right from the start.'

'I'll help you out as much as I can, Ma. Miss Eleanor was always good to us boys too, when we were growing up and I know she helped you and Dad to set up and get started right, here in London. But it's not just a friend you lost, is it? You've lost your job now that she's not here. That means no money coming in, 'cept what you get from Dad's army pay; that's only seven shillings a week and you've got an extra mouth to feed now too.'

'Oh, don't fuss boy. I'm getting' government

44

allowance on top of that, twenty-five shillin's while your pa's away, that'll feed us both and I'll find something else soon enough. Plenty of jobs for women now that our menfolk are all away.'

'That's true, but you won't want to leave Agnes alone in the house all day while you're working. She doesn't even have a school to go to right now. When Dad comes back … Ma, nobody knows how long this war going on for. It's been three years already. We never thought it would last that long. France has been occupied by the Germans for nearly three years. Nobody knows if they'll ever leave either.'

'I thought the Americans comin' over was going to finish up this war real quickly now,' objected Dilly.

'Oh, the Yanks.'

'Americans boy, don't be disrespectful.'

'No, you're right, Ma. We've got more of a chance of winning the war now. Everyone's more hopeful now they're here. We just don't know how long it will take.' There was a pause, then he added, 'I can send you some more of my pay. I've been saving it for after, but I'm not spending much. That's one good thing about being in a war,' he gave a wry chuckle , 'there's not much to spend your money on in an army barracks or at the front line.'

'Don't you worry, darlin', I'll find another job. We'll manage till then. I'm trying to put your father's pay by for him for afterwards too. Who knows what jobs there'll be?'

Agnes flushed. She had only been thinking of herself all day and Dilly had lost her job and the person she had called 'the best friend she ever had'.

There was a pause, then Dilly added, 'No, boy, the money isn't no bother, but I am worried right enough that they might come and take the child away from me.'

'What do you mean, Ma?'

'I've heard the orphanages is fillin' up with children who've lost their parents an' I don't think the authorities is goin' to leave Agnes here with me if they find out she an orphan.'

'But surely they'll let her stay here with you, Ma?'

'Well, I don't know, but I doubt it, son. I'm not no relation of hers and I'm not gettin' no younger. Besides that, I is the wrong colour. Least, that's the way they'll see it. It would break the child's heart to be in an orphanage, it would. Still, we'll fight that problem when it comes. "Don't go lookin' for trouble," as your dad would say, "it'll come lookin' for you soon enough." I isn't goin' to say nothing to the child for the time bein'. She's had her fair share of problems for a while yet.'

Agnes had crept to the top of the stairs the better to hear this conversation. The staircase rose directly from the front room where Albert and Dilly were sitting and she could now hear everything they said as if she was in the room beside them. Her heart seemed to stop as she listened to Dilly's words. She had not for a moment considered that anyone might try to take her away. But she had seen it happen; Charlie Henderson who lived a few streets away and had gone to the country as an evacuee, had become an orphan when his parents were both killed in an air raid some months ago. Granny had told her that he had been sent then to an orphanage in Kent. They had intended to visit him soon.

Agnes suddenly found that her teeth were chattering and she was shivering all over. She was only in her nightie, but it wasn't just the cold. She crept down the stairs which creaked as she neared the bottom. Dilly and Albert both turned to her at the sound.

At other times, when Agnes had stayed, she had always marvelled at the tiny size of the house and how much was crammed into it. The only lavatory was outside in a little shed at the bottom of the garden. All the houses in the street had little sheds at the bottom of their long thin gardens. If you looked at the front of the house it was almost indistinguishable from its neighbours. The street was a long block of red bricks, punctuated by different coloured front doors. Dilly's stood out, it was painted shiny red and she was proud of it. They had paid for their house and it was their own. The house and family stood out in other ways; they were the only coloured family in the street, even in the neighbourhood. There were very few non-white families in London at that time. Dilly's husband and his father had come over in the early 1930s to work as seamen on the new steamships which crossed the

Atlantic. Samuel, Dilly's husband, was in the Navy and all three of Samuel and Dilly's sons were fighting for the country they were born in.

Now Dilly sat forward as Agnes came into the room, 'What you doin' child?' her voice rose with gentle concern as she saw her. 'Come here, love. Why you're freezin' cold, probably hungry too. You eaten nothing today. You wait there a moment an' I'll fix us some hot milk'.

As she busied herself with heating milk in a pan on the cooker in the little back kitchen, she continued to chatter to Albert, while Agnes curled up in an armchair, nudging the tabby cat over to make room.

'When exac'ly you leavin' boy?'

'I've only got a few days, Ma, we'll be meeting up at the barracks in South London on Thursday.'

'Where are you going?' Agnes interrupted.

'Down to Kent – the unit's moving,' Albert replied. 'Actually' he went on, addressing his words more to his mother than to Agnes, 'although we are there as a defence unit on the coast, I think there's more going on that anyone's admitting to.'

Dilly appeared around the corner from the kitchen with a tray of mugs containing steaming milk.

'What d'you mean?'

'Well, officially there's no boats going between England and France now, but people say there's plenty of small boats disappear out to sea at night.'

'Why's that then, son?'

'Don't rightly know, Ma, but one day we'll have to invade France, get it back from the Germans, and the only real way to do that is by sea. Nobody knows where, or when though. Reckon they're doing reconnaissance in preparation.'

'Re-conny-sants, chile', what's that when it's at home?'

'Well, spying out the land, Ma, you know, looking for the best places to land and how many German troops are there to guard different points, that sort of thing.'

There was a responding 'hmm' from the kitchen, then Dilly's head appeared around the door.

'Thing I can't understand,' she said, 'is why they Frenchies don't try harder to get the Germans out.'

'There's too many of them, Ma. Germans that is. They're a very powerful army. But I think the Frenchies are doing more than you think, some of them at least. Others are getting their bread well buttered by the Germans. But there's all kinds of stories of Resistance groups in France. You know, people working secretly against the Germans.' He paused, and Agnes put in,

'Yes, my godfather told us that.' She remembered that she had been told then not to repeat what she heard and she waited till Albert continued with what he was saying.

'There's a fair number of Frenchies here in London – there's old what's-his-name, de Gaulle, for a start. Setting up the Free French army. Speaks on the radio every week to people listening in France he does. Reckon he's hatching all kinds of plans.'

'Hmm,' Dilly was interested, but the intricacies of war strategies were distant and hard to comprehend. As if reflecting her thoughts, Albert added in a more subdued tone, 'It's not going to happen tomorrow though, is it? I mean, it's not just England, Germany and France. There's fighting going on all over the world. It's going to take a while to sort all this mess out, whichever way it goes.'

Agnes drank her hot milk and went back to bed. Her mind was swimming with all that she had heard. She felt sad at the thought of so many men's lives in danger, while at the same time, she had a feeling that with all that was going on in the war, nobody would worry too much about her and that was a good thing. Besides, she could not believe that anyone would seriously want to take her away from Dilly who had looked after her all her life. Surely they had more important things to worry about. But Dilly had lost her job, she would have to look for another; rations were short and she was just an additional burden to Dilly's stretched resources. Whatever happened though, Agnes was quite certain she was not going to be put in any orphanage.

No, she would live here quietly with Dilly till the end of the war. If there were more bombing raids, well there was the Morrison, or the Underground station where she and Dilly had had to take shelter on other occasions. It wasn't far to run. Perhaps then, at the end of the war she would want to go and find her grandparents, or perhaps Dilly would adopt her and she would just stay here. Anyway, why would the authorities trouble themselves to come looking for her? It was very unlikely to happen.

This was Agnes' feeling and as those early, numb days turned into weeks, she became more certain and confident of it. It was a very different life that she and Dilly had to get used to now, but they comforted each other through it. Before he left at the end of his leave, Albert took Agnes to the nearest Public Library and enrolled her as a member. After this, she took out as many books as she could on each visit and spent much of her time reading at home. Dilly found work within a few days. It was just for the mornings, in a local grocery shop and it did not pay very much, but it was something.

Agnes stayed at home. She tried to help. She did the ironing and made the beds while Dilly was at work. When Dilly came home, she found her little jobs to do, like chopping vegetables, or bits of sewing, not because Agnes was very good or quick at these things, but because it helped to be busy. Both of them felt a dull ache inside them which weighed them down and made them feel raw and vulnerable, as if anything they touched might bruise or burn them. They both tried to chat about unimportant things. Dilly told Agnes about the people who had come into the shop that day and what was in short supply and how people shared recipes to make something interesting out of the few available ingredients; carrot cakes were especially popular as the carrots were sweet, but getting the texture just right was never easy, they were soggy if you put too many carrots in. Agnes told Dilly about the books she was reading or about how she had rescued a mouse that the cat had caught in the garden and was playing with.

But in the evenings, when they had eaten and Dilly at last stopped working and sat down, Agnes would often crawl into her lap, or onto the sofa beside her, burying her head against her and crying silently. She missed her grandmother more than she could possibly express. Eleanor had been everything to her; had shared so much of her own life with Agnes and had been an example in every part of Agnes' life. Agnes wondered suddenly how she could ever now grow up without Eleanor's wise words and guidance, as well as her always gentle and constant love. Dilly had few words of comfort to offer; she wept too and hugged and patted Agnes, but she was worried about the future.

There was no school of course, for Agnes to attend, and she saw nobody except those friends and neighbours of Dilly's whom they met at the allotment or who occasionally dropped in and Agnes missed the camaraderie of the boys she used to play with too.

But despite her unhappiness, there was a routine and a warm and safe home. And there was Dilly, who with her big, comforting arms was always ready to give her the love she needed, and who cooked delicious dishes to tempt her to eat.

And then, one morning, when Agnes had almost forgotten to worry about the prospect of being taken away, there was a knock on the door which would change her life.

Eleanor had worked in the Home Office and the Red Cross and had many other friends in influential positions. It was inevitable therefore, that people should be genuinely concerned about the granddaughter whom they knew Eleanor had adored.

Agnes had slept fitfully again that night and then as dawn was breaking, she had fallen into a deep sleep. She awoke to an urgent knocking on the door. Dilly had gone to work and the house was quiet. Agnes didn't move, thinking that whoever had knocked must have gone, but then they knocked again. It must be important. Perhaps Dilly had been taken ill, or had had an accident. She ran down the stairs in her nightie and opened the door.

On the step were a warden and an officious-looking woman in uniform. She had a beaky nose on which perched horn-rimmed glasses and iron-grey hair. She was surprised to see Agnes in her nightdress so late in the morning.

'Oh! You must be Agnes.'

Agnes hesitated then adopted her street tone.

'Who wants to know?'

The warden broke in, 'None of your cheek my girl. This lady has been looking for you all morning. Come all the way from Westminster, she has.'

The woman brushed aside the warden's effort at assistance however and carried on.

'You are Agnes, aren't you? Of course you are. My name is Mrs Egerton-Bass. May I come in? I'm really here to see Mrs Roberts.'

'Oh, Dilly, Diligence, you mean? Um, she's gone to work.'

'I see. Well, it's really about you I've come, my dear.' At this point the woman, not waiting for Agnes to answer her question, pushed past her into the house and turning to thank the warden, closed the door behind her.

'Me?' echoed Agnes, feeling suddenly wary. 'What about me?'

'A number of people have been very worried about you, my dear. Friends of your grandmother's, you know. We didn't know where you were for a time until someone had the idea that you might be with Mrs Roberts. We had a terrible time finding out her address; we had to go through the army to find out who her husband was. That's why it's taken us this long to find you.'

'You really shouldn't have gone to so much trouble,' Agnes protested politely. 'I'm very happy here and I am being perfectly well looked after and I am going to stay here until the end of the war when

I shall go to visit my French grandparents and see if they want me.'

The woman from Westminster looked taken aback at Agnes' assured and lengthy statement, but after a pause she went on gently.

'I'm afraid there's no question of you staying here, Agnes. Mrs Roberts is no relation of yours and it would not be … appropriate.'

'Why not? What do you mean?' Agnes' heart was beginning to beat faster, but she knew she must keep calm.

'Well my dear, a Jamaican lady bringing up a little English girl…it's just not….'

'But she's looked after me all my life, at Grandma's house…and I've often stayed here before. Grandma wanted her to look after me,' she finished lamely.

'Mrs Roberts should not have left you alone in the house this morning for a start,' said the lady from Westminster losing her patience. She had had a long morning trying to find this place in the East end of London and had not expected to be argued with, by a child, at the end of it.

'And besides, why aren't you in school? Children have to go to school you know.' Agnes didn't answer and so she went on, 'You are a very lucky girl because friends of your grandmother's have found a place in a very nice children's home in Suffolk. You will be looked after properly there and have lessons with the other children. You can stay there until the end of the war. Then we can see about these French grandparents.'

'I'm not going,' Agnes said, and the minute she had said it, she knew it was a mistake. The woman from Westminster gave a sharp intake of breath.

'I'm afraid you have no choice, my girl. A lot of people have gone to a great deal of trouble for you, and they have had far more important things they ought to have been getting on with,' she finished sharply.

Agnes hesitated. She realised she'd have to be more subtle to get rid of this woman. She had come with an objective, which was to take her away from Dilly and she had, in her own words, gone to 'a great deal of trouble' over it. She wasn't likely to leave without her unless she had good reason to.

'If you took me away now, Mrs … ' she struggled to remember the woman's name. It had been a complicated one.

'Egerton-Bass,' the woman reminded her helpfully. It gave Agnes a moment more to think.

'Yes, Mrs Egerton-Bass. Well, if you just took me away, Diligence would get the police out when she came back and the whole of London would be looking for me and that would really be wasting people's time. Besides, this afternoon she is going to take me shopping to buy some clothes. She's had to go and get special clothing coupons for me and it's taken this long to get them. I've only got my nightie to wear you see because the house was bombed. I can't go anywhere without some clothes, but by tomorrow I'll have some and I can ask Dilly, (Mrs Roberts), to pack them up for me to take to Suffolk. I suppose it would be rather nice,' Agnes went on, as if she was thinking carefully about it, 'to be amongst some other children and go to school again.'

'Yes, quite right dear,' said Mrs Egerton-Bass, encouraged. 'But what a nuisance, really, to have to come back. Still, I suppose I can't take you without talking to Mrs Roberts first. Leaving a note just wouldn't do and she may as well buy you some clothes. It will save someone else the trouble. What a nuisance,' she repeated, 'Well, tell her I'll be back tomorrow morning to put you on the Suffolk train. I suppose she doesn't have a telephone?' she looked around the little room as Agnes affirmed this. 'Never mind, I'll leave you my telephone number. She'll have to telephone me from a box if she has any questions.' She wrote out her name and a number in a little notebook she had in her handbag and tore out the page, 'Give this to her and make sure you tell her I'm coming back tomorrow morning and have everything ready to leave.'

She paused, remembering that this child had just lost her grandmother, and was, apparently, an orphan. A little more softly, she added, 'No more nonsense, Agnes. You'll be very happy in Suffolk. It's a lovely home and there are lots of other little boys and girls in the same position as you and a nice school to go to.' Her eyes swept around the tiny but colourful front room once more with a look of distaste until, with a final 'Hmph', she opened the front door and let herself out. Agnes closed the door behind her and hastening to an upstairs window, she watched as the woman walked to the end of the street where the warden was still loitering. After talking earnestly for a few moments, they parted company and were lost to sight.

Agnes' fingers were white, so tightly was she holding onto the rim of the sash window. Her heart was thumping painfully, but she was certain of one thing. She was not going to go to an orphanage.

There was no time to lose. If she told Dilly what had happened, Dilly would insist that she went with the woman from the Home Office. As much as she loved Agnes, she would want to do what she felt was right and would not disobey the authorities.

She dressed quickly and hunted about for a piece of paper and a pencil.

'Dear Dilly' she wrote. 'A woman came to try and take me away. I'm sorry to be a nuisance, but I'm not going to any children's home in Suffolk. I'll be all right. Don't worry. I love you, Agnes. P.S. You can show her this note because she ought to know you looked after me really well and she should have just left me with you. Love, Agnes x.'

There was nothing else to do. She had almost been truthful about the clothing. She had only what she had been wearing on the day they returned to the house and her nightdress, teddy and toothbrush. She pushed these hastily into a bag. There was a loaf of bread in the kitchen from which she cut two slices and looking around for something to wrap them in, she picked up one of the chequered squares of cotton that Dilly wore as a headscarf knotted under her chin when she went out, from the top of a neatly ironed pile. She hesitated in front of the photograph of her mother that Dilly had stood on a table near the door, having carefully removed the shards of broken glass. After a moment's hesitation, she removed the photograph from the frame and put it into the bag. Then she slipped quietly out of the front door. It was one o'clock and Dilly would be home soon.

Chapter 3

On the Run

What candles may be held to speed them all?
Not in the hands of boys, but in their eyes
Shall shine the holy glimmer of goodbyes.
Anthem for Doomed Youth *Wilfred Owen*

Agnes knew her way around London from the last few years of taking buses with Dilly or Eleanor. She had no clear plan in mind, just an overwhelming desire to go home. There was no home, of course and as she neared the street where her home had been, she realised that this was the first place that people would look for her. There were streets nearby with ruins she knew well however, and she headed for these, wondering if she would meet some of the boys in her gang. But the streets were quiet and Agnes settled into the corner of a ruined building, listening to the distant sounds of traffic and the occasional ambulance siren.

She must have fallen asleep, her head on her knees, for when she awoke it was dusk. She rose stiffly and walked the short distance to her own street. She approached the house cautiously, but there was no sign of any warden, or anyone else on the pavements in front of the large white houses with their tidy front gardens. There was the gap, like a missing tooth, pulled painfully from a row of white, sturdy teeth. The rubble had been moved off the road and the pavement, but lay in heaps about the few remaining walls of the house. She clambered over it, to reach the back garden where most of the wall still stood intact.

Stepping carefully amid the bricks, broken glass and plaster which slid and resettled as she walked on them, she watched carefully where she put her feet, afraid of making too much noise. The light was fading fast, but there ahead of her was something that was not bricks or plaster, a small object she recognised. She pulled it out and dusted it off. It was a little wooden statuette, about six inches high, that had stood on the table in the upstairs hall. Eleanor had once told her it was a copy of the statue of a knight from a famous Spanish story, Don something, she had called him. It had been her father's and was the last gift he had given her. She held it closely against her; it had been worth coming back just for this.

Just at that moment she heard voices from the front of the house. They drew nearer, edging carefully around the side of the house and clambering noisily across the rubble.

'They seem to think she'll come here,' said a man's

voice, 'though I can't see as there's much to come back for.'

'Oh, well, you never know with these young'uns,' said a second voice that Agnes recognised as the voice of a local warden, the one who had met them on the day of the bombing. 'Come back to where they know, don't they? Like all them evacuees who've run back to London.'

As they approached, Agnes stepped as quickly and as quietly as she could away from them and slipped in through an empty door frame into what had been the laundry room, next to the kitchen. There were two complete walls offering a dark corner between them, though there was nothing but sky above. Agnes pressed herself into the shadow of the corner. She could hear the footsteps of the men approach and a beam of torchlight which swept across the jumble of ruined building and back out across the garden.

'No, she can't be here,' said the first man's voice. 'I'd better come back and have another look in the morning. Meet me here at eight o'clock, will you?'

'Very good, Constable,' the Warden's voice answered. 'I'll ask the neighbours to keep an eye out for her too.'

The men's voices and clambering footsteps distanced themselves again and it was quiet. Agnes emerged from her hiding place and out beyond the rubble, to find, in the centre of the garden, the apple tree unharmed, with its swing, still and waiting. She sat on it, gazing at the dark shadow that was the ruined house. Tears flowed freely down her cheeks. There was nothing for her here now.

Later, she lay in the soft grass under the tree, looking up at the stars she could see in a cloudless sky through the trellis of leafy branches. She would spend this one last night in her garden, and then she would go. She would go to France. Somehow. All that remained of her family was there. She did not know how she would get to France, but she had heard someone say that on a clear day you could see France from the white cliffs of Dover. Dover was at the end of the line on the train she had often taken to her grandmother's house in Kent, before the war. So she would go to the railway station and get on a train to Dover. She had no money. Agnes' plan faltered here. Well, she would just have to see what she could do when she got to the station. Nobody on the buses had asked her for money. They had been crowded and she had been lucky, avoiding the eye of harassed conductresses and sheltering behind motherly looking women as if she belonged to them. Perhaps she would be lucky again. She must leave early, at dawn, though, before the warden and the police constable thought of coming back.

At first light, the birds woke her. The dawn chorus which she had sometimes heard from her bedroom if she had woken early. Now, they were right above her in the apple tree and other neighbouring trees. They filled the silence of the morning and lifted

Agnes' spirits. She shivered. The grass was damp with dew and she had slept very little and ached from the hard ground.

At least the streets were quiet. Nobody was about. The blackout curtains were all drawn in the other houses. The sky had clouded over and soon a steady drizzle started to fall. A few streets along she passed a milk delivery van, but the milk lady had her back to her, distributing bottles to doorsteps. At length, she reached busier streets and a bus stop. The rain was falling more heavily now and people kept their faces down, or under umbrellas, and nobody gave her a second glance. Again, she slipped, unnoticed, onto crowded buses, standing behind adults near the doorway at the back and watching the grey streets flash past. When she needed directions, she asked at the bus stops, finding the right numbers on the front of the buses, till at length the third bus she had changed onto drew up at Charing Cross Station.

Inside, the station was busy. Rivers of people flowed against each other in different directions; many arriving for their day's work in central London, from outlying districts, hurrying towards the Underground or out towards buses or the street beyond; others making for trains bound out of London. Among these were several groups of soldiers, while others stood or sat on the floor, in groups, smoking cigarettes and talking quietly, waiting for their train to be announced. All had large khaki rucksacks and their black boots were well polished. Several officers in peaked caps stood, slightly apart and deep in conversation.

Agnes moved quickly through the station, anxious not to draw attention to herself as being on her own, but looking at the destinations marked up above the entrances to platforms. At length she found one marked 'Dover', listing a number of other stations along the line, just as she had hoped. It was due in soon at the same platform where she had often boarded the train for Kent, before the war and it was therefore still vaguely familiar. As luck would have it, too, a small group of children were standing dejectedly at the far end of the platform. Agnes approached them carefully, noticing their little suitcases and a few anxious mothers standing by them. Some of the children clung to teddies, some to their mothers, who were offering last minute words of wisdom or encouragement, or simple comfort; some held hands with each other. A strap crossed the chest of every child from which hung a cardboard box containing their gas masks. Her gas mask! Agnes had forgotten it. This was a further reason not to draw attention to herself. It was a valid excuse for anyone to stop her and ask her why she was not carrying it and what she was doing there. But there was nothing to be done about that now. These children bore all the tell-tale signs of evacuees heading out to the country. Perhaps some had been home to London for a visit, or else they were 'escapees' being returned to safer homes in the country after running away back to their families in London. At the front, a woman with a pasteboard and a list of names parried questions from the adults. Agnes waited, loitering behind a pillar, until the train arrived with a great puff of steam. Then, in the confusion of carriage doors opening, people leaving the train to hurry off along the platform and whistles blowing, the children gathered closer to the train, collecting up bags and belongings, making hurried last goodbyes, and Agnes quietly joined the group unnoticed.

The woman at the front called to them, 'Come along now, children. Finish saying goodbye and hurry up. The train will be leaving again in a minute or two.' She showed the ticket collector standing by the door a handful of tickets which he took and carefully punched them all through with a neat hole, before waving the children on. He didn't count them. Agnes was safely on the train and in a narrow corridor with small compartments to one side. The children all headed on towards the end of the corridor and the two empty compartments which had been kept for them, but Agnes, turning back and looking through the corridor windows of the compartments chose one that was already filling up with soldiers who were stacking packs on the racks above the seat and making room for others at their feet.

'Is there any room for me in here?' she asked politely.

'I expect we can squeeze you in, love', said a large soldier with an open, cheerful face. 'Here, shift, Watson,' he gestured to a soldier just installing himself by the window to move over and make space beside it for Agnes, settling himself in the seat opposite. The compartment was full and they pulled the sliding door shut, pulling down the blinds on the windows into the corridor and lighting up cigarettes.

'Off to the country then, are you love?' said the friendly soldier.

'Yes, I'm going to stay with my Aunt,' Agnes invented effortlessly.

'Oh, you're a lucky one then, ain't you,' he commented. 'There's lots go to families they don't like. My kid brother included. Ran away three times he did. My mum's given up now. Kept him at home. Third time lucky according to him.'

Agnes smiled. She looked at him and the other soldiers briefly. They were all very young, probably new recruits.

'Where are you going then?' she asked.

'Training camp, near Dover,' the big soldier replied. 'First time out of London for some of us too.'

Agnes nodded and turned to look out of the window as the train had begun to move slowly out of the station. It was a tight squeeze between the window and the rough khaki uniform of the soldier beside her and the air of the compartment was beginning to thicken with cigarette smoke already. As if sensing this thought, the soldier opposite stood up and opened a small sliding window at the top. He fell into a quiet chat and banter with the others. Some seemed excited at this new adventure in each other's company. One, who looked even younger than the rest, sat quietly, his face pale, leaning against the corner farthest from her. He soon fell asleep. Agnes did likewise, resting her head against the window and closing her eyes. Soon, soothed by the gentle rhythm of the train, the warmth of the compartment and the soft rain against the windows outside, and tired from the poor rest she had had that night under the apple tree, she fell asleep. As she drifted out of consciousness the thought ran through her mind that if she could just get to Dover, she was a step nearer France and hadn't her godfather, George, said something about small boats going back and forth across the channel? Perhaps she *could* go to France after all.

Sometimes there is an advantage in not knowing too much about a situation and if Agnes had had any idea of how dangerous it was to think of going to France, or what life was really like there, she would never entertained this idea as a possibility.

About two year ago, when Germany had invaded France, the allied troops had had to retreat to the coast and try to get home to England. Thousands of soldiers and sailors had died as German planes bombed British ships at Dunkirk. These ships had been replaced by flotillas of fishing boats and privately owned boats as brave people sailed, motored and even rowed across the channel from England to rescue the stranded soldiers.

Since then the German army had controlled the west coast of France and there had been no official traffic across the channel.

Except that what George Meredith and Albert had both hinted at was true. There was some traffic, of a very secretive nature, and boats were being run by extremely brave men. Many of them did bring back English soldiers or airmen or escaped prisoners of war and many took other heroes over. Reconnaissance and spying was a vital part of the Allied effort to undermine and eventually overthrow, the German occupation of France. Few people knew about the comings and goings of these boats and it was better that way. They left from rocky coves away from the harbours of towns and villages. They kept well below the radar and as far away as they could from any warships patrolling the channel. In France they landed at even more remote and hidden places; spots, moreover, where they could hope to be met by a few trusted French hands to help them ashore. For members of the growing underground movement which stretched across France, secretly fighting the Germans was a vital part of this dangerous return journey. They were known as 'The Resistance' or, in France, as 'Le Maquis'. They helped British spies safely on their way; they brought other passengers, rescued pilots or prisoners, returning them safely to England, at agreed meeting points and they risked their lives to give the boatmen warning, if necessary, if it was not safe to land that night.

When Agnes got off the train later that afternoon, it was already dusk. The children must have left the train earlier and the soldiers had descended at the stop before Dover. Scores of them milled about on the platform of a small country station as harassed sergeants barked orders at them. The train had slowly pulled away and Agnes had caught the eye of the youngest, quiet soldier, who had sat in the corner of the carriage opposite her for the last three hours. She raised her hand to him hesitantly and he gave a brief smile. She felt lonely in the empty carriage, but stayed on, past Dover town, to the very last stop, Dover docks. Here she stepped down quickly from the train the moment it drew to a halt and out through a gate from the platform into the street before anyone in the station had time to ask her any questions.

She was on the outer edge of town which was largely deserted. The blackouts were up in people's windows and a chill wind was blowing off the sea. She could smell it; salt and seaweed and another, oily smell that went with it. It wasn't raining here, but it was cloudy and overcast, although a sharper light and an open space of sky told her instinctively which direction the sea was in. She headed towards it.

The front was deserted. A grey concrete wall separated the pavement from the shingle beach and huge rolls of barbed wire lined the beach between the wall and the dark, softly lapping water. She walked along the beach towards the western edges of the town.

Hunger gnawed at her stomach, causing it to grumble painfully. She had had nothing to eat all day, having finished her two pieces of bread in the garden last night. The daylight had faded quickly and the windows of buildings, as she approached, were already blacked out for the night. A small side-street branched away, uphill and Agnes caught a waft of the smell of fried fish and vinegar. Light spilled out momentarily from a doorway a few yards up. Two boys came out onto the pavement eating chips out of cones of rolled up newspaper. Agnes had no money; for the first time now it struck her how hard it would be to manage without money. She had nothing to eat and nowhere to sleep. Now she would have loved to buy a bag of chips. She approached the boys, catching the sharp scent of vinegar on hot potato.

'Hey, do you live around here?' she began.

'Who wants to know?' replied one, the taller of the two, a lad of about thirteen. She recognised the tone; street talk: it was much the same whether in London or Dover.

'Give us a chip?' She approached them cautiously. There was a faint glow from the doorway, despite the blackout, which allowed them to see each other more clearly.

'No, buzz off. Buy your own.' This was the response Agnes had expected.

'Can't. Haven't got any money. Go on, just one. I'm starving'. She had, nonetheless aroused the boys' curiosity as she had hoped, as the smaller one continued, 'Who are you anyway? Ain't seen you around here before.'

'No. My name's … Ann. I've run away from a home in London.' The boys looked interested. The bigger one offered her a chip.

'Go on then. What you doing here?'

Agnes took a deep breath, 'Look, I need some help. The police are after me.'

She was taking a great risk. Either boy could turn around and fetch the nearest adult and she'd be under arrest and frogmarched back to a children's home in Suffolk. But she was a reasonable judge of character from her time with the boys collecting war relics amongst the ruins in London over the last two years and these two wouldn't let pass a good story, however daft it might sound, if there was a chance of getting involved in something out of the ordinary.

'What for? What did you do?' said the smaller boy and at that moment there was the sound of adult voices as the door of the fish and chip shop opened again and light began to spill onto the now dark pavement.

''Ere,' said the taller one quickly, 'we can't stop 'ere. Let's go down to the beach and talk.' They moved off quickly, Agnes following the boys as people came out onto the pavement behind them and walked away in the other direction. After a few minutes walk they were at the sea. It was impossible to go far onto the beach however. The huge coils of barbed wire prevented that

72

and there were signs posted regularly along the wire and facing inland which read 'Danger. Mines.'

Beyond the tangle of wire, Agnes could glimpse the still, black expanse of water stretching away. Her heart sank. The moon was hidden behind clouds and cast only a dim light. The boys climbed onto a low wall and dropped down onto the narrow band of shingle beach which lay between the wall and the barbed wire.

'We're okay here,' one of them said, as Agnes hesitated. 'There's mines and tank traps all along, but they're further out.'

They crunched a little way along the shingle, keeping close to the wall, until they reached some upturned boats, pulled up to the wall and chained to metal rings set into it. Swiftly, the boys settled down between them. They were completely in shadow. Agnes sat beside them.

'Nobody'll see us here,' said the tall boy, 'by the way, I'm Tom. This is Matt.'

'My mum'll kill me if I'm late home again tonight,' Matt said.

'Na, she'll be all right,' Tom assured him. 'A couple of pints of beer and she'll have forgotten you're not there.' Matt did not look too reassured by this statement, but Tom ignored him and went on, 'So, have you really run away from London? You're not one of them evacuees is you? They normally run the other way round – back to London,' he laughed. 'Ain't been many round already, mind you. It's dangerous enough here. We'll be the first to get bombed, or shot, if the Germans invade England.'

'They'll never!' exclaimed Matt vigorously, his mother's instructions forgotten once more. 'But why're the police after you? Why've you run away?'

Agnes took a deep breath. 'I need to get to France,' she said. 'Do you know anyone who can help me?'

'You're off your rocker!' exclaimed Matt.

'Why d'you want to go to France?' Tom added. 'It's full of Germans, you know!'

Agnes was good at inventing stories. She'd told herself stories for years, lying awake in bed at night. She'd even written some of them down and given them to her grandmother. Eleanor had loved them. She'd talked about them with Agnes, before putting them away safely in her bureau. All of that, the bureau, the stories, her whole life with Eleanor, was nothing but a wasteland of rubble now. The sadness in Agnes' voice was real, if her story was not.

'I've got to rescue my dad. He's being held prisoner in a castle in France. He knows lots of secret information the Germans want to get, about the English army and their weapons and things.' Agnes felt herself on slightly shaky ground here, so she moved swiftly on. 'He's being tortured every day, but he hasn't told them anything. He's pretending he's French and he's lost his memory. I'm the only one who can rescue him, because I'm going to tell them he's a farmer and he really has lost his memory and I'm his daughter and I've come to fetch him. We both speak French, see.'

'So, why are the police after you?'

Agnes thought quickly. 'I stole a secret file on my Dad, to find out where he was being kept, and they found out, so they're after me. Don't worry though, they think I'm still hiding in London.'

The boys were looking a little doubtful. They didn't quite believe her story, but it was too good to waste.

'If you can really talk French, prove it.'

'*Il faut que vous m'aidez. J'ai besoin d'aller en France. Y a-t-il un bateau je peux prendre ? J'ai faim et je veux manger vos frites*. Okay? D'you believe me?'

'What did you say?'

'I just said, "You've got to help me get to France and find a boat and that I was hungry and I wish I could eat your chips." '

The boys looked impressed and passed over the remains of their chips. They had no real reason to help or befriend this girl with her rather far-fetched story, but nothing of much excitement had happened recently and their lives had been disrupted too.

'My dad's in North Africa,' said Tom, 'ain't seen him for two years. And Matt … Matt's dad copped it right near the start of the war. Killed in France.'

Matt hung his head and Tom went on, 'That's why his mum drinks too much now. What my mum says anyway. She's got five children to look after. Hey Matt, let's help her, if she wants to rescue her dad, eh?'

Matt shrugged. 'Don't see how we can.'

'We can ask around. Some of the bigger boys know things.'

'But you've got to be careful,' Agnes said quickly. 'If adults find out I'm here, they'll just send me back to London and I'll be arrested. Then my dad will die a painful death under torture and no one will rescue him.'

'Yeah, we understand. We'll be careful. Can you meet us here tomorrow? As soon as it gets dark. I'll see what I can find out.'

'Thanks, Tom, Matt. Yes, I'll be here.'

The boys rose to leave.

'We'd best be going or they really will start looking for us. Where are you going to sleep?'

'Don't worry, I'll find somewhere.'

'Okay. 'Night, Ann,' they called softly as they turned to crunch across the gravel.

'Ann'. Agnes had forgotten she'd changed her name. But it had perhaps been a wise precaution. And despite the boys assurances they would not speak to any adults about her, Agnes thought it best not to sleep there, where they might find her if they changed their minds. She trudged further along the beach for twenty minutes until she found a small huddle of abandoned beach huts. The locks had been broken on them and they had been raided of anything useful. There had been no seaside holidays for three years now after all. In one, however, she found a pile of old blankets and wrapping them around her and crooking her arm under her head for a pillow, she settled down on the floor to sleep. If she had not been so exhausted by all that she had been through in the last days and weeks, she would no doubt have been kept awake by the sudden loneliness that swept over her as she shivered under the frail warmth offered by the thin blankets, but the profound weariness she felt, combined with the gentle swish and suck of the waves on the shingle a few yards away, lulled her quickly into a deep sleep.

She was awake again, early, stiff from the hard floor. She would not meet the boys again until later that evening, so there was a day to find out what she could for herself. Making her way further down the beach away from the town, she soon found a rugged path to clamber up to the cliff top, from where she could see much further down along the coast. There were one or two sheltered coves, but mainly the coast wound its way gently along offering few hiding places for boats to land or leave from. She did not think that anyone would set out from this stretch of coast if they were trying to avoid detection. She walked back slowly towards the town. There were a few market stalls along the main street. Food was short here as everywhere in England, but there were locally grown vegetables, a butcher's van, a man selling freshly caught mackerel from a large tray on the front of his bicycle, and a bread stall. Agnes was now ravenous; the chips she had eaten the night before had hardly satisfied her.

She loitered around the baker's stall tantalised by the smell of still warm buns. The lady baker was watching her suspiciously, but the moment inevitably came when her back was turned while serving and chatting to some other women. Agnes chose that moment to seize one of the buns and run for it. Instantly, the baker turned.

'Oi, stop! Come back you little, thieving varmint!'

She went on shouting for some time but nobody gave Agnes chase and soon she was out of sight and hearing, her heart pounding. She didn't stop until she was well away from the streets again and up on the cliff path. She sat on the grass. She felt no satisfaction in her successful raid and although she was so hungry, the bread stuck in her throat as she tried to swallow it. What a very long way she was from her grandmother's house and garden, with Dilly cooking in the kitchen and gently chiding her for tearing a dress climbing out of the tree or calling her to scrape clean the bowl where she'd mixed a cake.

There was a strong breeze and small white clouds were scudding across the sky. Away in the distance, across the sea, Agnes thought she could make out a long shadowy strip which might be the coast of France. There was no one nearby, only a few sheep grazing the rough, grass behind her. The sea looked blue today and the grass she sat on was an emerald green. The colours fractured into prisms of bright light as her eyes filled with tears. She sat with the sun and the wind on her face drying her cheeks.

She reached into the little bag she had kept with her and pulled out the little wooden statuette which she had added to her few belongings. 'Don Someone', as she mentally referred to him. She held him in her hand looking at him.

'It's no use me crying, is it, Don Someone? It's not going to bring anyone back; not Eleanor, nor Mummy and Daddy. Nobody asked for this war and so many people have died or lost people they loved. It's not just us, is it?' She looked out across the sea. 'If I can only get to France,' she continued, thinking aloud. 'If I could only find my grandparents. I'm sure they'll be happy to see me.' A note of doubt crept into her voice here. She didn't know them after all, or what had happened in their lives since the war started. 'I've just got to be brave now,' she went on, 'stop thinking about London and everything that's happened.' She looked again at the statuette. 'I'll take you with me though. We'll do this together.'

She had reached a turning point and she knew it. If she stood any chance at all of reaching France and finding her grandparents, she would need to be strong and brave and keep all her wits about her, and not think too much about the past, at least for now.

She wrapped the statuette in Dilly's chequered scarf and tucked it into a large inside pocket in her coat, along with the photograph of her mother and her toothbrush. If she did reach France, she would not need anything else, particularly anything that might look English.

Chapter 4

Alone

Fair stood the wind for France
When we our sails advance,
Not now to prove our chance
Longer will we tarry.
Agincourt *Michael Drayton*

It was at least an hour earlier than planned when Agnes began to make her way back towards the meeting point she had arranged with the boys. She thought if she sat a little way off she would be able to see them as they arrived and make sure they had not changed their minds and brought any adults with them. But to her surprise they were already there, sitting on the shingle at the top of the beach and watching for her. As soon as they saw her, they stood up and started walking quickly towards her.

They were obviously excited and had news to give her, but before they spoke, they gestured to her to turn back the way she had come. They hurried along beside her till they were all out of sight of the town again and this was probably just as well, Agnes reflected, now that she had become a recognisable bread-stealing criminal.

As soon as they had rounded a bend on the beach, the boys' pace slowed. There was a wooden barrier the length of the beach from the wall to the sea, designed to stop the shingle drifting too far with the tide. They clambered over it, turning to offer help to Agnes. She ignored them and jumped down.

'Here,' Matt said, 'we can sit here. Nobody will see us.'

'We've got some news for you,' Tom said, conspiratorially. 'But first,' he went on, opening a canvas bag he'd been carrying over his shoulder, 'we brought you something to eat. We thought you'd be hungry.'

'Wow, thanks boys.' Agnes was touched. 'You're right, I'm ravenous.' She tucked into the cold slices of spam and bread he handed her, unwrapped from a tea towel and as she ate Tom continued, 'Matt found out something important for you. His uncle's a fisherman.'

'Yeah,' Matt took up the story. 'My cousin Pete told me that he'd heard his dad talking to another man and it seems that when they go out fishing at night, when the tide's in, they go in a little fleet, see, a few boats at a time. Most of them stay close to the coast but as soon as they're out of sight, one of them peels away and heads off for France. Then they wait for another boat to reach them, coming in the opposite direction, from France. So, there's always the same number of boats go out and come in, in case the coastguard's counting, but one of them's a different boat. Pete goes with them sometimes and he's seen things like that happen, 'cept, when he asked his dad what was going on, his dad just gave him a cuff round the ear and told him not to be so nosy.'

'So how does that help me?' Agnes prompted, puzzled.

'Well, if you could get into one of the boats that is going to France, you could get a free ride. Obviously,' Tom explained to her patiently.

'Right,' Agnes agreed. 'But how do I find out which boat – you said they went out in a fleet – which one is going to France and not just going fishing?'

'That's where Pete comes in,' Matt said. 'Last night he heard his father say "We've got to get him over to France tomorrow". We don't know who "him" is but he's going to try and find out which is *the* boat, before they leave tonight. He's allowed to go with his dad tonight, see, so he can hang around with all the fishermen while they're getting ready to leave.'

'Tonight? That's wonderful. But,' she hesitated, 'how do I get into the boat?'

'Well, that's the hard part,' Tom agreed, nodding, 'but we'll just have to get down to the harbour and see what we can do and what Pete has found out. It's important that nobody sees you though, or us, 'cos if you can't go tonight, we'll try again another night, but it may not be for a while.'

This was disappointing and worrying. She could not stay here for long, living on stolen bread or free handouts from the boys. She was bound to be caught.

'So where do the boats leave from?' she asked.

'Right there in the town, from the fishing port,' Tom put in, gesturing back towards the town. 'It's about a mile away and we've got to hurry. That's why we were waiting for you, hoping you'd come early. There isn't any time to waste.'

'That's fine. I'm ready. Shall we go then?' Agnes was excited and nervous all at once.

'In a few minutes,' Tom replied. 'We've arranged to meet Pete as soon as it gets dark, and he'll take us to the boats. He says it's dangerous though and if any of us gets caught, we're not to mention him. He made us promise.'

'I swear I won't tell anyone,' Agnes promised earnestly.

What a stroke of good luck it was to have met these boys who turned out to be so eager to help her. She could only hope that all that they had said was true.

Darkness fell soon and together the children made their way along the beach, keeping close to the wall on the beach side where the long drop on that side hid them from view. The tide was coming in fast and eventually they were forced to climb back over the wall. The streets were dark and deserted and it was not long before they had moved away from houses again and reached a long stone quay stretching out into the sea as one side of the fishing harbour. A number of boats were tied up to this and already men were busy preparing nets and pots and ropes in readiness for their fishing trip on the high tide. A tall boy stepped quickly out of the shadows at the end of the quay and greeted them.

'Is this her?' He looked at her doubtfully, 'I thought you'd be older.' He paused and she said nothing, waiting in case he changed his mind. 'I know which boat it is. I heard them talking. And we're in luck because it's moored on its own, down on the beach. Are you sure you want to go through with this?'

'Quite sure,' Agnes assented, quietly.

'Okay. Listen you three, we've got to be really quick. Come with me.' He led them along the top of the beach in the shadows and out of sight of the fishermen on the quay. 'That's it. The sailing-boat down there.' He pointed to where three or four boats lay, on the shingle, the tide just lapping around them, but only one was uncovered and its sails furled. 'There won't be much room, you're going to have to keep very still for a very long time.' He looked at her sharply now, 'Look, I'm doing this for Matt, my cousin, and Tom, 'cos they're my best mates, but if you get caught and give me away …' his voice trailed off, the threat left unfinished, but clearly he was nervous.

'Don't worry,' Agnes assured him. 'If I did get caught, I would never mention any of you, I promise. I'd just say I found my own way into the boat. And boys, thank you. Thank you so much.' Her voice was firm and low, but Agnes was aware that her knees were trembling.

'Send us a postcard,' Tom joked, but Pete ignored him and urged everyone on.

'Quick now, they'll be loading up soon. You two, you've got to go and distract their attention while I get her into the boat. Go on down the quay and say something daft to them. You'll be good at that. You'll be in trouble with my dad for being there, but you'll just have to deal with it.'

There was no further time for goodbyes and with a quick wave as Agnes turned, Pete led her away towards the other side of the harbour, as the other two boys began to stroll along towards the men loading the bigger boats. He hurried her down onto the beach in the shadow of the far wall. This beach was sandy and they edged along in the shadows quickly. Fortunately the night was cloudy and there was little light from the moon. They were soon up beside the sailing-boat. It was a sizeable boat, with at one end, a large heap of fishing net stowed.

'This won't be used,' Pete whispered. 'At least, I hope not. You'll have to hide underneath it. It'll be pretty uncomfortable. Quick, I'll give you a leg up.'

He hoisted her over the side of the boat and lifted

some of the net as best he could. Agnes burrowed her way down as Pete rearranged it over her.

'Thank you,' she whispered again, 'and say thanks to the others.'

'Good luck,' he replied softly, and then he was gone.

With a little wriggling, Agnes succeeded in making herself reasonably comfortable, wedged as she was, between two layers of net. The thick rope it was made from was slightly damp and smelt strongly of salt and fish. It lay heavily on her, but she could breathe quite freely. It was not long before she heard voices and footsteps and movements began to take place around the boat which was by now rocking gently in a few feet of water.

A minute more and the men began to push the boat out into the sea, clambering aboard as it lifted and slid gracefully onto the water. Another vessel seemed, a minute or two later, to be beside them; she could hear the men as they shouted across to one another. There was a small engine in the boat despite its sails and soon this was started up and joined by the sounds of other, bigger boats; those, no doubt, which had been moored on the harbour wall. Agnes could hear nothing above the sound of the engine and the sea being calm, the motion was a gentle one. She lay awake for some time, glimpsing, through the layers of net, tiny pinpricks of starlight in the night sky above her, feeling a mixture of apprehension and excitement, until presently, lulled by the gentle movement of the boat and the even throb of the engine and despite a creeping stiffness in her limbs already, from her cramped position, Agnes fell asleep.

She did not wake till hours later as the noise of the engines stopped. It was suddenly very quiet, the only sounds being the lapping of the waves against the bows in which she lay, and a soft exchange of words between the men on board. She listened carefully. She thought she could distinguish three voices, one of them possibly French, but she could not catch their words. The sails were up and their movement seemed swift through the water. Agnes felt very stiff and uncomfortable now. She had pins and needles in the arm and leg she had been lying on and moved them carefully and with difficulty. She longed to lift her head and see where they were. Were they within sight of France? How long had they been out at sea? She had to resist. It was still dark, but the sky had cleared and she could just make out pinpricks of light in the dark which were stars, through the layers of net, but it was agonising not being able to move and sit up. She shifted her position carefully to try and make herself more comfortable again, wriggling her fingers and feet to try and dispel the pins and needles and lay looking up.

When the men finally lowered the sails, the darkness had begun to lose its intensity and the stars to fade.

They might still be some way off shore, Agnes thought, but would have to take great care not to be spotted by German look-outs. The men spoke very softly now and they appeared to be drifting. Within a few minutes though, there was a new sound, that of waves lapping on a beach or against rocks and one of the men came forward, throwing a long rope to waiting hands on the shore and the boat was soon secured.

What now? thought Agnes. How do I get out without being seen? They'll kill me if they see me. The boat rocked as men jumped from the boat, standing on the rim of the deck to reach an outstretched, helping hand from the shore. She had to risk lifting her head to look.

The boat was tied loosely to a rocky outcrop in a sheltered cove, still some way from the shore beyond. Dark trees clung onto the rocks almost to the water's edge and five men stood talking in hushed tones, above her and under the trees. There were the three from the boat and two others. The three from the boat had their backs to the boat and hid the other two from view. There was not a moment to lose. Agnes climbed out from among the nets and over the edge, hanging on until she dropped into the water on the side furthest from the men. It was a longer drop than she thought and there was a small splash as she entered the water and a gasp, which she could not suppress, as she felt the coldness hit her.

'What was that?' called one of the men sharply. There was a pause.

'It was nothing' said another, with a strong French accent, 'just a wave against the boat.'

Agnes breathed again and stayed quietly treading water by the side of the boat until she was sure they were not listening for unusual sounds any more. A little further out in the water, about fifty yards away, there was a rocky outcrop which offered some shelter. She struck out for this, keeping her head low in the water and moving her arms slowly and carefully to make no loud splashes. She was fully dressed and still wearing her coat and shoes which made her movements heavy and slow. In addition, she was already tired and chilled through, her limbs stiff and hard to move in the cold water. But fortunately the sea was calm with only a gentle swell which helped her movement towards the shore.

Little had she thought, when Eleanor had encouraged her to do a life saving course in London that it would ever be so useful. Briefly she recalled the test where she had had to swim, fully clothed, a length of the pool. But that was a heated pool and very different from the freezing cold sea in April. She was a strong swimmer, though small, however, and as she distanced herself from the boat she swam more quickly and was soon holding on to the far side of the rocks, well hidden and out of sight. If only the men did not stay talking for too long; she could not risk trying to get to the beach while they were still there. She would, undoubtedly be seen.

It was, however, some ten minutes at least before

the boat moved off and the two men still left ashore disappeared amongst the trees. Agnes was shivering violently by now. She swam, as swiftly as she could with numb hands and the heavy weight of her saturated woollen coat and shod feet towards the rocks where she might climb out. Mercifully within a few yards her trailing feet scraped shallow rocks and she half crawled, half swam the remaining distance, pulling herself up and out of the water with difficulty on the slippery rock and with weighted clothes. As soon as she could, she stumbled, crouching, over the rocks, finally standing to run towards the line of trees around the edge the cove. Her legs felt very weak and were shaking and her sodden shoes squelched. She fell twice before she reached their shelter. Here she took off the sodden coat. Water was running from it freely. She carefully removed the statuette, her toothbrush and the photograph. It was wet, but still intact and she put it carefully between two dried dead leaves so that she could carry it safely until she found somewhere to dry it out. The coat she abandoned; no amount of squeezing seemed to make it any drier.

The darkness had lifted to become an opaque grey as dawn approached. It was possible that the men had not gone far and Agnes edged cautiously from tree to tree. The woodland did not seem to be very deep, just a narrow strip along the edge of the beach. There was enough light to see a narrow road, no more than a cart track, just beyond the trees and on the other side of that the land rose gently onto open fields. Crouching down by the trunk of one of the larger trees she waited, watching for any movement along the road, then when she was quite sure that the men must have gone, she stepped out onto the track and started to walk, keeping closely to the woodland edge.

A clear day was dawning and soon, along the rutted track, there were trees in pale green leaf. Amidst the grass grew stray wild flowers, mainly poppies. It seemed so peaceful after war-torn London. As the road sloped downwards and Agnes rounded a bend, she could see a village, the steeple of its church rising up from the surrounding landscape. She continued to walk towards it, but more cautiously now. Something did not seem right. It was too quiet. There was no sign of life; no farmers making their way out to the fields nor dogs in the street; no smoke from the chimneys, no smell of baking bread as there might have been on any normal morning. As she drew close to the first houses, Agnes could see why. The majority of houses had been shelled and were ruined or pock marked. Roofs had fallen in, windows were all broken. People had left in a hurry; front doors were wide open, belongings were scattered in the street or in the gardens before the houses. A long dead dog lay in the street, its skin draped over a skeleton frame. Agnes turned her head away and hurried past. It was as well for her that no-one was watching; her wet clothes clung to her and she was still shivering violently, her teeth chattering.

Despite the small size of the village there was a station for the railway line which ran through the fields nearby and curved away towards the coast. It was no more than a one-roomed office and a platform and, like the rest of the village, it was deserted.

She needed somewhere to dry out her clothes. A hundred yards beyond the station, a farm marked the outer edge of the village. There was a yard with a big barn and a door high above it onto the hay loft. The house seemed relatively undamaged and the door here too, stood ajar. As she stepped in, two chickens brushed her ankles with a squawk, as startled as she was.

She found herself in a large kitchen. It was dark and it took several moments for her eyes to adjust. A large dresser and a long oak table dominated the room which might still have been lived in. There were dried flowers and herbs hanging from the rafters, a kettle on an old fashioned hob and the table was set at one end with two plates and knives. But looking more closely, a fine layer of dust lay over everything on the table; a plate of what had been butter, but had turned green and black with mould, sat between the plates, with a pot of jam and a basket of hard, dried bread. The fire in the hob had long since gone out and the cooker was cold.

A door from the kitchen opened into a larder. Clearly much had been taken, but on the floor was a row of jars. She lifted one into the light from the kitchen door. Peaches! As light shone through the amber colour of the syrup surrounding the tightly packed peach halves. Agnes' mouth watered. She had not realised how hungry she was until that moment. She soon found a drawer with spoons and other cutlery and lifting the catch, she prised the airtight lid open, till it gave way with a soft hiss. She lifted out the first peach half, bit into it from the spoon. A delicious explosion of sweet fruit filled her mouth. It was so long since Agnes had eaten a peach that she could hardly remember the taste. But these were extra sweet with the syrup which had preserved them, soft, yet firm enough to bite into. The juices ran down her cheeks, but hungrily Agnes went on devouring the delicious golden fruits until she had eaten more than half the contents of the jar.

Upstairs there were three rooms, all with large and high wooden beds. There were further signs that people had left in a hurry; open drawers with clothes spilling out where others had been hastily taken and a bed unmade. She pulled off her wet clothes hanging them over a chair and over the metal foot of a bed. In a drawer she found a large cotton shirt which she put on. She felt overwhelming tired and giggled suddenly, nervously, in the silence, remembering Goldilocks. She chose the largest of the beds, climbing onto it and pulling the folded quilt up and over her head to shut out the light. She had slept very little for several nights past and the comfort of the bed and her weariness soon overwhelmed her and she slept deeply.

If there was any life in the village, or any passing

traffic on the road that day, Agnes heard nothing, for it was early evening when she awoke. Though her shoes were still damp, her clothes were nearly dry, but the woollen dress seemed to have shrunk and grown stiff from the sea water. After further searching in the chests of drawers she found a skirt to add to the shirt she had already taken. It came almost to her ankles and was too large around the waist, but there were some safety pins on the dresser. It would have to do. She stepped out into the yard. It was eerily silent and empty – no sign even of the chickens, but a pitiful mewing came from behind the shut door of the barn. Agnes opened it and a small tabby cat pushed quickly between her legs, then turned and rubbed itself against her ankles, mewing vigorously. The cat was very thin and bony. Agnes bent to stroke it but it darted away, back into the barn, then stopped a yard or two from the door and looked back. It seemed to want Agnes to follow. She ran quickly into a far corner of the barn where the floor was covered by loose straw. As Agnes followed, she already had an inkling of what she might find. Nestled among the straw were four kittens, their eyes still shut and their tiny bodies covered by a soft down. Another, smaller kitten lay some way off. It was dead. It had either wandered away and died, not being able to find its way back, or its mother had moved it from the nest after it had died. The four remaining kittens latched onto the mother's teats, but she clearly had no milk left to give them. She herself was starving. She must have been shut into the barn and unable even to get out to forage since she had had the kittens. She mewed continuously, watching Agnes intently, with a mixture of suspicion and desperation. Gently, Agnes bent down and picked up the dead one. She would take him out and bury him where he would no longer distress the mother and then find the cat something to eat.

In the pantry, she had noticed some tins of meat. She took one of these now and chopped the meat onto a plate, carrying it back into the barn. The cat wolfed it down quickly, allowing Agnes to stroke her and the kittens, as she ate. Agnes knew she must not give the cat too much food at once or she would be sick, not having eaten for so long, but she would feed her again in the morning, and leave the barn door ajar so that she could get in and out. It was the cat that had made her decide to stay that night. She could have tried to travel in the safety of darkness, but she would wait and feed the cat again and try to find out a little more about where she was, tomorrow.

In the event, Agnes stayed for four nights. When she awoke the following morning, heavy rain was beating against the window. It was the first day, she reflected, that she had ever woken up in an empty house, with nobody to talk to. A great rush of loneliness and longing for Eleanor washed over her. But she got up quickly, brushing the tears briskly from her cheeks. There were the cats to look after.

Outside, the yard had turned to mud. She stepped quickly and carefully across to see the cat, picking her way between the puddles and runnels of soft mud. It ran to meet her, rubbing itself against her legs and mewing. Agnes tipped more meat onto the plate and the cat ate it quickly again, crouched in front of it with her bony shoulders hunched and her ribs showing as dark shadowed stripes. For herself, Agnes had found a jar of white haricot beans which had been cooked with tomatoes and garlic and herbs. She ate them cold having no means of lighting the wood in the range cooker and being afraid that any smoke might attract attention. Between the beans and the peaches she ate till she was full. So did the cat. By the afternoon the rain had stopped and a watery sun came out, but there was a cold wind from the sea. Agnes stayed in bed, reading old magazines that she had found in a pile downstairs, and sleeping. She fed the cat three times a day till she lost the desperate look that she had had at the beginning and the kittens seemed to be feeding more successfully from their mother, sleeping soundly in between and she spent several hours each day with them, nestled into the straw beside them.

On the fourth afternoon, she ventured out into the village. Perhaps, she thought, she could stay here for the rest of the war, then move south to find her grandparents. There was food here, enough, in the farmhouse to last her several weeks and no doubt there would be more in the other houses. She had a comfortable bed to sleep in and was warm. Most importantly, there was no-one around to ask her questions.

But it was strange having no-one but the cats to talk to all day and the village felt lonely and sinister. The dead dog was still lying in the street and doors banged in the wind. People had clearly left in a hurry, but why? Where had they gone? What had happened to them and why had they taken so little with them?

By the time she returned to the farmhouse, she had already decided that she ought to leave the next morning, but it was her first encounter with the German army that decided it.

She was tucked into the bed of the room which she had made her camp when she heard a distant rhythmical tramping sound which rapidly drew closer becoming, quite clearly, the heavy marching feet of a group of soldiers. Quickly, Agnes got off the bed and looked carefully from the window. The view was partly obscured by a tree near the entrance to the yard, but she could see the men as they passed, twenty or thirty German soldiers, heading into the village. As the sound of their boots passed and grew more distant, another sound could be heard; the engine of a car approaching and drawing up outside the farm. From the window Agnes could just see the front end of a large, black car flying a small red and black flag. Presently two men came into view. Their uniforms were grey and they wore peaked caps and high black boots, above which their trousers puffed out like riding jodhpurs. There was no doubt that they were German officers.

They talked for a moment in the road then one of them walked away, towards the centre of the village, the other turned and came into the yard. He was coming into the house! Agnes looked around quickly. There was nowhere to hide in this room. There was a large wardrobe in another room but to get there she would have to run across the hall and could be seen from the bottom of the stairs. Besides, both the floorboards and the wardrobe door would creak. She pressed herself against the wall behind the open door of the bedroom. The bed was unmade and rumpled where she had just climbed out of it, warm even, but it was too late to do anything about it now.

She had shut the door from the yard into the kitchen, but it rattled as the officer opened it. It stuck slightly, dragging on the step. There was a pause, then she heard the heavy tread of polished boots crossing the kitchen floor. The metal soles clicked loudly on the stone and then scraped once as he turned to the foot of the stairs. He started to climb the stairs, his boots loud on the bare floorboards. Agnes pressed herself more closely yet to the wall, her heart was beating so hard she was afraid he would hear it. She felt at any moment that she might cry out or be sick with fear and held her hands to her mouth.

Before he reached the top of the steps however, there came the unaccustomed sound of a train approaching and passing through the village on the nearby railway line. It was the first she had heard in her four days here. It slowed, evidently pulling into the little station. The officer stopped. From the step where he stood, he could see onto the landing and through the open doors of the three bedrooms. He paused. The moment seemed interminable to Agnes. Then he turned and clattered down the stairs and back out into the yard. Agnes moved quickly to the window and watched as the other officer also reappeared by the car. The car drew slowly past the front gate of the yard. There was a driver in the front and the two officers sat in the back, clearly visible as the roof of the car was down. It took long minutes before her racing heart slowed and a few minutes more till she heard the sound of the train pulling away from the station and growing more distant.

It was dangerous to stay. Others could be back at any moment. Perhaps the Germans were here to find places for their men to stay. A whole empty village near the sea might be an ideal place. Perhaps they used the railway line regularly. Agnes knew she must leave as soon as possible. She waited till it was dark, creeping out to feed the cat once more, an especially large portion which it did not manage to finish. She left the barn door slightly ajar so the cat could get in and out. It would have to catch mice from now on.

When she left, she took with her a shawl and a little cloth bag which she had found hanging on a chair in one of the bedrooms. She had wondered about the people whose home it was – an elderly couple she felt, farmers of course. She hoped that the motherly housewife who had so carefully prepared her jars of beans and peaches for the winter month would not mind that she had eaten some and taken the shawl and the bag. Perhaps one day she would come back and thank them. Perhaps. She took the wooden statuette and the photo which had both dried out and tucked them into the bag. Wrapping the shawl around her shoulders, she then tied Dilly's scarf around her head, knotting it under her chin. She looked in the mirror. With her dark eyes and hair, she could easily be mistaken for a little French country girl. Her face was thinner too and there were shadows under her eyes. She turned away from the mirror towards the dark staircase, stepping out into the night.

Chapter 5

Thief!

All my past life is mine no more;
The flying hours are gone
Like transitory dreams given o'er
Whose images are kept in store
By memory alone.
Love and Life *John Wilmot, Earl of Rochester*

Agnes walked for hours along the dark roads. There was just enough light from the moon, which dipped at intervals behind clouds, to see her way. She passed through another village, which also appeared to be empty and then another which was not. She heard the sound of laughter and loud voices, German voices, whose words she could not understand came from a café on the street just ahead of her. Light spilled out onto the pavement where a man in uniform talked with a girl and tried to kiss her. She pushed him away and he laughed, but still held onto her. Agnes turned quickly, back the way she had come till she could cut across the empty fields to skirt the village. From this village there was nothing for a long way and finally, tired from walking for hours, she dozed under some trees a little way from the road's edge.

It grew light early and, rubbing her face and her eyes into wakefulness, she stood up, stepping back onto the road and walked on. At length, a car passed going at speed; it was another black car like the one she had seen outside the farm house, this one enclosed, the occupants hidden. A little while later, a box shaped French car passed more slowly, bumping on the ruts of the road. It contained four nuns, who turned and waved at her. She lifted her hand to respond, uncertainly. At length, she heard the clopping of a horse and the roll of cart wheels approaching from behind. An old man sat on the bench in front of the cart, holding the reins of a great carthorse wearing heavy blinkers, who also seemed old and in no particular hurry. The cart was moving at little more than a walking pace and the old man called down to her as her passed.

'*Bonjour, Mademoiselle*. Where are you headed?'

Agnes said nothing for a moment, phrasing her reply carefully before she spoke. She could speak French fluently, but was conscious that this was the first time she had spoken it in France. She wondered if she would have a detectable English accent and whether she would make any obvious mistakes.

'I am going to the nearest town,' she said at length.

The man did not appear to notice anything out of the ordinary about her though. He merely remarked, 'I'm going that way myself. Off to the market are you? I'll give you a ride.'

Stopping his horse, he reached down to give her a hand and settled her on the bench beside him. Looking over her shoulder, Agnes saw that the cart was full of wooden crates of vegetables and wicker baskets with lids containing chickens.

'That was lucky,' the old man chattered on. 'You would have had a long walk. But there's no hurry, eh? Here, have some bread.' He reached into a canvas bag at his feet and brought out a baguette. He broke a large chunk from it and passed it to her. It was still warm to the touch, the outside of it crisp and golden, the inside soft and light as she bit into it. It was delicious. 'My son is the baker, back there,' he gestured with his thumb back the way they had come and named the village. 'We're lucky to have him, my wife and I. Good bread's hard to get nowadays.'

'Mmm. It's delicious. Thank you,' she said, eating hungrily.

'Eh, you're hungry,' the old man spoke as he chewed. He glanced at her sidelong. 'You're not from round here are you? Where are you trying to get to?'

'I, er, I'm looking for my grandparents. I thought I would find them here. We used to come here for holidays.' She couldn't help but feel that it sounded lame, making the story up as she went along, all the while thinking carefully about her French, but the old man didn't seem to notice.

'Ah, yes. So many people have gone missing. So many have had to leave their homes. No-one knows where anyone is any more.'

There was a silence, the old man seemed sunk in thought as he watched the road ahead, twitching the reins occasionally.

'I thought … I mean, if I could get to a railway station, I might be able to get a train to where my grandparents have gone. Is there a station in the town we're going to?'

'Yes, there's a station. But there aren't many trains. It depends, where do you think you will find them?'

'They are in the south … I think. That's where they live. In Provence.'

'In the south! Ah, you won't get there. There are no trains south, not that I know about,' the old man exclaimed. 'No, child, you will have to wait till this war is over. Some more bread?'

The old man did not seem too concerned with her plight and Agnes was grateful that he did not continue to ask awkward questions. Certainly he seemed to have no inkling that she wasn't entirely French. The old clothes she was wearing must help. She tucked her feet under the bench. Her English buckled sandals still looked rather smart and out of place. Besides, as the man said, the war had disrupted so many lives in France, that finding a child alone on the road did not seem as strange as once it might have done. From here, he chatted about his vegetables, grumbling at what a poor growing season it had been with all the rain they'd had, how difficult it was to find enough meat in many of the towns, since the German army was taking so much of the local produce and how hard it was for people with so little to eat and so little money to spend in the market.

They had soon drawn up in the market square, where other stalls were being set up. The old man climbed down and pointed up the street ahead.

'The railway station is there. You could ask.'

'Thank you, *Monsieur*. Do you want some help?' Agnes felt that it would seem ungrateful just to walk off and leave him as he set up his stall.

'If you like,' he answered, unlatching and lowering the side of the cart. 'Push those boxes of vegetables over here, will you? And the chickens, hand them down to me. Thank you.'

A woman with a shopping basket had appeared beside the cart.

'*Bonjour, Monsieur Rachet*. I've been waiting for you. You're later than usual. Did you sleep in?'

'Sleep in? Small chance of that,' the old man grumbled.

'Who's the little girl?' the woman asked, gesturing to Agnes and giving her a quick nod.

'Oh, just someone I picked up walking on the road. She wants to go to the railway station.'

'Oh yes?' the woman was curious. 'Where are you off to? Are you on your own?'

Agnes felt uncomfortable under the woman's scrutiny, but as she hesitated, the old man answered for her.

'She wants to get to her grandparents in the south. So she needs to get on a train.'

'To the south?' the woman exclaimed. 'There are no trains south, besides, even if there were, they would not go from here. No, you would certainly have to go into Paris first and then to another station. Where are your parents, child? Are you ...' she hesitated for the first time.

'Is she an orphan?' she asked the old man, though without lowering her voice.

'Yes, it seems so. I don't know.'

'You poor thing,' the woman turned back to Agnes, who had by now jumped down from the back of the cart and was looking for an opportunity to leave quietly without arousing suspicion. 'Perhaps I should take you to the Police Station, the Gendarmerie. They will help you. Maybe you will have to stay in an orphanage until they can get you to the south. At the moment, I think it would be impossible.'

Agnes felt a rising sense of panic.

'Oh, but you don't understand,' she said, thinking quickly. 'My aunt and uncle are in Paris. If I can just get there, they will look after me until they can send me south.'

'Oh, you have family in Paris too! Why didn't you say so?' the woman exclaimed. 'I am sure we can get you to Paris. Do you have any money for a train?'

Agnes' face fell at this question. It was difficult to hide the fact that she had no money.

'No, I expect you don't,' the woman continued, correctly interpreting Agnes' silence. 'Besides, there are people here, tradesmen who have to travel into Paris. Come with me. I will find someone who can take you there.'

'Really? Is it possible?' Agnes' heart lifted at this and for the first time, she was grateful for the woman's interest in her.

By now, the old man was serving another customer and as she left, Agnes waved to him and thanked him again.

'I'll be back in a few minutes for my vegetables,' the woman called back to him. She led Agnes through the market, calling '*Bonjour*' to several people on the way, until they came to a seller of cheeses on the other side of the town square.

There were no customers at his stall for the moment and the woman stepped up to him, while Agnes lingered behind. They were soon engaged in a heated conversation. She found it hard to follow, they were speaking quickly and in low voices.

'*Ah, non*!' she heard the man say. She stepped forward.

'Please don't bother about me,' she said , addressing

107

the woman, 'I can find another way of getting there if it's too much trouble.'

'Nonsense,' the woman put an arm around Agnes' shoulder and turned back to the cheese seller.

'Claude, I knew your father when I was young. He was a good man and kind and would never have refused to help a child in trouble. What would he think now, if he knew you were selling your cheeses to the restaurants in Paris for all the Germans to eat up?'

At this the man grew silent, looking both embarrassed and angry. He shrugged his shoulders, avoiding looking at either of them.

'Very well,' he muttered. 'I'll take her. Have you got identity papers?' He looked now at Agnes.

'Papers? I … no,' she stammered, 'I … I've lost them.'

'You see, she has no papers,' the cheese seller looked triumphantly at the woman, as if to say that his reluctance to take Agnes to Paris had been vindicated. 'What if we are stopped?'

'You won't be stopped,' the woman responded sharply. 'The Germans must know your van well enough.'

This remark seemed to finish the argument and it was arranged that Agnes would wait, sitting on a wall near the cheese seller till the end of the morning. The woman left, only to return a few minutes later with a roll of bread, to which at her insistence, the cheese seller added a hunk of cheese. She kissed Agnes on the forehead then.

'Goodbye, child. Good luck,' she said. She turned and waved briefly before disappearing into the now crowded market.

The morning wore on and at length, the crowds began to thin and the stall holders to pack up their remaining produce. The cheese seller loaded his trays of cheeses into the van and then gestured to Agnes to climb into the passenger seat.

He said nothing as they made their way out of the town and onto a main road, but eventually he asked 'Where in Paris do you want to go? Do you have an address?'

'I, um ... that is, I will recognise the street and the house when I see it, but I do not have an address. I know it is near the big station, the one where the trains leave to go south. If you can just take me there, I will be able to find my way.'

He glanced at her curiously. 'There are several big stations in Paris, but I suppose you mean the Gare de Lyon. Well, I will see what I can do.'

He retreated into silence and they drove for some time. Agnes began to doze, with her head against the window. Cars always made her sleepy. Some two hours later, she woke with a jolt as the van came to a halt.

The cheese seller had pulled over to the side of the road. There was a queue of cars and lorries ahead.

'Look,' he muttered. 'There is a road block. I cannot take you any further since you have no papers. I am sorry, but I cannot afford to get into any trouble. You will find another way. We are not far from Paris now.' As he spoke, he reached over and pulled the handle to open Agnes' door. 'You must get out. Now. Quickly.'

Glancing ahead, Agnes could see a German soldier walking down the line of cars in the road, peering into them as he passed. She jumped out and an instant later the cheese seller had pulled the door shut after her and moved out into the road, joining the queue. Agnes started walking swiftly in the opposite direction, keeping to the verge. Fifty yards or so back, there was a larger van parked on the verge. Nobody was in the cabin and walking around it, Agnes tried the handle of the two doors at the back. They were not locked and as they opened, she saw that it was loaded with wooden crates. They were crates of wine by the look of them. She had seen boxes like these delivered to her grandmother, Eleanor. She saw, briefly, names written on the side, *Chateau du* ... but there was no time to hesitate, she jumped in, squeezing herself into the small space between layers of boxes and with difficulty, tugging the doors shut behind her. As she struggled back through the boxes, to be better hidden, she felt the van jolt slightly as the driver returned and climbed into the cabin, slamming the door and starting the engine instantly. He pulled out into the road, but then immediately, Agnes felt the van turning as if crossing the road and pulling away. Away from the queue of cars, away from the direction of Paris.

She had a moment of panic, but then she thought, no, perhaps he was just taking another route to avoid the road block. At any rate, there was nothing she could do now, not till they stopped again. She squashed herself down as the van gathered speed, to sit on the hard floor, hemmed in on either side by crates.

Hours seemed to pass and this time Agnes could not sleep despite the fact that she was in darkness. Eventually the van slowed and made a series of turns and Agnes could hear different traffic noises, as if they were in a town. She stood up, feeling bruised and stiff and began to edge her way to the doors at the back. She might have to jump out and run for it, if she could not open the doors before the driver got there.

When the van finally stopped however, the cabin door slammed and the sound of the driver's footsteps seemed to draw away. Agnes pulled on the catch, pushing as she did so, on the doors. They burst open, sending Agnes tumbling out onto the street. Quickly she got up, rubbing a grazed hand and pushed the doors shut again, before walking swiftly away.

She found herself in a quiet, deserted side street. The van had stopped outside a wine shop and apart from this, she could see a small grocery shop and where the road seemed to join a main thoroughfare, a café on the corner. She walked in this direction, hearing the sounds of traffic and movement and found herself on a road which formed one side of a large square. An imposing building dominated the square on another side. It had wide stairs leading up to an entrance which was bordered by thick rounded stone pillars. Carved on the architrave above the pillars were the words '*Mairie de la Ville de Reims*'. Reims. Agnes recognised the name. It was a town, Eleanor had told her where champagne came from. She remembered the conversation because she had seen it on labels sometimes, on bottles of champagne and she had asked how to pronounce it. The English often pronounce it 'Reams' Eleanor had said, while to the French it sounded more like 'Rance'. '*Mairie*', as Agnes knew, meant town hall. The town hall of Reims. Then she was not in Paris at all! She tried hard to remember where the town was on the map of Paris. Was she closer, or further away, she wondered, from her grandparents? It was a large town, however and perhaps that meant it would have a big railway station. Maybe she should just stay here and perhaps she could run errands for shop keepers till she had earned enough money to buy a ticket.

It was all so hard. She wandered across the square towards the Mairie. On either side of the pillars, the façade was adorned with a long red banner, marked in black with the distinctive sign of the Nazi swastika, which hung like a giant spider. As she drew closer, she saw that there were German soldiers guarding the entrance and turned away, crossing the square to another street. The light was fading, but she could see that the buildings around the square were tall and formal and made of a pale creamy stone. There were decorative metal balconies on some of the upper stories and around the square the globes of street lamps were flickering into life, like soft, pale moons hung from ornate metal poles.

Few people were about, only some German soldiers and Agnes, deciding that it would be better to get out of their sight quickly, left the square, skirting around the town hall. To her surprise, a vast cathedral rose before her, almost immediately behind the town hall. She circled it, looking in wonder at the carved statues of saints in niches on the walls and the gargoyles which leered out from high above. She walked on, into smaller streets. Her stomach gnawed at her with hunger and she felt immensely weary. She had hardly slept last night and her short doze in the cheese seller's van had done little to rest her. Where could she sleep? She thought of the tramps she had seen in London sleeping on the pavements or in doorways, wrapped in blankets. She did not even have a blanket, but soon she found a quiet doorway down a side street in which there was no sign of life. It offered some shelter, however inadequate, as the sky had clouded over and it was beginning to rain. She sat with her knees drawn up and her head resting on them, her back against the wall and with her little bag tucked in against her stomach to keep it dry. In the morning she would leave at first light and try to find the railway station and then go and look for a way to earn some money. If only she had stayed at the farmhouse. She could have hidden in the barn whenever the Germans came. But perhaps the war would not go on too much longer.

She was to have little rest. Within a few hours, the rain had grown heavy and a wind got up, which swirled around the little streets, blowing rain into her doorway. Agnes was soon wet through and shivering. She stood up and walked through the rain, looking for better shelter, but the next one she found was little improvement and she could not sleep.

By dawn, exhausted, she had made her way back to the square where already vans were beginning to arrive and a market to set up. Quite soon, women and old men with baskets began to arrive and form queues at the stalls. Pangs of hunger gnawed viciously at her stomach and she felt nauseous and dizzy. She hated the idea of stealing bread again, but it was that, or begging and she did not want to draw attention to herself. She would have to be quick. There was a long queue at the baker's stall but the stall holder was busy with customers. She wandered up to the stall as if she was choosing from the array of baguettes, large round loaves and smaller buns and pastries and in a moment when he seemed most engrossed in conversation and with her back to the queue, she reached out her hand to a small bun. The instant she did so, a hand reached from behind her and seized her wrist in a vice like grip. Agnes let the bun drop. She had not noticed the stall holder's wife approach from another direction.

'Thief,' she screamed gripping her still tighter as

Agnes twisted and pulled to free herself. The woman turned away from the stall dragging Agnes down the line of stalls. She was still shouting, 'Thief, dirty little thief!' and Agnes was aware that everyone's eyes were on her. Not far away there was a policeman checking the stall holders' permits. Agnes pulled and struggled against her, but the woman was very strong.

Her fate was sealed.

The young gendarme had a kindly face. He held her by the wrist in case she tried to escape, but he said, 'We had better go and sort you out at the police station. Come with me.'

To her astonishment, the gendarme stopped in a bakery, pushing Agnes gently in front of him to keep her there, and bought her a brioche, a soft sweet bun. She ate it ravenously and thanked him profusely.

'If you were trying to steal bread, you were obviously hungry,' he shrugged, 'but still we have things to talk about.'

At the police station, a sour-looking secretary sat behind a desk, but nobody else seemed to be there. The gendarme took her into an office and sat her down, pulling up a chair to sit opposite her. He did not seem surprised that she had no papers, but asked if she had run away from home or if she had just got lost. Agnes explained as much as seemed safe. She was an orphan. She was trying to reach her grandparents in the south, near a place called Carpentras. In answer to his questions, she fumbled vague responses. Her parents had both died of an illness. She had stayed in their farmhouse on her own until the Germans had come. Now she just wanted to reach her grandparents.

He had taken his peaked hat off and looked even younger. He could have been her big brother, Agnes thought.

'Look,' he said, 'it will really not be easy for you to go south on your own at the moment. You have no papers and no proof of your grandparents' existence and the Germans would soon arrest you. If I write out a report and hand you over to the authorities, you will certainly be put in an orphanage and it will be very hard to contact your family.'

'But I can't go to an orphanage!' Agnes burst in. It was just what she had left England to avoid.

'Wait a moment,' the gendarme held up his hand, 'I know some people who I think will look after you. They already have some other children with them and I think they will do their best to help you. I shouldn't do this, but I'd like to help you and it would be better this way than your being registered an orphan.'

Agnes felt a wave of defeat wash over her and then a surprising sense of relief. Now the decisions had been taken out of her hands and if what the gendarme said was true, people might be able to help her.

'Where are they, the people with the children?' she asked.

'They are nuns. They have a convent just outside

the village where I live. You must wait here for an hour and then I will go home for lunch and take you with me. Perhaps you would like to have a sleep.' He gestured to an old leather armchair in the corner of the room and Agnes had no sooner curled into it than she was sound asleep.

Chapter 6

David

Here in the country's heart
Where the grass is green
Life is the same sweet life
As it e'er hath been
The Country Faith *Norman Gale*

They left the town, in an elderly box of a car, crossing a large river and were soon out into the countryside. There were fields and fields of vines on gentle slopes, with new green leaves creating a bright green haze along the rows. Here and there, Agnes spotted a large house, or chateau, perched on a hill, partly obscured by trees. A cross and an icon of Saint Christopher dangled from the rear view mirror of the car, swinging in front of the landscape as they drove. After several miles of empty, narrow roads, they drew into a village and slowly beyond it to pull up outside a pair of wrought iron gates set into a low wall topped by railings.

Beyond them was a short drive on either side of which stood large, leafy trees before the convent. It was a big, plain house in pale stone with rows of windows whose shutters were open and clipped back against the wall.

In answer to the gendarme's tugging on a bell by the gate, an elderly nun soon emerged. After brief words, she led them both into the building and to the Mother Superior's office. She too was not young, her face was gentle, but care-worn and tired. She rose and greeted the gendarme by name.

He explained briefly why he had come.

'I know that you have other children here, Mother Superior. Please take one more in. I do not trust her chances if the authorities get hold of her.'

'Philippe, you are not supposed to know that we are sheltering children here, though I know I can trust you personally. However, I do not know how long they will be safe here either.'

'But Mother Superior, this one is not …'

'I see that,' she interrupted before he could finish, 'but all the same …'

Not what? Agnes wondered, but the nun sighed and said, 'Oh well, she will be no worse off here than anywhere else, for the time being. But you must promise me, Philippe, that you will not say a word, not to anyone in the village, not even to your parents.'

He reassured her of his discretion, but added, 'It is known, in the village, that there are children here. You must realise that.'

'Of course I do,' the Mother Superior agreed, 'and some people have been very kind. They have bought us things for the children. But not everyone is trustworthy.'

Shortly after this, the gendarme left, wishing Agnes good luck in finding her grandparents and she was led by the Mother Superior along to a large dining hall. She had said little, except to respond to one or two questions as she was feeling shivery and a little feverish. She had been chilled through and wet during most of that night and had had little sleep in two days.

The spacious dining room was full of the chatter of children, who were eating with some of the nuns, at three long tables. They grew quiet as the Mother Superior came in and Agnes felt all their eyes upon her.

'This is Agnes, children,' the Mother Superior introduced her. 'She has come to stay with us. Sister Marie, would you give Agnes something to eat. She does not look very well. Take her upstairs afterwards and let her have a sleep.'

Sister Marie rose and came forward. It was the elderly nun who had opened the gate to them. She looked into Agnes' face, then put a hand to her forehead.

'You look feverish child, and your head is hot. Come and have a bowl of soup and then I will find you a bed.'

As Agnes ate her soup, she looked around. There were about thirty children in the room, most of them quite young, though a few looked her age and there was one who seemed a few years older than the rest. The Mother Superior sat down beside him to eat and they were soon deep in conversation.

After lunch, Sister Marie took her to a little room with three beds in it. Two were already made and clearly being used and the nun busied herself fetching sheets and blankets for the third. Agnes did her best to help her make the bed, but was shivering violently by now, with an aching head and she put up no resistance as the nun helped her take off most of her clothes and climb into bed. She was asleep almost instantly.

She slept throughout the rest of the day and as night fell, she was conscious of two girls who came in and prepared for bed, whispering and tiptoeing quietly around the room before climbing into their beds. In the morning, she woke feeling much better and said hello to the girls who smiled at her and said they hoped she would feel better soon. But Sister Marie insisted she stayed in bed that day and another, younger nun soon appeared with hot milk and bread with jam for breakfast.

'We have our own cows here,' she told Agnes, 'so this is fresh milk and home-made butter. When you are better you can come and help in the dairy. The children are taking it in turns to churn the butter.'

By the afternoon, Agnes was feeling much better and sitting up in bed. Sister Marie appeared at the door and behind her the tall boy she had seen in the dining room.

'I have brought David to meet you, my dear,' she said. 'David is the eldest here and has been a great help to us. He was anxious to meet you.' David came in.

'Do you mind if I come in and have a little chat? Are you feeling better?'

Sister Marie left them, 'I will just be tidying the linen cupboard down the hall if you want me,' she said as she went.

Agnes smiled and moved her legs so that David could sit down on the edge of her bed near the end. He was tall and dark, his face serious in repose, but with a twinkle that lifted his dark eyes readily and a crooked, good humoured smile. His voice was calm and gentle and there was an air of authority about him which made him seem even older than he was.

'Sister Marie has spoken to me about you, Agnes. She wanted me to come and have a quiet word with you.' He paused and Agnes looked puzzled, saying nothing, so he went on, 'When you fell asleep yesterday afternoon, you were feverish and Sister Marie came and sat with you for some time.'

'Did she? I didn't know anyone was here.'

'She is very kind and caring. They have all been good to us, but some of the nuns find it harder to be with children all the time. Sister Marie has endless patience. They are all used to a quiet and sheltered life, however and we have brought them many problems, some of which they don't know how to deal with. That is why they talk to me about things. I try to take some of the burden of responsibility from them.'

Agnes felt that he had not yet reached the point of his visit, so she waited as he paused, until he was ready to continue.

'You were talking in your sleep, Agnes, talking in English, and so much and so fluently, that she is sure you are English, or partly so. Is this true?'

Agnes flushed, 'Yes,' she said quietly.

'That means you are as much in danger here as we are.'

'As you are?' she queried. 'I don't understand. Why are you all here?'

'All the children here are Jewish, Agnes. Do you know what that means?'

'Well, I know that it means you go to synagogues instead of churches. There was one in London.'

David shook his head, 'Yes, but I meant, do you know what it means in terms of our position in France at this time?'

Agnes shook her head, 'No, I don't understand.'

David sighed and as if gathering his thoughts he paused before he continued in a sad voice, but with a touch of anger in it now as well, 'All over Europe, the Nazis are persecuting Jewish people. They are throwing them out of their jobs and seizing their homes, for Germans to move into. It seems they herd the Jewish families into sections of a city which they then wall up and call a ghetto. There they are guarded and their lives controlled.'

'I didn't know,' Agnes said, very quietly and David continued.

'It is not openly admitted but I had heard my parents speak of it for some time past. Then more recently, there was talk of Jewish people being sent to prison camps far away, on the eastern side of Germany or in Poland. They are taken away on trains and are not heard from again.'

'But I still don't really understand,' Agnes interrupted, 'do you mean this is happening in France? Is that where all your parents …?' Her question was left unfinished as she saw the look of anguish cross David's face.

'We do not know where our parents are.' David's voice was even quieter now. 'We used all to live in Paris. One day I arrived at school late, as I had been to the dentist. When I got there, the yard was full of Nazis. The children were being divided up into small groups. All my friends had already been taken, they had gone, so I was put into a group with some younger children, the ones who are here. We were all taken away. My group were lodged in a house belonging to a woman who had nothing to do with the Germans or with us. We were just forced upon her as she had space in the house. She tried her best to feed us and care for us, but she resented us too. I tried to get news of all our parents, but there was nothing. The Germans told us that they had all been taken to Germany, to work there, "to assist the war efforts of the Third Reich". Of course we cannot believe them. Somehow my parents would have got word to me if they were safe and my older sister too. She disappeared at the same time.' He paused again before he said, 'No, I am afraid sometimes, that we may never see our families again.'

'But that can't be true!' Agnes exclaimed passionately. 'It's too horrible to be true. Why would the Germans do such a thing to innocent people?'

'You are right, Agnes, it is too horrible and I cannot tell you why. It makes no sense to me either.'

He said nothing more for a long moment, his head down and his gaze fixed on the floor.

'I'm so sorry,' Agnes said softly. Then after a pause she added, 'How do you all come to be here?'

David drew himself up again and managed a weak smile at her.

'My parents had … have … a good friend who is a Catholic priest. You may think this strange, but my parents are very liberal. They are both doctors and they frequently worked with Monsignor Laurence giving voluntary care in some of the hospitals and homes of those who could not afford to pay for medical treatment. When my parents and my sister disappeared, Monsignor Laurence found out where I was and did his best to make our lives more comfortable. In Paris, we were all kept in two rooms and could not go outside. It was very unhealthy. Besides this, he was constantly afraid that the Nazis would come back for us. Eventually he smuggled us out of Paris in a lorry and brought us here. He has risked his life to help us. The nuns too, are perhaps risking their lives. Do you understand, Agnes?'

'I think so,' she nodded. 'And me, being English is just as bad for them, isn't it?'

'Sister Marie thinks we should not tell any of the others, not even the nuns. We will just have to hope you don't talk in your sleep any more.' He smiled at her. She liked the way one side of his mouth went up more than the other when he smiled. 'Perhaps you will tell me now how you come to be here.'

Agnes told him her story as best as she could. He listened attentively and sometimes he interrupted her to ask a question, to clarify a point or fill in some detail she had missed. When she had finished he said gently, 'You should never have come to France, Agnes. It has been divided in more ways than one by the Nazis. Nothing is the same as it was before and there are many French people who cannot be trusted. It will not be easy to find your grandparents either, I suspect, but we will talk to Monsignor Laurence the next time he visits us and see what he can do to help.'

He put his hand, which was large and strong, over hers lying on the cover and gave it a gentle squeeze.

'You have had a great deal to suffer and I am happy fate brought you here, despite the dangers.' He was quiet for a moment, then added, 'My parents loved going to London. We could all speak English in our household, as well as Hebrew and even some German. In fact, the last birthday present my parents gave me was an English book, *The Oxford Book of English Verse*. Do you know it?'

Agnes shook her head.

'By chance, I had it with me the day I was arrested. I had taken it into school to show my teacher of English who had asked if he could see it. I will show it to you sometime, when no one else is about, of course.'

'Thank you, I'd love to see it.'

David's voice was brighter as he changed the subject and told her, 'We live very busy lives here. We help in the dairy and in the kitchen gardens – the nuns grow all their own vegetables – and in the kitchen and laundry and the older children take it in turns to watch over the little ones. We are like a big family. Would you like to do these things with us?'

'Of course I will and I am happy I have come here too,' Agnes replied sincerely.

'You look tired now,' David stood up, 'I will leave you to rest again and perhaps tomorrow you will feel well enough to get up.'

After he had gone, Agnes spent a long time thinking about all that he had told her and her sad, hot tears were as much for the other children as they were for Eleanor and all that had happened. When the other two girls, whose room she shared, came in to see her, bringing soup and bread, however, she chatted to them cheerfully and soon felt they would become firm friends.

David was right. The days were busy and time passed quickly. Agnes was soon absorbed into the routines of chores and daily life. There were meals to be prepared and cleaned up after; there was work in the dairy and in the garden and constant washing which the nuns were most insistent on, to keep the children clean and healthy. Agnes enjoyed the work and quickly came to feel that she belonged to the little community and was not an odd one out. When she got into bed at night she chatted with the two other girls, Hannah and Sophie, who were about her age, until they fell asleep, weary from their active days. It was not hard for Agnes to hide the things she couldn't talk about. All of them instinctively avoided mentioning their families and their past lives. They talked instead about the nuns and the other children or the jobs they had been doing throughout the day. All the children had been brought up in the city and the work of the countryside was new to them. Hannah, a large, solid girl found that she was especially good at milking the cows. She found it, she said, very soothing and calm to rest her cheek against the warm flank of the cow as she had been shown, while she milked it. Agnes had tried, but she did not have the touch, the cow grew fidgety and impatient with her and yielded little milk. They all enjoyed the sweet, creamy milk though, a luxury which they had not been used to in Paris. Sometimes the girls discussed books they had read or games they used to enjoy playing with their friends, but if the conversation strayed too close to their old lives, they grew quiet until one of them changed the subject. In the daytime it was they, the older ones, who tried to keep the little ones happy and clean and busy and in the evening they helped to put them to bed. Inevitably there were times when one small child or another cried pitifully for '*Maman*' or '*Papa*', but as the weeks went on, their memories of home were fading.

Many, though not all of the nuns were elderly and grateful for the help the older children could offer. While not used to caring for children, they were kindly and patient on the whole. They rose very early every day to go to morning mass in their chapel. They did not ask that the children attend their twice daily services, but they frequently reminded them to say their prayers at night, sitting with the little ones as they did so and adding their own blessing.

The weather was growing steadily warmer and drier. The nuns took advantage of the sunny days to get the children outside as much as possible and give them small chores to do in the garden. Everyone began to look healthier and lose the sickly pallor they had had when they first came from Paris. One morning Agnes offered to trim the laurel hedge which protected the kitchen garden on one side and snipped away peacefully in the sunshine. There was birdsong in the trees, wild orchids and cowslips in the field beyond the monastery garden fence and Agnes felt happier and more at peace than she had done for a long time.

In the middle of the morning Sister Thérèse brought out some bottles of water and biscuits for the children and called them all over to sit on the grass with her. Little Samuel, who had been 'helping' weed between the vegetables, tripped as he ran along the garden path and sprawled headlong, where he stayed, howling loudly. David was there to pick him up and brushing him down he said,

'Two grazed knees. That's not too bad, nothing broken.' He reached for a bottle of water and took a folded clean handkerchief from his pocket, but Samuel now sitting with his legs stretched out and gazing at his muddy, slightly blooded knees, was still howling. David quickly washed the grazes till they were clean. Only a few scratches were still visible, but Samuel was not to be comforted.

'Oh dear, Samuel,' David said gravely, 'if your legs are hurting that much, I think we'll have to chop them off. What do you think?'

Samuel stopped crying and looked interested, enjoying the attention. 'Yes!' he agreed decisively.

'Right we are. Agnes, pass me those shears would you?'

As Agnes well knew the shears were very blunt, but David opened them up and appeared to be considering Samuel's legs carefully.

'Where do you think they should come off, Samuel?' he asked in a serious tone, 'here, or here? Which bits don't you need?' He measured off places on Samuel's leg, till the little boy rolled away and jumped up shrieking with laughter.

'He was going to chop my legs off,' he shouted happily, jumping up and down.

'I think you have effected a miracle recovery, David, praise the Lord!' Sister Thérèse laughed.

Agnes marvelled not for the first time, at David's way with the children. They all loved him and trusted him.

'I am going to be a doctor,' he had told her during one of their conversations. 'Like my parents and my older sister. I suppose I never really had any choice. It's in the genes.'

'My parents were both doctors too, but science was never my strong point. I don't think I'm destined for medicine unfortunately.'

He smiled, 'What do you like best at school, then?'

'Oh, writing stories, and history,' Agnes responded. 'But I liked reading the books my grandmother had at home best, I mean I think I learnt a lot from reading Charles Dickens and Jane Austen and other people. My grandmother thought I was a bit young for some of the books in her library, but she said as long as I enjoyed it she wouldn't discourage me from reading anything.'

He smiled his half smile, 'She must have been

lovely, your grandmother.' He paused. 'I must show you my book of poetry soon,' he said, remembering his early promise.

It was a few days later that an opportunity arose. It was an unusually hot day and the nuns had suggested that the children take a rest after lunch, as they themselves would do. Agnes had chosen to carry a book out to the shade of a tree. A kindly neighbour had delivered some old children's books to the nurse. The one Agnes had was a little young for her, but it was good for her French she reasoned. She was lying comfortably on her stomach when David approached.

'Am I disturbing you?' he asked.

'No, please join me.' Agnes sat up as David settled with his back against the tree.

'I've brought my book of poetry out, would you like to have a look?'

'Yes please,' she replied, taking the book carefully. It was a sturdy volume, bound in blue cloth, with blue leather corners and spine. She read the words in gold lettering, '*The Oxford Book of English Verse.*' She handled it with care, knowing that this book was very special to David.

She recognised some of the poets' names and even some of the poems as she gently turned the pages. After a few moments, he took the book back and looking through the pages found some poems which he read a few odd verses out to her.

'Thank you,' she said, feeling suddenly shy. 'I can

see there will be years of reading in there. It is the kind of book Eleanor used to call a "literary companion".'

'Yes, this is certainly my literary companion,' he agreed, then he asked, 'Do you have anything left from home, Agnes? I remember you had a little bag by your bed, when I came in to talk to you that first day. I wondered what you had in it, after you'd told me your story.'

'Yes, I'll fetch it.' Agnes jumped up, running in to fetch her bag from where she kept it, under her pillow. She was glad to have something to share with him too.

Once back in the shade of the tree, she drew out the little statuette first.

'I found him in the rubble of the house, after the bomb,' she said. 'He's called Don someone, I can never remember his name. He belonged to my father.'

David took the wooden figure and looked carefully at his long face and stiff pointed beard and the sword he held upright, its tip between his feet. He smiled.

'Don Quixote, I would say.'

'Yes, that's it, I'm sure it is. How did you know that?'

'He is just how Don Quixote ought to look.' David continued to inspect the little carved figure, with a smile on his face.

'Who was he?' Agnes asked.

'Don Quixote was the hero of a very famous Spanish story by Cervantes. He was a Knight, but not a very good one. He spent much of his time attacking windmills.'

Agnes laughed, 'Why was he such a hero then?'

David paused to reflect, as he often did before

133

answering a question. 'Well, he was an idealist. He always followed his heart and his dreams, no matter what people thought of him. He thought that you should see life and people as they should be and not as they really are. Not a bad lesson for life. He had a very devoted servant too, called Sancho Panza. They are usually pictured together, in illustrations. It is a good book, but very long, a great classic in Spain. You should read it one day.'

Agnes put Don Quixote back in the bag and more hesitantly drew out the picture of her mother, now sadly creased and stained. He looked at it carefully.

'She was very pretty, like you,' he said and Agnes felt herself blushing as he looked from the photograph to her face.

'You told me they were working in Africa. Do you know what exactly they were doing?' he continued.

'Only that they had set up a hospital in a very poor area. It served thousands of people. But I don't know very much about it.'

'I would like to do something like that once I'm qualified as a doctor. My father was always excited by the important medical research being done in hospitals here, but once I have got some experience it would be good to get out of Europe too, to do something really useful. Will you come with me if I go to Africa?'

Agnes looked up at him in surprise at the question. His expression was serious, but his eyes had that twinkling light they sometimes had as if there was laughter behind them.

'I wouldn't be much use to you, I'm afraid.'

'Nonsense, you're very good with the little ones. I've watched you. You have a great deal of patience and a kind heart, Agnes.'

'Well, but I wouldn't have any practical, medical skills.'

'No, but you'll make a good wife!' He was smiling now, but Agnes felt herself blush again. Then he added more wistfully, 'Who knows what will happen, when the war is over. But it is good to think there may be things to look forward to in our lives.'

Agnes met Monsignor Laurence, the priest who had brought the children there, only two months or so after her arrival. David had mentioned him once or twice, surprised that he had not visited them before. When he came he looked tired and drawn. He spoke for a long time in private with the Mother Superior and then to David. He did not stay long, having greeted the children briefly, saying that he must hurry back to Paris.

After his visit, David seemed worried and preoccupied for several days. At last, Agnes had the chance to ask him what Monsignor Laurence had said. David looked at her for a long moment, sadly, considering whether or not to burden her with his worries, but finally he said, 'He does not think we will be safe here for long. The Germans and the French

Police know we are no longer in Paris. They could not get much information from the woman whose house we lived in, as she was not told where we were going, but she knew Monsignor Laurence was involved. It seems they are looking for us.' He took a deep breath, looking at Agnes intently.

'Perhaps I should not have told you this, Agnes. But it might be better for you to leave. You are not implicated in this. Your case is different.'

'I'm not Jewish you mean?'

'Yes. Of course you are in danger too, because you are English. But no-one would know that now. Your French is fluent. I suspect if you talk in your sleep now, you do it in French.' He gave her a weak smile.

'I'm not leaving you,' she said firmly.

'Selfishly, I'm glad,' David smiled at her again, this time with more conviction. 'But I think we should keep very quiet about this. There is no point in worrying the other children. We really have nowhere else to go.'

After this conversation, David did not refer to it again and though Agnes caught his pensive, worried expression from time to time, things seemed to continue as normal. The children had grown so used to their life with the nuns and felt so secure in the gentle routines, that they had begun to believe that they would stay there for ever, or at least until the war ended and their parents came home. If the nuns were concerned, they hid it well and continued to treat the children just as before.

It was true that in the early days, they had been more cautious about allowing the children to be seen by outsiders, taking the little ones down to the orchard to play, where their voices could not be heard from the road. But, inevitably the word had soon got out. As the young policeman who had brought Agnes there had said, in a small village it was hard to hide things. Besides, there were deliveries sometimes made to the convent by people from further afield. The children could not remain hidden all the time. As summer came, they were outside for hours, their voices drifting over the walls of the garden as they played or worked. Many local people had brought clothes or contributions of food. But the nuns knew, in truth they had always known, that for every kind soul in the neighbouring villages, they might be another more interested in saving his own skin, or perhaps, for his family's sake, who might choose to give wanted information to the Germans. They gave no sign of their anxieties to the children however, not wishing to hurry the end of whatever time of safety and comfort was left to them.

Chapter 7

The Gift

We that did nothing study but the way
To love each other, with which thoughts the day
Rose with delight to us and with them set,
Must learn the hateful art, how to forget.

A Renunciation *Henry King*

It was on a morning in early August that the Germans arrived. The children had been in the convent for nearly three months. The settled fine weather meant that each day started clear and bright, with a promise of heat to come. They had got into the habit of getting up early and taking their breakfast into the garden, then having a rest after lunch during the greatest heat of the day. It was too early now, however, for most of the children to be up. A few, already awake, heard the sound of a heavy vehicle drawing up before the gates of the convent. Agnes and Hannah were up and dressed, Hannah ready to go down and help with the early morning milking, Agnes to prepare breakfast. The nuns, as usual, had started their day much earlier having held their morning mass and started their own routines for the day.

Hastening to a window in a passage which looked out over the yard, Agnes and Hannah watched as German soldiers descended from the truck whose arrival they had heard and two officers got out of a car which had pulled up behind the truck. The officers approached the gate. The loud and unaccustomed clatter of the bell echoed through the yard. Hannah gripped Agnes' hand tightly. David, too, came out into the corridor, as one of the younger nuns, Sister Thérèse, appeared.

'Quickly,' Sister Thérèse's voice shook. 'We must get all the children up and out of the back gate.'

Hannah and Agnes turned to obey, but David spoke quietly.

'It is no use our running away, sister. We would not stand a chance.'

The bell clattered angrily again. Slowly, the Mother Superior made her way across the yard.

'Mother Superior will deal with them,' said Sister Thérèse desperately. She was shaking. Agnes could feel her trembling as she stood by her. The Mother Superior, taking a large key from her pocket, unlocked the gate slowly, but the German officer was shouting and the moment the gate was unlocked, he pushed it open roughly and continued to shout at her. They could not hear his words, nor her response, but after a brief exchange, he pushed past her, followed by the other officer and made towards the building. As he approached, he barked an order to the soldiers waiting by the truck, who followed him towards the building.

'They have come for us,' David said simply and Agnes had never heard him sound so desolate.

They could hear German voices now in the hall downstairs, their words echoing up the stairwell to where the children and Sister Thérèse were standing.

'*Schnell*. Quick. Get the children up. Get them out here. Now!' Other nuns had appeared beside the children from elsewhere upstairs. David turned from the window, looking at Agnes, then to Sister Thérèse.

'Sister, Agnes is not Jewish as you know, she was raised a Christian and the Germans should want nothing with her on this count. She does not have to be part of this. Please, hide her,' he whispered urgently.

'No, David. I want to stay with you,' Agnes protested in a fierce whisper.

'I cannot.' Sister Thérèse shook her head, trembling all the more violently.

'I will take her.' It was Sister Marie, who took Agnes by the arm firmly.

'David ...' Agnes turned to him, beseeching.

'Agnes, go. For God's sake,' he told her.

There were heavy footsteps on the stairs already, Sister Marie gripped her elbow firmly and pulled her away down the corridor towards the back staircase. As they reached the top of the stairs, the Germans stepped onto the landing by the main staircase, shouting at the children and the nuns huddled within sight, by the window.

The back stairs were narrow and wooden and led directly down to a passage outside the scullery behind the kitchen. From here, there was direct access to the farmyard where the cows came in. This could only be reached by a back gate into the neighbouring field which was used for pasture and another gate on the far side, where a rough track led down to the road, emerging at some distance from the main driveway. There was no-one in sight here.They waited for a few moments by the cowshed to see if any Germans were on their way around to this entrance, then Sister Marie approached the farm gate, motioning Agnes to stay still and silent. She looked carefully across the field towards the farm gate and the road. There were no vehicles in sight. She beckoned Agnes forward.

'Quick,' she said, 'you can go out through the farm gate. Wait by the trees till the Germans have gone. We will see what happens, but you must stay hidden.'

Agnes was shaking. Her legs felt weak, but she slipped out, crossing the field amongst the cows carefully and quickly. The cows knew her and did not stir from their grazing. She reached the trees, four large oak trees, on the far side of the field near the gate connecting the two fields. From here, she was roughly on a level with the front of the building and she had a partial view of the courtyard and the gate where the truck and the car were parked. She positioned herself in the shadow behind the large trunk of one of the trees.

It was some minutes before anything happened and then children began to emerge from the building, into the yard. The German officers continued to bark orders and the soldiers stood guarding the children with guns as if they were dangerous criminals. It did not take long till they were all gathered. From the gate, the first to emerge was the Mother Superior. She was being held by the arm by one of the German officers. He was still shouting and his voice carried clearly.

'Is this all? Are you hiding any more? We will search the building you know.'

'You have *all* the children who came from Paris here.' The Mother Superior's voice was quite audible on the still air too, though she spoke calmly. She stressed the word 'all', careful not to tell a lie for she could see that Agnes was not among them.

'So, you have been keeping these children here for so long now. They are prisoners of war, you know. You will have much to answer for.'

'They are children!' she exclaimed firmly. Calm as she was, she could not keep the outrage and horror from her voice. 'They have done nothing wrong, nor have we, in caring for them.'

At this, he seized her arm, pushing her into the back of the car and the rest of his words were lost. The children began to emerge from the gateway next. The little ones were crying, the older ones silent, holding them by their hands. Agnes strained to catch a glimpse of David. All at once, she saw him. He was apart from the others, standing by the railings above the low wall surrounding the yard a little to the right of the gate. She saw him push something between the metal rails quickly and it fell amongst the grasses below. A glimpse of blue. She knew what it was. There was a shout and a German soldier gave David a cuff across the head, peering through the railings as he did so. Fortunately, he could see nothing. He was the last out. The others were already being hoisted roughly up into the back of the truck. She saw him shrug away the helping hand of the German soldier and climb into the back. He did not look out towards where she might be. He and the others were swallowed into the shadow of the covered truck as the armed soldiers climbed in behind them. As the engines started and the sight of the lorry and car were enveloped by the dust from the driveway behind them, Agnes sank into the grass behind the tree, her vision blurred into a sea of green and brown.

For an hour or more Agnes found it impossible to move. She felt numb, shocked beyond credulity. The world had been shattered and suddenly there was no point of reference to help her decide what to do next. At length she remembered the book. She walked down the slope from the trees to the front of the convent, approaching cautiously in case any of the German soldiers had been left behind to guard the convent.

But the place was deserted. There, in the grass, just where she had seen him drop it, was David's book. He had left it for her she knew, hoping that she would see him drop it; thinking that she would be watching if she could, or hoping that someone else would find it and give it to her. It was a great sacrifice that he had made. She would take care of it until he came back, for years, forever if necessary. This he would have known, she was sure.

She made her way back to the farmyard entrance and so back into the scullery. She could hear the nuns in the kitchen. There was the sound of weeping and urgent, anxious words in low voices. Sister Marie came out, spotting Agnes immediately, she put a finger to her lips.

'Thank God,' she whispered. 'Come outside. I have been watching for you for the last hour.' She took her out once more into the farmyard. 'Listen Agnes, my dear. They have taken all the children and the Mother Superior, but they will be back to keep an eye on us. We will be lucky if we are not all arrested. You must go. It is not safe for you here anymore. Not safe for any of us.'

'I understand,' Agnes said quietly. 'What will happen to them, sister?'

'I do not know, my child. They are in God's hands now.'

'What will happen to Mother Superior?' Agnes persisted.

'I cannot tell you that either. She is in God's hands too. She is a brave woman however, Agnes. You must not concern yourself. You must look after yourself as best you can. We can do no more for you here. Try to go south, try to find your grandparents. God willing, there may be good people to help you along the way.'

'I understand. Thank you, Sister Marie.' There was a huge lump in her throat which made it hard to speak and she was shaking still. But suddenly remembering, she turned back. 'Sister Marie, I have a bag upstairs. May I fetch it? It has a few things from home, a photograph of my mother. Please.'

Sister Marie looked anxious, 'I will fetch it for you child. Hide in the cow barn, just inside the door. Where will I find it?'

'It is underneath my pillow.'

In a few minutes, Sister Marie was back, breathless and nervous. She gave Agnes the bag, just inside the barn door, saying, 'You must go now, child. Quickly. It isn't safe to linger here.' As they moved out into the sunlight, she added, 'God bless you, Agnes, and keep you safe.'

She stood and watched for a moment as Agnes set off back towards the trees and the gateway across the field and out onto the road, then she turned back into the convent.

Agnes walked along the road away from the village, not knowing and not thinking about where she was going. The last words she had heard David speak echoed through her mind. 'Agnes is not Jewish. The Germans should want nothing with her on this count.' What he had said implied that the other children were all wanted by the German army, all at their mercy, simply for being Jewish.

She walked all day. Frequently she was racked by sobs, and tears flowed freely down her cheeks. The suddenness and the roughness of the children's arrest were hard to make sense of. At one moment, their lives had seemed safe, secure, even happy, the next, everything was gone, nothing was the same.

If anyone passing noticed her, she was not aware; she just kept walking. She was fortunate that she was on very quiet country roads. They seemed to lead nowhere but across a series of slopes with endless rows of vines stretching away into the distance and the occasional copse or house. When night fell and she was too tired to go on any further she stopped and slept in a ditch; she was heedless of danger for the moment. It did not seem to matter what happened to her.

Where *had* the Germans taken all the children? Perhaps it really was to join their parents in Germany. But no, this made no sense. Agnes remembered all that David had told her about what had happened to the Jews; the fearfulness of Monsignor Laurence; the caution of the nuns and finally, the way the Germans had behaved towards the children and the nuns. They had been harsh, rude and rough; there had been nothing of kindliness or concern in them. These were men who wished the children ill. In her heart Agnes feared for their lives, wondered if she would ever see any of them again, ever see David.

In London the war had meant bombs, ruined houses and sudden deaths and disappearances too, her own grandmother's among them. But people were all on the same side and kind to one another on the whole. The ever present danger which they shared gave them a feeling of solidarity, often a sense of duty to be cheerful with each other and to help other people in trouble. Here in France the war meant something different. People could not trust one another, not knowing for sure whose side they were on. People were afraid of the Germans and even of other French people living amongst them. They lived in their own country which had somehow been taken from them, just as their freedom, their food, their right to travel had all been requisitioned by the German army. There was no London cheeriness to be found here. There was sadness and fear.

Before dawn she started to walk again. She tried to remember how to look for her direction. 'The sun rises in the East and sets in the West,' she thought, watching as the sun came up on her left hand side. Good, so far, that meant she was heading south. But from what she remembered of her French geography and the map she had looked at it the railway station, oh, all those months ago, it could be seven or eight hundred miles to the south. She did not really know where she was except that the nuns had confirmed they were in the region famous for making champagne on the eastern side of France, east, anyway, of Paris. The Alps were on the eastern side of France too, of course, but she could not see any mountains from here. Champagne – she had seen her grandmother drink glasses of champagne before the war – delicate, rounded, cocktail glasses of biscuit-pale wine with lines of tiny bubbles which seemed to stream up from the bottom of the glass. She had watched as one or another of her grandmother's men friends had pushed the fat cork gently out of the bottle neck using his thumbs, then quickly tipped the frothing bottle to a waiting glass, and how the champagne had bubbled up and then subsided quickly so the glass could be filled. Eleanor had let Agnes sip, once or twice, from the top of her glass, to try it. It tasted slightly bitter to Agnes, but the flavour was subtle and complex; the bubbles went up her nose and made her laugh, but she liked the tingle of them on her tongue. When she thought of champagne, she thought of parties and laughter. The rolling, deep laughter of men, the higher, musical laughter of some of the ladies. Sometimes she would sit at the top of the stairs when Eleanor was having a dinner party and listen to the sound of chatter and laughing, until Dilly or someone else came and chased her into bed. That was in London, or the country, but before the war. It was years ago.

It was another world. Here was Champagne, the place. Here were the vines where the grapes grew to make champagne. Here, children were stolen by the Germans and disappeared.

Chapter 8

The Maquis

Still let my tyrants know, I am not doom'd to wear
Year after year in gloom and desolate despair.
Emily Bronte – *The Prisoner*

Agnes walked for three days. She passed through
several villages and a sizeable town, but she did not
attract attention. She looked like a little French country
girl with her second-hand French clothes. She had had
nothing to eat for three days but the hunger had stopped
gnawing away at her, leaving a sort of numbness. She
had been well fed at the convent and with all the fresh
air and exercise which had been part of those weeks,
she was strong and healthy. Nonetheless when she
drank water from a village fountain, it made her sick.
By the fourth night she was feeling slightly delirious,
dizzy and with new shooting pains in her stomach.

The landscape became less flat, with undulating
slopes and patches of woodland. She had wandered

well off the road looking for shelter and found a small copse of trees that bordered a stream of clear water. It was shallow at this point where it flowed over rocks, making a soothing, trickling sound. Here she drank and the water was sweet and clean tasting. Moving a little way into the band of trees, Agnes curled up in the crook of a tree's roots and slept, comforted by the gentle sound of the stream.

She had not been asleep many hours when she was awoken by a loud noise which seemed to be directly overhead. It was dark and she could not see it, but the engine sound and its proximity, immediately told her that there was a small plane, apparently in trouble and very close by. The noise was intermittent, it sputtered and cut out for a few seconds, then started again, then stopped. There was a longish pause then a loud, but distant crash which was quickly followed by an explosion. She crawled out from the trees. The moon, though passing intermittently behind clouds, allowed some light and beyond the trees she could see a wide empty meadow. There was no sign of the plane, but all at once she could see a small figure, black against the sky though close to the ground, beneath a white parachute which glowed with a strange luminosity. He landed with a heavy thump, falling sideway to lie on the grass. The parachute settled gently behind him. He did not get up. Agnes hesitated. What should she do? Was he dead?

Within the seconds it took her to deliberate, two

more men appeared from the trees, like hares put up by a hound and racing towards the prone figure. Swiftly they cut the man loose from the parachute and began to drag him back towards the trees. Almost at the same moment, the sound of a car engine, and the beam of headlights came from a road on the opposite side of the field.

'Blast! The parachute,' one of the men hissed anxiously. They were half way back towards the trees, but they were struggling with the weight of the unconscious pilot. Without thinking further, Agnes ran out, passing them. She bundled up the huge cloud of parachute silk, half carrying, half dragging it back towards the trees. It weighed very little but it was bulky and difficult to manage. Her feet became tangled in it as she tripped over lagging cloth, then stumbled on. She reached the shelter of the trees, just as the men got there with their far heavier load and one of them turned back quickly to help gather the parachute away under the trees. Just as they did this, a huge arc of light swept the field. There were German soldiers on the opposite side, near the road. The powerful beam swept across the field several times, lingering in the corners and along the edge of the trees. The two men ducked instinctively and one put out an arm to Agnes, pulling her roughly down beside him. The light seemed to play for a long time at the edge of the trees; it seemed almost impossible they would not catch sight of them or catch a flash of white from the parachute. After several minutes, the light went out. There were voices and the sound of an engine starting up again and the car leaving.

'We haven't got long,' said one of the men. 'They'll be back. Come on.'

The other turned to Agnes, 'Who are you?' he asked, then without waiting for a response, 'it doesn't matter, you'll have to come with us. Can you manage this?' He wrapped the parachute up into a much smaller and tighter bundle, winding the loose, hanging cords around it and put it in her arms. It was surprisingly light and easy to manage now.

'Yes, it's fine,' she replied. One of the men hoisted the pilot, who was still unconscious, over his shoulder in a fireman's lift and the other led the way, a gun in his hand. Agnes followed. They picked their way across the stream and over some fields on the other side, keeping to the shelter of walls and hedges wherever possible. Within a few minutes they were in a farmyard and entering a large barn. With difficulty the men carried the pilot up a ladder into the hay loft.

'You'd better come up here too,' one of them said, taking the parachute from Agnes and helping her up the ladder. 'Who are you anyway? What are you doing here?'

Agnes had strong evidence already that these men, who had just rescued a pilot, would not be on the Germans' side and also that she had better give them some good reason to know that she was not to be mistrusted.

'I'm English,' Agnes said, 'at least, half English. It's okay, I'm on my own.'

'*Zut!* This is all we need!' the man muttered. 'How on earth did you come to be here? Never mind, now. Look, you'll have to stay here with this man. Here, take this water,' he said, removing a flask which hung on a strap across his chest. 'If he wakes up, give him a drink, but just keep him quiet. We'll have to move you both as soon as possible. The Germans will be searching for him. They'll be everywhere as soon as it's light.'

It was only a matter of minutes before the pilot woke up. He put his hand to his head.

'Holy …' he looked at Agnes, 'Holy Moses, where am I?' He spoke in English and his accent was strongly American.

'Shh,' she warned, replying in a whisper. 'Some men rescued you, you came down in a parachute. The Germans were looking for you. They're hiding us here, in a barn, till they can move us.'

The pilot scratched his head with both hands, then looked at her again. He was a young man, in his early twenties perhaps, with fair hair and a fresh face.

'We're in France right?' he asked.

'Yes, your plane crashed.'

'So how come you speak English?'

'I am English. Half English, anyway.'

The pilot shook his head from side to side as if he could not believe what was happening.

'Jeepers,' he took the bottle of water which Agnes

offered and drank deeply and at that moment there were steps on the ladder again.

'He's woken up? Good. Quick, we've got to get out of here.'

'What's he saying?' asked the American. Agnes translated.

'He doesn't speak any French?' asked one of the French men.

'No, I don't think so,' Agnes replied.

'Well, that's great!' the man exclaimed in a low growl, 'you might come in useful then, you'll have to translate.' He hurried them down the ladder as he spoke. His manner was brusque and nervous. As Agnes came out into the yard she saw that there was a third man, keeping watch towards the farm entrance. The three men wore dark clothes and caps. They were solid men, two young, one middle aged. All farming people she guessed by their clothes and manner. The man who was keeping watch beckoned, leaving the main gate and setting off into a field on the other side of the yard. They followed quickly and in silence.

They went at a brisk pace but when possible kept to the hedges and low walls where they moved, crouching. After half an hour they started climbing a wooded hill. They were close to the summit when the guide stopped. They were standing under pine trees and could just see between them, back down the hill across the vineyards to the farm buildings in the distance.

'Is it here?' asked one of the other men.

'Yes, wait till I find it,' answered the guide. He took out a small torch and flashed it briefly at the surrounding trees, moving a few yards to his right. Suddenly he began to stamp his foot on the ground. There was the muffled sound of leaves on earth, then suddenly, as he shifted between the trees a dull, slightly hollow sound.

'Here, take the torch,' he passed it to another man who held it very low to the ground as the other had done. Immediately he bent down and scraped back leaves and some loose earth, uncovering a trap door. He pulled it open. The torch shining down revealed a rough wooden stepladder descending at an angle into the hillside.'

'Go on, quick,' one of the men said, 'take the torch with you. We'll close up and cover the trap door.'

Agnes followed the guide, feeling her way backwards down the wooden steps, as they had done. The other two men stayed behind, closing the trap door quickly above them. They heard the sound of earth and leaves being scraped back across it, before they reached the bottom of the steps. Though the last to come down the ladder, she could see as she turned around at the bottom, by the faint beam of the torch that they were in a low and narrow passage whose walls and ceiling appeared to be made of earth and wooden beams. It sloped steadily downwards into the hill. The air smelled damp and musty. The American turned round to her, holding out his hand.

'Here kid, you go ahead of me. I can see over your

head.' He pushed her gently in front of him, keeping a hand on her shoulder to steady either her, or himself, she wasn't sure which. The three of them walked on for a long time till they reached a door, which the guide unlocked. They found themselves then in another tunnel, but this one had bricked walls and an arched ceiling and lamps hung from hooks on the wall at long intervals. The walls on either side were lined with row upon row of bottles, the green indented circles of their bases facing outwards, dusty for the most part, but here and there catching the light from a lamp in an emerald glow. They proceeded quickly along a series of tunnels which seemed to go on forever, until at length Agnes became aware of more light ahead of them. There was a door, standing ajar and beyond it a huge cavernous room filled with rows of wooden casks and dim lights hung from the ceiling. There was another man in the room; he pushed shut the door behind them and rolled a cask in front of it. Looking back, Agnes saw that the doorway was invisible. It was cut into the panelling that covered the end wall.

At the other end of the chamber was a table with a pair of benches on either side of it. The man beckoned them over and gestured to them to sit down. Brief explanations were made in a few words, then the man they had joined said to the pilot and Agnes in broken English, 'You wait here. You eat now.'

Some food was produced, bread, cheese and red wine. The two French men helped themselves to the food, passing a tumbler of wine to the American pilot and one to Agnes. She took a sip and coughed. It was strong and harsh and she pushed it back towards him. The man smiled and poured some of the wine into his own glass, adding water to Agnes' and giving it back to her. This time it was drinkable and it spread a warm feeling down her throat as she drank it. The pilot was not hungry, and drank only a little wine, but Agnes was ravenous and ate at great speed. One of the men noticed and passed her more bread and cheese.

'Eh, you're hungry. Have some more. You'd better, or the wine will go to your head.'

A few minutes later one of the men they had left behind on the hillside arrived. He came in by another door, which he shut hastily behind him. He came over to the table.

'They're everywhere, the Germans. He must be important, this bloke.'

'What's he saying?' the American asked Agnes.

'He says you must be important.'

'You bet!' said the American, visibly more relaxed after his first glass of wine and helping himself to more. 'Ask them how they're going to get me out of here.'

Agnes translated the question, but the man seemed edgy and impatient and without replying, he spoke again to the other men,

'Look, you'll have to get him into the back room. This isn't safe enough. As for the kid, what can we do

158

with her? Who the hell is she? We can't keep her here.'

The other men looked embarrassed. They turned away slightly from Agnes and tried to speak more quietly.

'Well, we can't just turn her loose now, can we? She's English. What do you want to do, throw her out to the Germans? Besides, she knows us and this place now. If she was picked up, they'd force her to talk.'

Agnes, racing in her mind, to keep up with what was going on and what they were saying, wanted to protest that she would not talk, no matter what 'they' did to her, but she was frightened by the tone of what they said and kept quiet.

'We'll have to keep her here until the American's moved on, then we'll see what we can do with her,' the guide acceded, finally.

One of the other men ruffled Agnes' hair. She was looking pale and scared. Her stomach was hurting again from the food she had eaten rather quickly and she did indeed feel dizzy from the diluted wine. His tone was kind as he said, 'Don't worry little one, we're not going to eat you. You'll just have to keep the American company for a few days while we find out how to get you both out. We'll talk about it later. For now, we'd better get you both out of sight.'

From the cellar with casks and the long table, they passed through a door into an office; a fairly large room, well lit, with a desk, a smaller table and some chairs and a pair of bookcases containing files. The ceiling here was of arched brickwork and much lower than in the previous cellar. As soon as they entered the room, two of the men pushed one of the heavy bookcases aside. It moved easily, seeming to glide on hidden rollers. Behind, was what appeared to be a solid brick wall. One of the men pushed carefully on a brick which loosened. Reaching in he appeared to lift a catch on the inside and a door then swung open; a door whose brick façade had seemed to be part of the wall. Beyond this was a short, pitch-dark corridor and at the end of that a small room behind another door. Agnes and the pilot were hurried into the dark corridor. An oil lamp was brought and they were shown the way into a tiny, cell-like room, sparsely furnished with a bed, a chair and a small square table.

'You'll have to stay here, both of you,' the guide said gruffly, addressing his words to Agnes, who translated to the American.

'Ask him how long?'

'Two days, maybe three. Till we can find a way to get him out,' the guide responded. 'Tell him we'll try hard to get him out quickly, but it does not depend just on us. We will have to contact people. But the sooner it happens, the better it will be for us too. There are lots of Germans around at the moment and they're looking for him.'

One of the other men had come back with the remains of the bread, cheese and wine which he put on the table and, pulling a pack of cards out of his pocket, he put that down too.

'Look, we'll bring you food and twice a day we'll get you out to go to the … you know … there's a toilet by the office, but we've all got to be very careful. The Germans don't know about this wine store – yet, but they could find out at any time.' He turned back to the others, 'Some of us had better get home to bed in case they search our houses.'

Agnes translated all of this as the men left and the American gave her a wry grin. 'Great. Don't know what I'd do without you, kid. What's your name anyway?'

'Agnes.' She pronounced it in the French way, 'Ann-yes,' because she had got used to that over the last few months.

'Hi, Ann - yes,' the American said, 'mind if I call you Annie? Like my kid sister. I'm Frank. Pleased to meet you.' Frank held out his hand and they shook hands.

'How do you do?' she said. He smiled and she couldn't help but smile at him too.

'Do you know who these men are, and where we are?' she asked him. 'They seemed to be waiting for you.'

'Well, I don't think they were waiting for me in particular. Probably just out keeping watch. I can't say for sure, but I'm fairly certain we've been picked up by the Resistance, which is pretty lucky for us. They've been rescuing Pommie soldiers and pilots (sorry, Annie, British to you) for a while and helping them get back to Britain, or 'Blighty' as the RAF guys call it. Guess that's why they were nearby. I'm kinda hoping that's what they'll do for me. Lucky escape. Could have been picked up by the Germans real easy while I was lying there unconscious. D'you wanna tell me exactly what happened while I was out cold?'

Agnes related events as best she could, including an account of how she had become involved when she had run out to collect the parachute just before the Germans arrived.

'They were there so quickly,' she said, 'they shone the searchlights across the field and into the trees where we were hiding for ages. I suppose if they'd seen the white of the parachute in the field, they would definitely have come looking for us amongst the trees. It was lucky I ran and got it, probably.'

'You bet it's lucky. Gee, kid,' Frank whistled softly, 'you could get yourself into trouble running around rescuing G.I. pilots at night. You probably saved those guys' skins too. They owe you one. I guess they'll have to get you out too.'

Agnes changed the subject. She had no intention of going back to London, but did not want to have to explain that just yet.

'They think you're someone important,' she said, 'are you?'

Frank chuckled, 'Hell, no. Though I guess the plane was important. Lucky it blew up. No use to the Germans as a pile of burned scrap. No, I'm just a G.I.

162

pilot working for the RAF. One of the first party to get trained over here. I've been out of the U.S. four months – not long. This was our first reconnaissance mission over the north of France. Just my luck to be shot down on the first run.' He paused, 'But gee, you're a plucky kid, Annie. Crazy, but plucky. I'm mighty glad you were there.' He had picked up the cards and was shuffling them absent mindedly in his hands as he spoke. 'Here, d'you want a quick game of cards before we get some sleep?'

But Agnes' eyelids were drooping. The wine had made her very sleepy, particularly after four nights of very little rest. Her head had already sunk down onto the pillow where she sat on the edge of the bed. Frank lifted her feet onto the bed, and taking a couple of blankets which he laid on the floor for his own bed, he took off his heavy sheepskin lined flying jacket and spread it over Agnes. She was already fast asleep.

The room they were in was far underground and with no access to natural light it was impossible to tell whether it was day when Agnes next awoke, but Frank had lit the lamp again and was lying on his blanket on the tiny patch of floor available, beside the bed, with his hands behind his head.

'Is it morning?' she whispered, looking at him without raising his head from the pillow.

'Sure is,' Frank replied, looking at his watch. 'Nearly eleven o'clock. We both slept late.'

'Thank you for giving me the bed, Frank,' Agnes said, 'I hope you weren't too uncomfortable – or cold.'

'No. I can sleep anywhere,' he replied, 'I'm kinda stiff this morning though.' He rubbed at the back of his neck with one hand as he sat up. 'Must have come down harder than I thought when I landed under the parachute last night. Guess that's what knocked me out.'

'Why don't you lie on the bed then,' said Agnes, getting up. 'I could make some breakfast for you.' She shuffled down to the other end of the bed in order to reach the table and assumed the kind of voice she thought a waitress might use, 'Would you care for some stale bread and cheese and a glass of wine for your breakfast, *Monsieur*?' She sawed through the hardened bread and cheese with the penknife which Frank had left on the table.

Frank grinned, getting up stiffly from the floor. 'Don't mind if I do thanks, Mam'zel. I'm kinda peckish this morning.' He took the food she offered, but declined the wine, drinking some water from a bottle on the table while he sat beside her on the bed.

'So tell me Annie, how do you come to be here and where are your folks?'

'It's a long story.' Agnes' tone was evasive. She was unsure of how much she wanted him to know and wary at the thought of what might come next. Certainly Frank would be looked after if these men could help. They had said they were going to try and get him back to England, but they had assumed she would want to go too. Where could she go? She had not been able to think clearly since she left the convent. She swallowed hard, trying to turn her mind to practical solutions to her situation. The prospect of ever reaching her grandparents in the south seemed very remote now. But neither did she want this young American pilot to feel responsible for her. She was aware that he was watching her, and waiting. At length, as he said nothing more, waiting for her to go on, she said, 'I don't really want to talk about my family now. I don't mean to be rude, you don't mind do you?'

But Frank replied gently, 'Sure, kid. No problem. Any time you want to talk, just talk, and if you don't, that's fine too. But if there's anything I can do, just let me know, okay? I owe you one. '

'Okay, and thanks. But I do just want to say that I'm not going to England. I'm trying to find my grandparents who are here in France.'

'Well, that's great, Annie. These guys will help you, I'm sure.'

Agnes was not so certain, but she made no reply. Instead she asked, 'Perhaps you could tell me about your family?'

'My family? Sure. Hey,' he paused, suddenly remembering something and fishing in the breast pocket of his jacket, 'have some gum.'

Agnes took the proffered stick of gum, wrapped in silver foil and with an outer paper label. She had heard of chewing-gum, but never seen any before. She followed Frank's example as he folded a stick into his mouth and chewed on it, while he told his story.

'I'm the eldest, then there's Mike, then Annie, about your age, freckles, bit of a tomboy, always up a tree or out playing on the street and in trouble. Mike's the brains of the family, does better in school than I ever did. Then there's Mom and Dad, of course, Dad runs a factory and Mom's a nurse though she doesn't work much now. It was tough on them when I joined up, but they supported me, especially Dad. We live on the East coast, New England. It's mighty pretty there, especially in the Fall.'

'Fall?'

'Oh,' Frank laughed. 'Autumn, you call it,' he pronounced it in an exaggeratedly English accent 'Orr-tom'. 'The colours of the leaves are beautiful in the Fall, red, orange, yellow – stunning. New England's famous for it.'

'It sounds lovely,' Agnes spoke thoughtfully, 'they sound nice, your family. I'm sure I'd like your little sister. I'd like to meet her one day.' She was anxious to keep him talking if it meant that he did not ask any more questions about her. She did not want to think about what had happened at the convent only four days ago. Besides, she was interested.

'Oh, you two would get on like a house on fire,' Frank grinned. 'Maybe you will one day. Maybe your mom and dad will bring you over to the United States for a visit when all this is over.' He was still sleepy and did not notice the shadow which crossed Agnes' face as he said this.

'I think I'm gonna snooze for a while, if you don't mind,' he yawned, rolling over to face the wall.

Agnes took out the gum and put it into the paper wrapper. It had turned tasteless quite quickly and made her thirsty. She couldn't quite see what all the fuss was about. Frank can't have slept that well on the floor, she reflected, since he was so sleepy now. She liked him. He was friendly and easy to talk to. He seemed kind too, not bothering her with awkward questions.

She picked up her little bag from the table where she had placed it the night before. She had been sleeping in the woods with the handles over her shoulder and had never taken it off, not even when she had run out and bundled up the parachute. She had opened it only once since she left the convent, to put David's book into it. Before she did that however, she had placed the crumpled photograph of her mother between its pages to flatten it and keep it safe. The sea water had left faded patches on it, but the picture was still clear. Besides that there was only her statue of Don Quixote, her scarf and her shawl. Now, she drew out the book. She held it carefully, then brushed the crumbs off the table before putting it down. She opened the cover. On the inside page there was an inscription written in an ornate hand in black ink. Underneath a date it read: 'To our beloved son, David ....' The words swam on the page and she quickly closed the book again before any tears fell onto the writing and spoiled it. She replaced the book carefully in the bag which she lay in her lap, and folding her arms on the table she laid her head upon them, closing her eyes.

A few hours had passed when Agnes became aware of sounds at the end of the tunnel which meant that the men were returning. She had been dozing, but became aware that there was an urgent and tense sounding discussion going on in low voices outside the door to their little room. Frank stirred into wakefulness as three men entered the room. Two of the faces were familiar. They were the guide and the man who had been in the cellars last night, but the third was someone they had not seen before. He had a heavy, dark beard and a cap pulled low over his forehead. He spoke softly, but angrily, and the other men seemed cautious and respectful of him. Beside him stood a dog, a tall, lean and long grey-haired deerhound who kept his slender nose close to his master's thigh.

'What did you bring the girl here for? It's not safe either for her, or the rest of you now. What if someone catches and interrogates her?'

'She helped rescue the pilot. If she had not been there, he would have been picked up. The Germans were right behind him. And she has acted as interpreter, she speaks English.'

As Agnes lifted her face to the man, a look of confusion, or even fear, seemed momentarily to cross his face, then it resumed the impassive expression she would come to know. He stared at her for a long moment, however and as Agnes returned his gaze stolidly, she saw a glitter of hard sadness behind his eyes.

'Who are you and what are you doing here? In this area, I mean?' he asked, in a softer tone than he had used with the men. For some reason, Agnes felt that she must trust this man. She should tell him the truth, as far as possible and he would know if she did not. Besides, he might be able to help her. She hesitated only over her name.

'My name is … Ann. I come from London, but I am trying to reach my grandparents who live in the south of France.'

He said nothing for a few moments, staring closely at her, the cap shading his eyes under the dim bulb above their heads.

'Why did you not stay in England?' he said at last, his tone was harsh now. 'It is safer than France for the moment.'

'My grandmother died in an air raid. My parents are both dead too. I wanted to go to my grandparents in France. They are my only family now. I do not want to go back to London.'

She spoke quietly and calmly. The man continued to look at her, long and hard. He said nothing and after a few moments he looked down at the floor. He seemed to be thinking about what to do. The other men were looking at him anxiously. Agnes was sure that her fate rested with him. It would be him that would make the decisions. It would be difficult to escape if he decided to send her back to England. Or perhaps he had something else in mind … she represented a security risk to them now.

'You say you have grandparents in France. Where do they live?'

For the first time, Agnes' voice faltered. She did not know precisely where they were, she had no address for them and was conscious that she would sound foolish to have taken so great a chance on finding them.

'I don't know exactly. But it is near a town called Carpentras, I think. They have a farm. I will find them. And I know what their name is, it is the same as my own surname because they are my father's parents.'

'Do not say your surname,' the man interrupted, speaking brusquely and impatiently. 'We tell no-one our real names here.' The other men looked at him nervously again, as if fearful of his anger. Then one said, 'It is hopeless. She will never get to her grandparents. Perhaps she means Carpentras in the Vaucluse, but there is no chance of her getting there. It is much too far away. We must send her back to London with the pilot.'

Agnes started, about to protest, but the bearded man spoke sharply again, addressing the other who had spoken.

'No. That would put the pilot in danger. We must follow the plan for him and send the girl out of the area quickly. There is a way.'

He turned again to Agnes. 'We will help you, but we will demand your total co-operation. You must take orders and do exactly what is asked of you and tell nobody anything. Do you understand?'

'Of course.'

'It was dark when you were brought here, I suppose?'

'Yes, it was the middle of the night.'

'Yes, that's true. She couldn't see anything, at least, very little that she could recognise,' one of the men agreed, as if trying to help her.

'Good, so she could not find her way here again. When we take you out of here, you will be blindfolded. Do you agree to this?'

'Yes.'

'Good. And now, you both need to get some rest. Tell the American that we will move him tonight. We have a pick up for him. He is lucky. All being well, he will be back in England in two days' time. You can translate all that?'

'Yes, of course.'

As Agnes followed this first order and explained about the pick up to Frank, she could hear the men who had moved out into the passage arguing with the bearded one. She felt sure it was about her. She too was lucky, he had had a sudden change of heart about sending her back, but clearly the other two men were nervous. She would never tell anyone about them or their hiding place, she thought fiercely, not even if the Germans tortured her! But how could she persuade them of this? How could she really know, herself, what she would do, if tortured?

At length they came back in, one of the men addressing Frank for the first time,

'Okay? Tonight?' one said in halting English.

'Tonight,' confirmed Frank, 'at what time?'

The men held up eight fingers, '*Huit heures.*'

'Okay, eight o'clock,' Frank echoed. 'Thanks, guys.'

The bearded man turned to Agnes, speaking in French. 'You be ready too. At eight.'

'*Oui, Monsieur.*'

Chapter 9

Into Free France

For Knighthood is not in the feats of war
...but in a cause which truth cannot defar
And no quarrel a knight ought to take
But for the truth or for the common's sake.
The True Knight *Stephen Hawes*

Agnes and Frank were both sitting on the edge of the bed in the light of the oil-lamp which burned on the table beside them, when Frank's wrist-watch showed a quarter to eight. Frank had put on and fastened his sheepskin-lined flying jacket and Agnes too, sat with her shawl wrapped around her. Despite the fact that it was summer, the underground passages and rooms were cold. Agnes was nervous. She hesitated. There was something she very much wanted to say, something that had been weighing on her conscience since last night, when she had known that Frank would be going back to London, but she had been afraid it would give rise to too many questions. Finally she said, rushing her words, 'Frank, could I ask you to do something for me in London, please? It's very important or I wouldn't ask.'

'Sure, kid, anything I can do, I'd be happy to.'

'Well, I can't explain exactly why, but I'd like you to take a message to someone. Someone who will be very worried about me, and just tell her that I am okay.'

'Of course, Annie. Just give me their name and address. Do you know the address?' Agnes did. Frank had a little notebook in his shirt pocket, with a thin propelling pencil which fitted into its spine. He drew it out and Agnes wrote down Dilly's name and address for him. 'Oh, and by the way, my name's pronounced "Agnes" in English.'

'Okay, Annie. You're still Annie to me,' he joked, returning the notebook to his pocket. He checked his watch nervously. It was eight o'clock now. By ten past, no-one had come.

Twenty minutes later they heard voices once again, but one of these was a loud, German voice and they were coming from the room at the end of the passage. They were trapped. Quickly, Frank jumped up and blew out the lamp on the table, then putting his finger to Agnes' lips, motioning her to be absolutely silent, he took her hand and led her out into the passage. The voices were muffled slightly by the fake brick wall between them and the office but the words were audible.

174

'What are you doing here, now, in this place, in the night-time, I would like to know?'the German shouted, in a heavy accent.

'*Monsieur*, if you will permit me, I will explain,' came the quiet, calm reply. It was Jean or Luc, by the voice. 'I am here because it is necessary for someone to be here all the time. The fermentation of the wine is a very delicate process. We have to check that the temperature of the wine does not rise too high as it will ferment. Also, the bottles need to be turned daily. Or else it will be spoiled.'

'You think I can believe this,' the German still spoke rudely, but his voice was calmer than before. 'We are in August now, I think. The fermentation of wine in the autumn is taking place, a little after the harvest. We have good wine in Germany too, you know. Mine family in the Rhineland also wine makes. I know all about it so, you see.'

'In that case *Monsieur,* you will understand when I explain that this is not ordinary wine. This is champagne. There is a second fermentation, which takes place in the bottle.' The Frenchman explained patiently and politely. 'It is what makes champagne petillant ... with bubbles. It is this second fermentation that we have to watch.'

'Ach so? This is how you make the champagne?' the German replied. The detailed explanation seemed to have captured his interest and gained his respect. The Frenchman had treated him properly, as someone who understood the making of wine. 'So. Explain to me zis second fermentation. How do you make it in the bottle happen? Explain.'

'We add a spoonful of sugar to each bottle, *Monsieur*, which then turns into alcohol. It is a very delicate business. The process of fermentation makes the bubbles, which are trapped in the bottle. The turning of the bottles is also a skilled process which must be done by a *remuer* such as myself. If you are interested, I could show you where this takes place. If you could come in the daytime, I will get the men to show you how it is done. But perhaps you would like to try a bottle now? There is some excellent, young champagne in the neighbouring room; it is ready to be labelled.'

'Ach yes, why not? Since we are here und you have explained to me, I am interested.' The German was talking now in a friendly tone. The voices moved away, presumably to the big room nearby, where they had first come in.

Frank put an arm around Agnes' shoulders. They were both trembling. He led her back into the room and they sat down again, side by side in the dark.

'Translate,' he requested in a whisper. She explained, as much as she could remember.

'The German was shouting and saying what was he doing here at this time of night and the French man was explaining about how to make champagne. He said someone had to be here all the time. I didn't understand all of it, but then he said he would give the German some champagne to drink in the next room.'

'Guess he'll be trying to get the German drunk enough so he'll go home happy,' Frank whispered.

'How long will that take?' Agnes asked. Frank did not reply except with a short breath out through his nose, as if he was smiling in the dark. He put a hand on hers, reassuringly and they sat silently in the dark for a long time.

At last, after what seemed like hours, there was a quiet scuffle and low torchlight out in the corridor. Luc appeared in the doorway, casting his torch at Frank and Agnes where they sat.

'Quick,' he motioned to Frank. 'There are Germans everywhere. It is dangerous. You stay here,' he added nodding at Agnes, 'the Wolf himself is coming to collect you soon.'

'I have to stay here. You have to hurry. He says it's dangerous,' Agnes translated quickly for Frank. He put a hand down and ruffled her hair.

'Good luck, kid. I'll be seeing you, and I'll get that message to your friend.'

Then they were gone. With scarcely a sound, the secret door at the end of the corridor was opened and closed again.

Another hour passed and then the sound came again. Low torchlight and another man, this time the bearded one they called 'Le Loup' or 'The

Wolf'. He beckoned to her, his finger to his lips and taking her by the hand, he put out the torch. They felt their way out of the passage, closing the door behind them. There was no need for a blindfold, Agnes could see nothing, but this man evidently knew every inch of the rooms and passages he now led her along. She did not recognise it as being the same way they had come the previous night; this was a series of long and very narrow passages. The air was close and stuffy.

After many minutes, she felt cool air on her face and at last they emerged from between rocks into the night air. It was much lower down the hill than where they had entered and they were almost in the valley and out of the woods, but hidden by a series of giant rocks, which they threaded their way between. As they emerged, the Wolf gave one low whistle and in a few moments there was the soft rustle of dried leaves from nearby and the soft sniffing of the dog that had been with him the day before. It had been waiting for him nearby and keeping watch.

It was a very dark night; there was no moonlight, but the Wolf knew his way and picked a route carefully between trees and across fields until, eventually they arrived in a farmyard and entered a large barn.

All this time, the man had held Agnes' hand in a tight grip, leading her along without a word and when at last he let go in the barn, she rubbed at the numbness with her other hand. She was scared. She had no idea where they were going or what he was going to do with her. He had said that she was a danger to them all. He had fetched something from further back in the barn, lighting a lamp as he did so. He held out something to her. It was an old pair of boots.

'Here, you must put these on. You must look like a French country girl.'

The boots were big for her, but sturdy. They would be good for walking in. She laced them up. They felt comfortable, more comfortable than the buckled sandals she had worn since she left London. Her toes had grown up against the ends of them in the months since she'd been in France and they were scuffed and worn.

'I have a scarf,' she offered, reaching into her bag for Dilly's scarf. She folded it and tied it under her chin.

'That's good,' the man nodded briefly. 'What else have you got in the bag?' He made as if to take it, but Agnes clutched it to her chest.

'They're just some things of mine.'

'Look,' the man replied impatiently, angrily even. 'Both our lives are at stake. I need to know that you haven't got anything in there that would give your identity away.'

'No, it's just a book, and a ... doll,' she didn't quite know how to explain the statuette.

'What book?'

'Just poetry. I got it from a friend. He gave it to me a few days ago.' She felt a lump in her throat and did not go on. Besides, it would have been too complicated to be more precise, and it wasn't the moment to try.

'Okay.'

He turned his attention back to a cart filled with hay in the barn, to which he beckoned her.

'Climb up onto the seat at the front there.'

He opened the large doors of the barn and disappeared into the darkness, returning a few minutes later leading a huge, heavy horse which he backed and harnessed into the shafts of the cart. He gave a brief whistle to the dog, which jumped up onto the back of the cart. At length the straps were all tight and the Wolf led the horse slowly out into the yard, pulling the cart. A dim morning light was beginning to brighten the sky as he climbed up onto the bench beside her.

'If we are stopped, you must say you are my daughter and your name is … Ann, did you say? We are on our way to a stable in Reims with this hay, if anyone asks, and I am taking you to market.'

'Okay.'

He said no more and within minutes they were away from the farm and out on the empty road. Light was just beginning to break in the east and birds were singing in trees by the roadside. They had not gone far before Agnes' head lolled against the man's shoulder and she slept. She had been up all night. She did not see or feel it, but the man called Wolf shifted his arm, putting it around her shoulder to make her more comfortable and secure against him. He was not, after all, such a hard man. It was the war that was hard.

The closer they got to the town, the busier the roads became with people going to market; many of them were using horses and carts, or were on bicycles. Petrol was strictly rationed and its use was mainly restricted to the German military vehicles which were greatly in evidence. There were no barriers in place on the outskirts of the town and though they were passed by several jeeps and a large black car, which hooted loudly, ploughing its way between the traffic and up the centre of the road, forcing carts and vans to pull off the road and almost into the ditch, they were not stopped and seemed to draw no particular attention.

At length, the Wolf directed the horse into the courtyard of an old coaching inn, passing under an arched gateway. There was a stable on the far side at which he drew up, jumping down just as a thickset man emerged from a side door of the inn.

'*Salut, comment va*?' The innkeeper held up a hand to steady the horse which was shaking its head, causing the harness to jangle.

'Who's this?' he asked next, catching sight of Agnes and nodding towards her.

'I'm taking her down to Grenoble. Her family is around there. She was involved in a rescue the other night.' The Wolf spoke rapidly, in a low voice, unbuckling the horse as he did so.

'That's dangerous,' the innkeeper muttered. 'A kid, she could talk.' His voice was low too, and the men had turned their backs towards Agnes, but she caught the drift of what they said.

'On the contrary, she's a good decoy for me. What could be more natural than a father taking his daughter along on a delivery during the school summer holidays?'

'Well yes, I suppose so. It's a reasonable disguise. But for God's sake, be careful. You can't afford to be arrested and let her say anything she shouldn't.'

'I'll make sure that doesn't happen.'

Agnes shivered. She wondered what lengths these men would go to, to protect themselves and each other. Again she gained the impression that this man, the Wolf, was obviously important. Everyone seemed respectful of him and concerned for his safety.

At length, the Wolf led the horse away from the cart and to a water trough where it drank deeply and noisily through its halter bit, and then into a stable whose door the innkeeper swung open. Agnes climbed down from the cart.

'Don't forget your things,' the Wolf nodded towards her bag under the seat at the front of the cart.

Agnes gasped. 'Oh yes,' she *had* nearly forgotten. She reached up for it.

'Is the van ready?' the Wolf asked the innkeeper.

'Yes, but before you go, come and have a cup of

coffee. We have managed to keep a little real coffee for ourselves. Come into the kitchen.'

The kitchen was big and busy looking, with two large cookers, and a long heavy table in the centre of the room on which the innkeeper's wife was chopping vegetables to make soup for the day. She had recently had several deliveries of food from people supplying the market. There were piles of bread, packets of wrapped cheeses and paté for the day's menu. Lunch time at the inn was always busy on market days, despite the war and the general shortage of things. Having German clients brought benefits and the inn was lucky to receive regular supplies of coffee, bread and meat.

She kissed the Wolf on both cheeks, and then Agnes, giving her a hug, although they had never met before. She asked no questions except to offer them coffee. It smelt rich and strong and rare after the ground chicory and barley substitutes that most people were forced to drink nowadays and which Agnes had drunk in the convent. As she put it on the table – a small cup with black coffee, for the two men, a large cup of hot milky coffee for Agnes, all with sugar, she said, 'You have a long drive ahead. Why not have some soup? See, I've a pan here of lentil soup almost made. It will be ready in a few minutes.'

It was only when she smelled it that Agnes suddenly realised how hungry she was; it smelt delicious.

'No, we must get on,' the Wolf responded but

Madame, catching the look of disappointment on Agnes' face, persisted.

'It'll take you ten minutes. Look at the little one, she's hungry. And while you are eating it, I'll wrap up some bread and paté and tomatoes for you to take along.'

They were soon bent over steaming bowls of lentil soup with vegetables. It was thick, fragrant and delicious and the Wolf ate with no less relish than Agnes, although it was still only mid morning.

'Here you are, child,' Madame said as they finished, handing Agnes a basket filled with bread, fruit, and other small packages, along with a bottle of wine and a bottle of water. She kissed Agnes again, as the men went out into the yard.

'*Au revoir, Madame, merci beaucoup.*'

'*Au revoir, cherie.* Take care of yourself.'

She was reluctant to leave. She wished she could stay in that kitchen with the motherly wife of the innkeeper. It was the first glimpse of a normal home life she had had for a week, since she'd left the convent. But she was out into the courtyard again. The men had opened a barn door and there was a little Citroen van with a domed roof behind the small cab. The innkeeper drove it out, carefully, between the narrow doors and Agnes read the lettering on the side: *Jean Petit*, Purveyor of Champagne and Fine Wines.

'The papers are all in the glove box,' the innkeeper said quietly to the Wolf as he got out of the driver's seat. 'Certificates for the transport of wine, your identity papers. Everything's in order. There are no papers for the girl of course. I wasn't told she was coming.'

'That'll be okay. Don't worry,' the Wolf answered, gesturing to Agnes to go round to the passenger door and climbing into the driver's seat himself, but not before he had motioned the dog to jump into the space between them. A wolf-like dog for a man named Wolf, Agnes reflected. But the dog sniffed her in a friendly way and settled down putting his head on his master's leg.

'When can we expect you back?' asked the innkeeper.

'I could be a while. Maybe ten days. There are people in the network I have to make contact with down there. It's important, to pull everyone together now. You know what I am talking about.'

'Yes, good. Well, good luck.' With a wave he had turned away and was heading back to the house, as the van rolled out of the courtyard and turned left out onto the main road, heading south.

As they turned out, the Wolf said quickly,

'If we are stopped, your name is Ann Petit. I am your father and my name is Jean Petit, as it said on the side of the van. Did you read that?'

'Yes,' Agnes nodded assent.

'Good.'

'Where are we going?' No-one had told her this.

'I am a wine merchant. That is, Jean Petit is a wine merchant. We are delivering wine for the German headquarters in Lyon.'

'To the Germans?' Agnes did not understand.

'Oh yes, it is the Germans who take all our best wine and champagne these days – at least what we have not hidden. You saw perhaps, the stores of bottles in the underground cellars?' he glanced at her. 'Perhaps not. Still, at least they pay something for it this way.'

Up ahead, the traffic had trailed to a stop.

'*Ah, zut*! Our first barricade. Don't say any more than you have to.'

The Germans had blocked off half the road and were checking peoples' papers as they went through, whether on foot or in vehicles. A German car ahead was waved through quickly as the soldiers at the barricade saluted smartly, and next a farmer's van ahead of them.

'What's the dog's name?' Agnes whispered, a sudden thought occurring to her that a German soldier might ask her this.

'Panza,' the Wolf replied.

'Panza,' Agnes repeated. The dog turned his nose towards her at the sound of his name, and gave her ear a friendly lick. Then it was their turn.

There were about six soldiers, heavily armed, at the checkpoint. The Wolf said nothing, but handed out the papers from the glove compartment. Three soldiers bent over them, spending several minutes reading and checking them.

'Get out of the van,' one of them ordered the Wolf. Agnes felt the blood drain from her face, but the soldier merely wanted him to open the back, so that he could look in. Another peered in through the window at Agnes.

'Who are you?'

'That's my daughter,' the Wolf spoke from beside the soldier before Agnes could say anything. 'She's coming with me for the ride.' He paused, not rushing his words, 'It's the school holidays, you know. Her mother's busy.'

The soldier was uninterested. He scribbled something on the Wolf's papers and handed them back. The other soldier slammed the back door, having satisfied himself that the van was full of wooden cases of wine and they were on their way.

There were two more stops like this before the morning was over and then they were out on open roads through the countryside. The Wolf's face was grim. He did not like to have his face seen and known by the Germans, even if it was with a false identity. Agnes sensed that he would not welcome her chatter, so she kept quiet, only asking at one moment, 'How far is it to Lyon?'

'A long way. Five hundred kilometres. It may take us two days. It is late already. Those checks have delayed us.'

'Do we have enough petrol to get there?'

'Yes, I have some cans in the back. Behind the cases of wine. Luckily the Germans didn't find that.' Again, a grim smile played at the corners of his mouth.

For some time the countryside they drove through was covered with vines, in full leaf at this time of year. They spread across the hillsides in neat rows, looking like rippling waves running up a beach. Some had bushes of red roses at the end of the rows and sometimes Agnes could catch a glimpse of dark purple beneath the green, as the grapes were ripening.

They kept to small roads and they met little other traffic and no further road blocks for a long time. At length, the vines petered out and then for many hours there were forested slopes, occasional rivers that rushed along beside them, or which they crossed on small bridges. It was a hot but pleasant summer's day and they sped along the empty roads until, in the heat of the mid afternoon, they finally pulled off the road, up a forest track.

'Where are we going?' Agnes asked.

'I have to see some people briefly. They live at the end of this track. You can stay in the car. I'll only be a few minutes.'

Pine trees grew in closely on either side of the track, until, rounding a bend, they were suddenly upon the house. There was a confusion of people by the front door. In the next instant they took in what was happening. Two men were being led out of the house by German soldiers. They were handcuffed with their hands behind their backs and were being jerked roughly by the elbows, two soldiers to each man, while a German officer stood by barking orders and gesturing towards a military truck, parked behind a car outside the house.

It was too late for the Wolf to flee. The track was narrow and the car would have to be turned before they could get back down it and the military vehicle was taking up the only available turning space. But there was still a moment, while everyone looked up at their car, but had not moved towards them.

'Get out,' the Wolf hissed at Agnes. 'Open the door and crouch. Hide in the trees. Whatever happens, don't come back.'

Agnes obeyed instinctively at his first order. She heard the remaining instructions as the door closed behind her. Her side of the car was on the opposite side to the house and it was just possible that no one would see her. The car covered her path in the moment it took to reach a tree large enough to hide behind.

The officer was approaching rapidly, echoing the Wolf's order, now to the Wolf himself.

'Get out!' he shouted. 'Get your hands up!'

This track led to nowhere but the house. If a car came down it, it could be for no other reason than to see the people in the house. If they were being arrested, if they had been caught as members of the Maquis, then the Wolf would instantly be implicated as well. They would guess that he was also part of the Maquis. The German was asking questions, shouting and waving a pistol. There was no time to lose.

Agnes stepped out from behind the tree and walked towards the officer. She saw the two men look towards her; the expression on the Wolf's face was one of shock, dismay, even anger, as he too saw her; the German's face was simply puzzled. Agnes yanked on the sides of her skirt as if pulling up her pants and taking no notice of the German, she approached and in a high, whiny voice said, '*Papa*, my stomach's hurting. Let's go. I want to get to *Tante Marie's* house. There's no paper here. It's disgusting.'

The German officer had dropped his pistol. One of the soldiers had come up, having put the other men into the truck. He asked the officer a question in German and the officer responded, translating what Agnes had said. The soldier laughed and the officer stuck his pistol back into its holster. He jerked his head, gesturing for both of them to get back into the car.

'Go on. You can turn around here.' He indicated a space between the trees and watched as the Wolf backed into it and turned. As they drove out, Agnes found she was shivering violently. She glanced over and saw that the Wolf's knuckles were white as he clenched them on the wheel. No sooner were they out on the road than he turned to look at her, his face furious.

'What in God's name did you think you were doing? I told you to get out of sight and not to come back, whatever happened. You could have got us all killed.'

Agnes' response was equally, one of outrage, 'I

saved you! What do you mean? Why are you so angry with me? If I hadn't come back and behaved as if I was your daughter, they'd have arrested you.'

'You were lucky, that's all I can say, extremely lucky!' the Wolf was not to be appeased; he was still very angry with her.

'But I don't understand,' Agnes went on, not willing to let the matter drop. 'When we were at the inn, where we started, you told them that I would be a good decoy … that it would look like a normal father taking his daughter on a trip in the summer holidays. If I hadn't come out and pretended to be your daughter, they'd definitely have arrested you. If they had arrested us both, it would still have been better for you. You could have stuck to the story about the father and daughter on a car journey.'

The Wolf took a deep intake of breath, speaking slowly as if trying to control himself.

'Do you think for one moment, that I would have put your life at risk in order to make my own chances a little better?' He did not wait for an answer, or expect one. 'The point is … Ann …' he continued, 'you disobeyed my order and that was entirely unforgivable. Nobody disobeys orders in the Maquis. It would cost too many lives. Do you understand now?'

'Yes. I'm sorry,' Agnes' resentment subsided. She understood his point about obeying orders, but nonetheless she was puzzled. His only real concern then, had been for her safety, even at his own expense.

Why? Why should he really concern himself about her?

She sat silent beside him, feeling more sorrow than anything, sorrow that she had lost his respect in some way. It mattered to her.

They said nothing for several kilometres. At last he asked, his voice returned to normal, 'How's your stomach?'

Agnes looked at him quizzically and saw that there was a hint of a smile at the corner of his mouth. Then, in a serious tone, he said, 'Despite what I said before, you are a brave girl and you thought very quickly.' Then after a pause he added, 'But I'm sorry for those two men, they will be in for a very hard time now.'

Agnes said nothing. She knew that there was a danger there to the Wolf still, if under torture the men confessed to knowing him, which was why, she realised, he had not wanted anyone to see her with him at all. But the German officer had seemed convinced by the idea that he had simply turned off the road to allow his daughter to do what she had to do in the shelter of the trees and if they were lucky, the Germans would not connect them to the two men at all.

'I was going to stop so that we could have something to eat,' the Wolf said, 'but I think we should just keep going now. In a while when we turn off this road, I'll pull over for a few minutes to put some more petrol in the tank and then you can make a sandwich for us both, from the basket.'

* * *

By early evening they had travelled through another region of vines and again into more rugged countryside; Agnes was feeling very sleepy in the warmth of the sun and had dozed off again, when the Wolf shook her gently and pointed out of the window to his left. She gazed in wonder, instantly awake. In the distance to the east, the white peaked caps of mountains rose majestically. She gasped at their size and splendour as the snow and ice sparkled in the late sun.

'Where are we?'

'Those are the Alps. Didn't they teach you geography in London?'

She was surprised. It was the first time he had mentioned anything about her background.

'Yes. But I wasn't very good at it. And they didn't teach us much about France anyway.'

'Perhaps that explains why you thought it would be easy to cross France and find your grandparents,' the Wolf's tone was ironic and Agnes smiled sheepishly, wondering if he was really angry with her, or just thought her a fool.

'It's true. I had no idea France was so big.'

'So what did they teach you in Geography in London?' he continued.

'Mostly just about Britain. And Africa. I learnt all the countries of Africa. I was interested in that, you see, it's where my parents were.'

The Wolf did not respond and when she glanced at

him, Agnes saw that his face was set with the grim expression he normally wore. His moment of friendly curiosity seemed to have passed and they continued in silence.

'I should not say anything about my own past life,' Agnes thought to herself, 'he doesn't want to know. He said it was better that people didn't know too much about one another.' Still, she had perhaps saved his life back in the forest and she felt less of a burden to him than she had previously. She was even a little irritated by his unfriendly manner.

The journey continued in silence. Agnes watched as the setting sun in the west picked out the upper slopes of the mountains in the east until darkness fell.

'I am going to push on and finish our journey tonight. I have some friends we can stay with, but they are still a few hours away yet. It is risky, but I do not need to use headlights,' the Wolf told her, as the sun had finally disappeared. It did not grow really dark; it was a summer night and there was a moon rising.

'Try to get some sleep.'

Agnes complied. She wrapped her shawl into a bundle and propped it against the window, crooking her hand under her head, and slept.

Hours later, when clouds had drawn over the moon and the night was dark, she did not wake as she was lifted gently from the van and laid onto a bed, her boots removed and a blanket laid over her.

Chapter 10

The Wolf

Balow, my babe, lie still and sleep!
It grieves me sore to see thee weep.
Anon *16th C.*

It was still early in the morning when Agnes woke and found herself in a small, truckle-bed in what amounted to little more than a cupboard. From the next room she could hear voices talking anxiously, even heatedly, in low tones. There were three, two men's and a woman's, as well as that of the Wolf.

'There is no time to lose,' one of the men was saying to him. You have to get away from here as soon as possible. They're on to us, the Gestapo. At least, they are suspicious. They took Jean-Claude last week and tortured him, but he didn't give anything away.'

'How do you know this?' It was the Wolf's voice.

'We have someone inside the Gestapo office. She's

working as a secretary there. She's an excellent source of information, she has access to some of the plans they are making to move further south, to take the rest of France. The man she is working for is a bigwig in the army. For that reason they are going all out to get the Maquis in this area. She's a very important link for us this girl, we cannot risk putting them on their guard about us.'

'What about the wine? They are expecting the delivery today from Reims.'

'No problem. I'll drive it in. You'll have to give me the papers, including the identity,' one of the men replied.

'Wait a minute. They wrote on it, at one of the check points that I had a child with me.'

'Blast! No matter, I'll say I dropped her off at her aunt's, in … where did you go through?'

'In Chalon, perhaps. There are no Germans stationed there, they are not likely to chase it up.'

'In Chalon then. By the way, what are you doing with this girl?'

'I'm taking her to the mountains. I'm going up to the shepherds. We have some important men there – links in the chain south. I need to see them. I'll leave the girl with them. She's going south too.'

'How is this project going? Are we nearly there?' It was the woman's voice.

'It's about as airtight as it's ever going to be. There are a few details and people I need to make sure of, which is why I'm here. But I think we can be sure that this will be the most important escape route we have across France – all the more important if the Germans do take the south. Any one of us may need it some day soon.' The Wolf's voice was serious and earnest and the others were quiet, till one spoke again.

'You must go. Take the old Renault. We'd best get the kid up.'

As he spoke, Agnes opened the door into what proved to be a small kitchen.

'Ah, you're awake. Good,' the Wolf greeted her brusquely. 'We have to leave at once. Get your things.'

'I have them here already,' Agnes showed the little bag in her hand. The other people in the room said nothing to her and she had no time to look at them as she was hastened out of the door towards a battered little car outside. The delivery van of Jean Petit was parked beside it. Panza jumped into the back of the car as the Wolf opened the door.

'Down boy, stay on the floor.' The Wolf motioned to the dog to get down between the front and back seats so that he could not be seen. There was a wave from one of the men at the door, as the Wolf turned the car and headed away down the dirt track that led to the farmhouse where they had spent the night. They turned out onto the road and had not gone more than a hundred metres when a black car passed them. It bore the insignia of the Gestapo. The Wolf slowed and in their wing mirrors, they could both see the car turn into the dirt drive leading to the house that they had just left. The Wolf said nothing, but Agnes saw his jaw clench. He stopped and began to turn the car.

'Why are we going back?' Agnes asked, alarmed.

'We're not, but the car passed us going in one direction. In case they come back for a second look, we'll have gone in the opposite direction.'

Agnes held her breath as they passed the end of the drive, but the path turned and they could not see the house, or the black car from the road. At the first crossroads, they took a left turn and then a series of further turns, though always heading eastwards. They did not begin to breathe freely again for at least an hour, when Panza, whimpering, reminded them that he was still crouched on the floor behind them.

'Okay, boy. You can get up.' The dog jumped onto the seat, pushing a grateful nose towards his master's ear and then to Agnes, who turned and patted his head.

'Will they be okay?' she asked, 'those people in the house?' She had not dared to ask the question before.

'I don't know. If they are lucky, they will just be questioned, then left alone. Certainly, it was very fortunate that we were not there for a few minutes longer. The outcome may have been very different then, for them and for us.' He said no more for a few minutes, only looking at the road with a grim expression.

Panza pushed his nose forward again, whining softly for attention.

'He's so good,' Agnes said, turning to pat him again. 'He always does what you tell him.'

'He's a good soldier,' the Wolf replied. He changed the subject abruptly, 'Now, you are no longer Ann Petit. You are Ann … think of a name.'

'Ann … Dumas?'

'Good. Ann Dumas, and I am Jean Dumas. We are on our way to visit my mother, (your grandmother), who is ill. She lives in the mountains. Okay?'

'Okay,' echoed Agnes with a smile, till the Wolf reminded her, 'We are not out of danger yet. We are still in German occupied France and we have no papers which is enough to get us arrested. Just pray that we don't get stopped.'

They drove on for some time, along increasingly small and remote roads and once or twice along dirt farm tracks which crossed fields and farmland. Stretching back behind them and to their left were the Alps, but the land in front of them began to rise steeply as the roads climbed into the foothills of the mountains.

'That's it,' the Wolf said at last. 'Theoretically, we are in Free France now. We may not be out of danger, but we can breathe a little more easily for the moment.'

He stopped the car. They were on a tiny road which led steeply into the mountains, zigzagging its way high above them. To either side stretched grassy meadows of wild grasses and flowers and above them, pine forest stretched upwards towards invisible peaks.

'Come, Panza. Let's stretch our legs for a couple of minutes.' The dog jumped down from the car and bounded out into the meadow, enjoying the space and the warmth of the sun and fresh mountain air. Suddenly Agnes felt she had to run too. She spread out her arms and ran, laughing, after the dog. Panza ran back to her, circled her barking and ran along beside her across the meadow and then back towards the Wolf. He was watching the two of them, the girl and the dog, as they came closer and Agnes could see him smiling slightly. It was the first time she had seen him smile.

Some time later, and off the road down a series of bouncy tracks, they came to a shepherds' lodge, a hut roughly made of stones piled one on top of another and with a slate roof. The Wolf parked the car behind it and left the keys on a shelf inside the otherwise empty hut.

'We must walk from here,' he said. Agnes had only her little bag to carry and the Wolf a small satchel which he carried over his shoulder. They had no food, having left the basket and what remained in it back at the farmhouse that morning, in their hurry to leave. He set off up a steep mountain path at a swift pace until Agnes was struggling to keep up and even the dog was lagging beside her, his tongue lolling out in the heat.

'Please can you tell me where we are going?' Agnes asked, raising her voice to reach the Wolf striding ahead of her. They had been walking for some hours and he had not looked back, except with an occasional glance to check that she was still behind him. She was very tired now. It was hot. They had nothing to drink. She had no idea in truth where the Wolf was taking her, or why they were heading into the mountains. She had heard him say something about shepherds, but he had said nothing to her. She felt that she might begin to cry and her face assumed a stubborn fierceness.

The Wolf stopped and looked back at her, then stepped back a few feet towards her.

'Look, I am trying to get as far away from danger as possible. There is a stream just there, where we can drink. We will stop when it grows dark and then we will talk. For now we must press on. This is not the time or place for tears.'

Agnes felt angry and humiliated by his harsh response, but the cold, clear water was delicious and refreshing and she felt better after the long drink which she, the Wolf and Panza all took from it. From there on she said nothing, but marched onwards with weary, but fierce determination.

At last they stopped. The light was beginning to fade and the air was cool. They were high in the mountains though still far below any snow line and could see nothing but peaks and rolling slopes around them. A fall of rocks had made a shelter against a slope, like a cove or natural harbour, and here they settled.

'I cannot risk lighting a fire,' the Wolf said, 'our smoke would be too obvious in this clear mountain air and possibly still visible from the valley. You will have to stay hungry too, I'm afraid. We've nothing to eat but a few biscuits I have in my bag, and here, there's some water too. I refilled the bottle at the stream.' He handed the bottle and some hard biscuits to Agnes and she bit into them hungrily, resting her back against the sun-warmed rock. They were tasteless however and sandy textured, their dryness sticking to the roof of her mouth and despite her hunger, she could not eat much, sharing them instead with the dog.

'It was important that we got as far as we could today. Now, I will answer your question, "Where are we going?" I am taking you up to meet some friends of mine in the mountains. They are shepherds who will take you south, towards your grandparents when they return to their homes. Have you heard of the "transhumance"?'

'No, what is that?'

'The transhumance is the journey the shepherds and their flocks make every summer, away from the hot, dusty plains and low hills of the south and into the mountains to graze the sheep where the pasture is fresh and sweet. They live up here for five months or so, and then, at the end of the summer, they go south again, back to their homes and families. It will soon be time for them to go home now. The nights are getting cold.'

'*Monsieur* Wolf,' Agnes asked, not wishing to make him angry again. 'Why are you doing this for me?'

The Wolf paused, then he spoke gruffly, 'You were a danger, left on your own. You had seen too many of the men I work with. If you had been captured, you might have given them away, even if you hadn't wanted to.'

'No, I would never,' Agnes protested fiercely.

'The Gestapo would not stop at torturing little girls,' the Wolf responded bluntly. 'No, it will be better if you can get to the south and lead a quiet life there till the war is over. You were lucky, I had to come this way to see some people.'

'I heard you say there was a "big project" happening. What is it?'

He looked at her sharply, but after another pause, he answered, 'You should not ask so many questions, but I will answer this one. You know your friend Frank, the American pilot who you helped to rescue? By now, he should be back in England, if all has gone according to plan. If he had been captured by the Germans, he would be in a prisoner of war camp by now, at best. At worst, he would be dead. All over France, people are fighting secretly against the German occupation. This is part of their fight, to help people escape. Sometimes it is necessary for the helpers to escape too, because if the Germans find them, they will shoot them. You see, people are putting their lives at risk every day. Even for you, people have risked their lives.' Agnes said nothing. There was nothing she could say. He went on, 'This project is only one of many things happening, but it is to establish an important escape route through the south, out to sea. It has begun already and we have taken many people out, but we are preparing for the day the German army occupies the south as well, as inevitably they will, and every escape needs a network of trustworthy people.'

He paused, 'I am not giving away any secrets, you understand. The Germans are aware of an escape route, but do not know how it is done, or who is involved.'

As he spoke, he stood up, more easily to remove his jacket.

'Here. Put this on,' he handed the jacket to Agnes. 'It will get cold in the night.'

'But what about you?'

'I'll be okay. The dog will stay close to me and keep me warm and I do not want to sleep anyway. I will keep watch. You must sleep now.'

Agnes tucked herself down as comfortably as she could among the rocks, pulling the jacket over her shoulders. She shivered with the cold. She was alone on a mountainside with this man who she ardently wished would not be so cold and unfriendly, so difficult to talk to, although he was not unkind to her. Somehow, though, she had no doubt that he wanted to help her, even that he had gone to a great deal of trouble to do so, and that he would protect her if the need arose. Yet she did not know why she was so sure of this and she had seldom felt more lonely than she did now. She ached from the climb and her stomach grumbled with hunger. Her last thoughts, before she drifted into an exhausted sleep were of her grandmother's perfume and soft cheek as she bent to kiss her goodnight in her bed at home in London, and a hot trail of tears ran down her cheek as her eyes closed.

True to his word, the Wolf started them early. Agnes still felt very tired and very hungry. There was a heavy mist in the early morning and they followed the paths which were no more than wild goat tracks, branching steeply uphill, seeing only a few metres ahead of them as they climbed. Soon, the mist lifted and the sun began to heat the path before them. At length, they found themselves walking beside a steep ravine; from time to time, rushing streams crossed their paths, tumbling over the edge into the ravine in long, narrow waterfalls. The path was steep and rocky alongside the ravine and presently Agnes tripped and fell. She had grazed her knee badly. It was the kind of thing that would not have bothered her for a moment back in London playing with the boys among the bomb sites, but she was exhausted and sat down on a rock beside the path, rubbing her knee. The Wolf relented. He cupped some water from a nearby stream and splashed it over the graze, dabbing at it then with the hem of her skirt.

'It is okay, there is no dirt in it, but you are tired. Sit there for a few minutes. I will go up a little way to see if I can find out exactly where we are.' He looked worried, exasperated even, she felt, at the way she slowed his progress.

He left her sitting on a rock beside the path. The sun was warm and the rock on which she sat was comfortable. He was gone for some time, longer than she had thought. At length, she opened her bag and drew out David's book. She opened it at random and began to read a poem. So absorbed was she that she did not hear the Wolf return until his shadow fell across her page as he bent over her shoulder to see what she was reading. All at once, he tried to seize the book from her hands.

'What is this?' he growled at her. 'This book is English. You little fool! We could all have died if the Germans had found this on you.' She hurriedly pushed the book back into her bag beside her, holding it close, but he snatched the bag away from her and in one gesture flung it out into the ravine below them.

'No, no!' Agnes screamed. Running to the edge of the ravine she peered over, but could see nothing other than the steep slope with a few scrubby trees and bushes which ended in a fast flowing river crashing over rocks a long way below. She turned on him.

'I hate you! I hate you!' Tears coursed down her cheeks. Everything that was precious to her was in that bag. It was all she had left of her past life. After a moment, the Wolf said more quietly, 'I am sorry, but you should have told me. You said it was a book you were given a few days ago. I assumed it was French.' Then after a pause he added, 'That was my fault, I should not have assumed ...'

Agnes said nothing. She stared down into the ravine, her vision blurred. At length, the Wolf tried to take her arm to lead her on. She pulled away from him and sank to the ground again. Suddenly everything that she had gone through seemed too much to bear and she bent her head into her hands, propped on her knees. Uncontrollable sobs racked her body. Losing her statuette, the last link with her home in London, the photograph of her mother and David's book was the last straw. She did not care if she never went any further.

After a few moments she became aware of a large, gentle hand on her head, as she lay face down in the grass. He stroked her head till her sobs subsided. Then he stood up and said quietly, 'There is nothing to be done now. We must go on.'

She stood and followed him as he continued to climb the path. After another half hour of slow walking in silence, they reached the edge of a gently sloping meadow. The Wolf stopped.

'You need a rest. Here,' he put down his bag and rolled up his jacket, offering it to her as a pillow. She lay on it. Her tears had exhausted her and the sun was warm on her body.

'Have a little sleep. I will be back shortly. Panza, you stay here. Wait with her. Stay.'

The dog whined softly but sat down at Agnes' side watching as his master disappeared back along the path. Agnes fell asleep. She did not know how long she slept, but the Wolf had still not returned when she woke. The dog was nearby, watching the path. He wagged his tail when he saw her awake and came over to her, giving her a brief lick on the hand.

It was another hour and growing late in the afternoon before the Wolf appeared. In his hand he grasped Agnes' bag. It was dusty and the strap was broken, torn away on one side from the seam which had held it, but it was otherwise intact. The Wolf bore a large scratch across his forehead and cheek.

He handed it to Agnes.

'Thank you,' she said at length, astonished. 'How did you get it?'

'I was lucky, it was caught on a tree not too far down, but it was very difficult to get to. I risked my life; it was crazy.' He spoke as if angry with himself.

She said nothing, so he continued, 'We must go now. I had hoped to reach the shepherds' encampment by nightfall, but I think it is further than I thought and we have lost some time. We will have to stop one more night.'

They walked another hour or two, but the sun was already beginning to sink towards the mountain tops and Agnes was lagging behind again. They had been climbing steadily and had now reached a kind of plateau of undulating, green meadows with long grasses and wild flowers and gentle slopes, although still surrounded by high peaks. The Wolf led them along beside a small stream which tumbled gently over rocks, till they found a sheltered hollow.

'We will stop here for the night,' he said. 'It will be safe to light a fire now if we can find some wood.'

There were pine trees not far away and leaving Agnes quenching her thirst from the sweet fresh water of the stream, the Wolf strode away and soon returned with enough wood to make a small fire. Next, he edged his way along the stream until he found a pool of water. A few small fish hovered there in the shade. Gently he lowered his hand in, so carefully that the fish only flickered briefly in mistrust before settling again. Slowly he began to stroke the stomach of the largest fish till it seemed hypnotised, then he grasped it firmly with one swift move and lifted it out of the water, hitting it deftly on the head with a stone. Agnes watched, astonished as he went on till he had four small fish. Next, with his knife, he cleaned and gutted the fish and skewered them with a long sharp stick, holding them over the little fire and turning them, till, a few minutes later they were ready to eat. Agnes ate one, carefully picking the fish from the fragile bones, then she did the same with the second one he handed her, but shared it with Panza who had watched the whole operation with great attention. He took the offering from her fingertips gently, with his teeth. The Wolf smiled.

'You will feel better for having eaten something.' He continued to eat in silence for a few minutes, then he said, 'You should check that everything in your bag is all right. Perhaps something may have been broken or fallen out.'

Agnes opened the bag, pulling out the book first.

'May I see?' the Wolf asked. He held out his hand.

'It's a book of poetry. It was given to me by a friend.'

'*The Oxford Book of English Verse*,' he read, looking at the spine. 'Who was your friend, the one who gave you this?'

'He was called David. He was taken away by the Germans. Him and the other children I stayed with in the convent. They were Jewish.'

'I see,' he said quietly. Agnes brought out the statuette.

'It's not exactly a doll, either,' she said. 'It's something I saved from home. Oh, his sword is broken'

The Wolf took the little wooden statuette of the old Spanish knight. Don Quixote held a long thin sword. It stretched upright, between his clasped hands and the little patch of wooden floor between his feet. The thin sword had broken in Agnes' bag, but the pieces were both there. He said nothing but looked at the figure for a long time. The late afternoon sun was still warm, but Agnes thought the Wolf looked suddenly very pale.

'I am really sorry about not telling you about the book. It is very important to me.'

He still held the wooden statuette in his hands.

'I will mend the sword of Don Quixote for you, as soon as I find some twine. Then you can glue it later.'

'You know who he is?' Agnes asked, surprised. When the Wolf did not reply, she added, 'David knew who he was too. He told me the story about him. Him and his friend, his squire … I've forgotten his name.'

'Sancho Panza. His squire was called Sancho Panza.'

'Yes, that's right!' exclaimed Agnes, ' "Panza", like your dog. What a strange coincidence.'

'Not such a coincidence,' the Wolf replied quietly, 'I am sorry. He reminded me so much of my own childhood suddenly. I too, grew up with the story of Don Quixote and his crazy adventures.'

'I see.' Agnes understood now, the expression on his face when he first saw the statuette. She was curious about him, but she knew better than to ask him any questions.

'Thank you for getting my bag back,' she said simply.

The Wolf's next words surprised her as much by the gentle tone as the interest he suddenly showed.

'I would like you to tell me all that has happened to you … Ann. Since you left London, or even, before then. If I am to help you to find your grandparents and keep you safe. It is essential that we trust each other, and tell the truth. You must tell me as much as possible. It may help.'

So Agnes sat down again. She told him her story. When she started, she could not stop; it came bubbling out of her with a force as irrepressible as the mountain river which had nearly carried away her bag a short while before. She did not leave anything out. She started with her life in London and her parents' departure early in her life, their death and then her grandmother's; she told him of Dilly and all she had meant in her life; of the boys in Dover who, along with Dilly's son Albert, had first told her about the Resistance movement in France, although neither she nor they had understood the scale of it then; about the children in the convent and her time with them; the sheltering nuns and the children's arrest the morning the German soldiers came; then her time living rough and her chance sighting of the pilot coming down in his parachute. From time to time as she talked, she remembered the wild stories she used to make up for the boys in the bomb sites and she wondered if the Wolf would believe this one, which was all true, but sounded a great deal more far-fetched. She did not leave anything out that she could remember and all the while she talked, the Wolf said nothing but sat with his head bowed, occasionally looking at her steadily for a few moments.

Finally she stopped.

'Now, here I am. I am not so far away now, from my grandparents I mean. I don't know exactly where to find them though, and I don't even know if they will want me when I get there ...' Her voice trailed away.

The Wolf still sat in silence for several moments more then, 'I cannot believe you have done all this and have come so far. You will find your grandparents and they will want you. This I am sure of. You have been very lucky Agnes, and there are many good people who have helped you.'

'I know…'Agnes was confused. 'Did you call me Agnes? How did you know that was my real name. Did I tell you?'

'You must have done. In any case, if it is your real name, you had better use it now. It may make it harder to find your grandparents with a false name. They will certainly not know they have a granddaughter called Ann, if they think she is called Agnes.' The Wolf smiled slightly, then said, 'For now you should get some rest. We have another long walk before us tomorrow.'

Agnes was suddenly very sleepy. Talking of everything she had kept to herself for so long, suddenly left her feeling tired with a deep weariness that she could not explain. She had scarcely time to take in the sweet smell of the grass as she lay down and the tinkling of the stream, before she was asleep.

The Wolf, sitting comfortably on a rock and smoking a pipe, picked up the book which Agnes had left out of her bag for him. There was scarcely any natural light left and only a little from the fire, but he could make out a few words on the page. He leafed through the book, without stopping long on any particular poem, until a page fell open more readily than the rest. He put down his pipe and picked out the little black and white sea-stained photograph of Agnes' mother, which had been tucked close to the spine of the book. He held it close to the light of the fire to look at it carefully. Then, replacing it gently into the book which he closed and laid down, he put his head in his hands and wept. Agnes slept on.

In the morning, they walked on, at a gentler pace, but steadily. The paths were less steep and they crossed meadows and valleys, heading southward. The Wolf seemed quieter even than usual, but at length he said, 'You are very like your mother, you know.'

'What?' Agnes was startled. 'My mother?' How could he possibly know?

'Yes. The photograph. There is a photograph in your book which I looked at last night.'

'Oh.' Agnes said nothing more for a moment, resentful that he had looked at something of hers that was so private, then, 'I don't think I am really. She was quite fair, you see, whereas I am dark, like my father.'

'No, but despite that,' the Wolf insisted. 'It's not just the colour of your hair. It's the whole shape of your face and your expression.'

'Oh,' again, Agnes was puzzled. He seemed to have drawn a great many conclusions from one small photograph. But she was pleased, nonetheless. Evidently he wanted to be kind to her. Everyone always said how beautiful her mother was and if she, Agnes, had something of her, then in a way, it brought her closer.

She could not see the Wolf's face as she walked behind him, but she thought he seemed sad. Perhaps, he too, had lost someone special to him. She would have liked to ask him, but felt shy. He was far less distant and severe than he had been when they first met, but still, there seemed to be a kind of wall around him which she could not breech. Another thought occurred to her.

'Do you know how to speak English? I mean, if you were reading the poems.'

There was a pause, then the Wolf said shortly, 'I can read it. Yes.'

He said no more, but walked on swiftly, seemingly lost in thought and at length, he started to whistle a low tune. From time to time they spotted a small flock of sheep or herd of goats, with a shepherd who would raise his crook to them from a distance. These were mountain people who lived here for most of the year, going down to the nearest villages in the valleys only when the snows began.

At last towards the end of the afternoon, they rounded a peak and stood on a steep slope looking down onto a valley. It was crossed by a fast-flowing stream and patched with copses of leafy trees. The grass in this valley was emerald green and the slopes surrounding it dotted with wild flowers of every colour. Many small paths led out of the valley in different directions to neighbouring slopes. Above the peaks surrounding it, the sky was a clear, deep blue.

Strewn across the valley were thousands of sheep and goats. They heard them even before they could see them, as many wore heavy bells around their necks, which clanked rhythmically as they grazed or walked, their intermittent bleating carrying on the clear mountain air. The sheep were being gathered from the surrounding meadows into the valley for safety in the night. From the farthest visible slopes, Agnes could see dogs herding small groups of sheep down towards the others. As they descended, approaching the gathering of people, the sun was beginning to set, sinking towards the tips of the western peaks. Down by the river a large fire was being built and people were gathering to cook the evening meal. Agnes and the Wolf beside her, watched for a minute or two.

'We'll go down to the river,' he said, after they had surveyed the scene below them for some minutes. 'We will find my friends down there, I am sure.'

Chapter 11

The Shepherds

Come live with me and be my Love,
And we will all the pleasures prove
That hills and valleys, dales and fields
Or woods or steepy mountain yields
The Passionate Shepherd to his Love
Christopher Marlowe

People were gathered near the large fire, helping with the preparation of food or bringing more wood to feed the flames. There were women and children among the many men and some young shepherds, only a few years older than Agnes herself. A small, wiry woman with grey hair seemed to be directing the major undertaking of feeding so many people. Her sleeves were rolled up and her hands bound in a cloth as she lent across to an enormous pot which hung from a tripod over the fire, prodding or stirring it with what looked like a long, pale stick. Those shepherds not directly involved in the preparations were sitting in groups, chatting quietly and puffing on clay pipes. Elsewhere, close by, dogs were being fed and feet, hands, faces were being bathed in the river.

As Agnes and the Wolf approached, people turned curiously towards them and returned their greeting cheerfully.

'I am looking for Jean-Loup … is he here?' the Wolf asked.

'Ah, *le loup*,' replied one of the men, 'he's over there, by the trees.' He waved an arm towards a small copse of trees a short distance away where a little group sat, smoking pipes and talking.

'You stay here,' the Wolf commanded. He strode away leaving Agnes standing on the edge of the group, feeling awkward and self-conscious as the others by the fire looked at her. But not for long.

'Are you hungry?' asked one of the women who was not engaged in stirring the pot over the fire. She beckoned Agnes closer, breaking a chunk from a loaf of rough, brown, flattish bread and passing it to Agnes as she spoke, while a young shepherd cut a slice from a big, round cheese and handed it to her on the knife.

'Have some of this. It is good sheep's cheese,' he invited. They spoke with a strong, musical, southern dialect which Agnes had not heard before. It was hard to follow as they spoke quickly among themselves.

'Come and sit down while we wait for our meal,'

said the young man who had given her the cheese. She sat down with him amongst a small group of young people. They were chatting and laughing and amongst them two were whittling at pieces of wood with a knife; another was blowing softly on a small flute-like whistle which he had evidently carved himself, testing the notes he could get from it. Agnes sat quietly with them, trying to follow their conversation and watching the skill with which they quickly shaped the pieces of wood. They asked her no questions and she soon felt quite comfortable with the simple way in which they had welcomed her presence among them.

'Here, try this,' said the young man with the whistle, passing it to Agnes. She had learned the recorder at school. She hadn't been particularly good at it, but she could play 'Three Blind Mice' and could reproduce it on this three-hole whistle. The others laughed.

'Bravo!' they told her, 'it works, Gaston. Not bad!'

A short while later, they were all called to eat. As they approached the fire, Agnes looked about her for the Wolf. It was growing dark, but she could see him approaching slowly with the men he had been talking with, to join the large group gathering by the fire.

'Agnes,' he called over to her, 'come. I would like you to meet my friend, Jean-Loup.' He introduced her to an elderly, but upright shepherd. His face was nut brown, with deep lines carved by long exposure to the weather, his hair and beard a thick, grizzled white. He was a quiet man with a kind, calm look in his eye. His hand, as he reached out to shake Agnes', was like the gnarled root of a tree.

'How funny that your name is "wolf" too,' she said. John-Wolf it would be in English.

'Ah yes, but Jean-Loup is my name. For the Wolf, it is his title,' the old man replied. 'It is different.'

Certainly Agnes soon saw that the young boys teased the old man for his name, as they would never tease the bearded stranger who had just arrived with Agnes.

'Ah, the wolf has been among the sheep all day,' they laughed, or 'Have some bread, *le loup*. A hungry wolf is a dangerous wolf.'

Agnes wondered if the shepherd might be offended by the fun made of his name, but Jean-Loup smiled kindly at them; he had probably heard the same jokes for many years, and evidently took them only in the affectionate spirit in which they were made.

Soon, all were seated around the fire, with metal plates and spoons and a rich goat-meat stew, well flavoured with wild herbs from the mountain pastures, and more rough bread. When all was cleared away and the darkness was deepening, on this late summer night, they began to sing. Their songs were folk songs from Provence and sung in the old language, so that Agnes did not understand them, but she was warmed by the spirit of these simple, friendly people, nonetheless. After a few songs, the young ones called for a story and story-telling began.

'In French, for the little one,' said the first story-teller, and Agnes realised he was referring to her and was going to tell the story in French instead of Provençal, for her sake. The story was about a mean and lazy miller who added dust to his flour to save money, until his trickery was discovered and exposed by a young shepherd. There was much laughter from the listeners.

Overhead the night sky had grown rich with millions of stars. Agnes had never seen so many, or seen them shine so bright. The tranquillity and beauty surrounding her and the good natured camaraderie of the shepherds, as well as a greater sense of safety and distance from the war than she had known for a long time, began to work a kind of magic on Agnes. A new sense of peace and happiness filled her heart, quite unexpectedly, in the company of these people. She was sleepy and lay down, resting her head on her crooked arm to listen. Before the story-teller reached the end of his tale, she had fallen asleep on the grass, between the two wolves.

From time to time, in the night, she woke and heard the bubbling motion of the river close by and the rhythmic clanking of sheep bells a little further off and these comforting sounds quickly sent her back to sleep on the soft grass.

The shepherds were gone early in the morning. It was to be a source of wonder to Agnes how they and their dogs could distinguish their individual sheep. By night the flocks mingled with each other close to the river and the safety of the fire in one enormous group. But somehow each morning, separate flocks gathered and were led away as each shepherd took his own sheep to higher pastures.

Agnes had slept late, worn out by the last few days of travelling and the sun was already warm when she woke. The Wolf was not far off. He was washing some of his clothes in the river, his shirt and his socks and talking to some women who were washing clothes too. He beckoned her over as he saw her get up.

'Agnes, it would be a good idea if you washed too. You stink after all that travelling; it must be a while since you had a bath.' He laughed, smiling at her and the women laughed too, and so did Agnes.

'Take all your clothes off,' the woman whose name was Ann-Marie handed her a bar of soap. 'Get in and wash. I'll wash your clothes.'

If Agnes felt self-conscious about undressing, she soon realised there was no room for this kind of modesty here. Women stood up to their thighs in the water, rinsing clothes and pots, their skirts tucked up, while several small children dabbled naked at the water's edge. Ann-Marie, hurried her along, helping her off with her clothes. The cold of the water was breathtaking for a moment or two, but soon her skin numbed and then grew warm. The sun was hot now and soon she was splashing happily and laughing in the sparkling, crystal clear water which raced over her.

If she sat on the bed of the river on the smooth stones, it came up to her neck. Ann-Marie and the other woman, Huguette, who had stirred the pot the night before, laughed at her, as they washed the clothes by bashing them against some larger smooth rocks, rubbing them with soap and dipping them in the water.

'Dip your head back, I'll wash your hair.' Ann-Marie, who was round and motherly, waded in, her skirt tucked up into her waist band, so that the water swirled about her bare knees. She scrubbed at Agnes' short, dark hair with the same soap and held her as she leant back in the water to rinse it off. Agnes was shivering by the time she got out and her skin had a bluish tinge. One of the women held out a rough towel to her and rubbed her vigorously till her skin shone red. She sat then on the grass by the two women and the sun soon warmed her through. Her clothes did not take much longer to dry, spread out on scrubby, aromatic bushes. Agnes felt she could never have imagined how delicious it felt to be clean after so long without a bath.

The Wolf had moved discreetly away while Agnes was bathing, and gone about some other business, but he returned when she was dressed. He sat in the sun, chatting to the women while he also, dried off.

'We'll walk up to the pastures and find Jean-Loup, shall we?' he suggested. He stood up. He too, looked clean and refreshed. He had taken off the hat he had worn pulled low over his eyes for most of the time she had been with him and his face looked younger and softened in this mountain air. His dark hair was fluffy from its recent scrubbing in the river and drying in the sun. The war seemed a million miles away. A little boy of two or three hung on to the Wolf's trousers, drawn to the one man not gone away with the sheep.

'Stay here!' the little boy commanded.

'Hey, little one,' the Wolf bent and caught up the small boy, 'where did you spring from?'

The little boy gurgled with appreciation and the Wolf tossed the little boy gently up in his arms while he shrieked with laughter and his mother laughed too.

'Always looking for attention, that one!' she exclaimed.

The Wolf was so different here. She looked up at his smiling face. The sun was behind him and his eyes were laughing. His big hands blotted out the dazzle of the sun for a brief instant. For a moment her heart seemed to stop. The force of a memory came back to her – it was in the garden in Kensington, the sun behind her father's head, as he tossed her up in the air. She turned away.

As they walked away from the river, the Wolf was whistling; it was the same tune he had whistled the day before, and presently he started to sing in a rumbling low tone which made Agnes smile. The words were Provençal and she could not understand them, but it was good to hear him happy.

* * *

'I am going to have to leave you tomorrow morning,' he told her, as they climbed a gentle path out of the valley, 'but Jean-Loup will look after you, and the women. They are good people. You will have to stay here with them until they go home at the end of the summer, but you will be safe, safer than you have been for many months. Jean-Loup will find your grandparents.'

'Does he know them?' Agnes asked eagerly.

'No, but he knows approximately where they live and he has many friends in the area. You must trust him absolutely.'

'I will.' Agnes did not know what more to say, but she felt, suddenly, as if an enormous weight had been lifted from her. At the same time she felt an unexpected regret that the Wolf was going. She had grown much closer to him over the last two days and felt she had misjudged him before. It was as if he had built a wall around himself so that she could not see the real person behind it. It occurred to her now for the first time that he would leave and she would never even know his real name.

They soon found Jean-Loup and his troop. The sheep were grazing in a meadow full of long sweet grass and tall wild flowers, giant daisies and blue and yellow flowers that stood up amongst the grasses. There were butterflies of many colours everywhere, fluttering above the flowers like tiny prayer flags blowing in the wind. All around soared peaks of mountains which,

225

at the very top were still white with snow. There was absolute peace. The bells and bleating of the sheep were softened by the vast space around them and the gentle hum of bees among the flowers was the only other sound. Agnes had never been anywhere as beautiful.

She spent the afternoon exploring the surrounding slopes and little streams that galloped over rocky beds and down sudden falls and she played with Panza, who fetched the sticks she threw for him. Sometimes though, he dropped the sticks in the sudden need to run at full speed, soaring over the grass like a hare, his legs stretched in great bounds. She laughed to watch his sheer joy at the freedom of the mountain meadows. The old sheep dog looked on, bewildered, but the Wolf and the shepherd, Jean-Loup, lifted their heads from their conversation and smiled at the girl and the dog in understanding. At length, both Agnes and Panza were exhausted and she flopped down, lying in the long grass and looking up at the blue of the sky while Panza lay panting beside her. The afternoon wore on and as the sun began to lower among the high peaks, the Wolf came to sit beside her. He seemed thoughtful and quiet.

'This has been a good day,' he said, at last. He seemed to want to say something else but was hesitant, weighing his words carefully. At length, however, he added 'Don't think too badly of me, Agnes, I have been hard with you at times I know. The war has made people tough; down below in France, away from these mountains, lives are in danger at every moment.'

'It's okay, I understand.' Agnes felt suddenly shy. 'I know you're not as … well, as … I know you care about me more than you seemed to at first. You have been very kind. Thank you for bringing me here. I don't know how I would ever have got to my grandparents without you. Sometimes,' she hesitated, 'sometimes you have made me remember what it would be like to have a father.' She wondered if she had said too much, if he would be offended by this, but he looked at her for a moment, searchingly, his expression sad again, very sad. At last he said, 'One day, when the war is over, perhaps we will meet again and then things will be different.' He paused again. 'Tomorrow, when I go, Agnes, I am going to leave the dog with you.'

'Panza? But you can't!' Agnes exclaimed. She was shocked. She had never doubted how much he loved his dog and how closely Panza followed him everywhere, gazing up at him whenever they were still.

But the Wolf continued, 'He will take care of you and keep you company and you will be doing me a favour, if you take good care of him. It is too dangerous for him to stay with me down there. I am too recognisable with a dog, particularly a dog which is as distinctive as this one. People remember him, and I cannot afford to be recognised, I still have important work to do. You understand this, do you, Agnes?' She nodded.

Suddenly she felt that she was going to miss him terribly. She turned and put her arms around him, kissing him on the cheek. The Wolf seemed to hesitate for just a moment, then she felt his strong arm around her, giving her a gentle hug in return.

'Thank you. I'll take great care of him,' she said quietly as he let her go. Again, he was silent and looking into his face she thought for a moment that his eyes were full of tears.

He looked out across the mountains for a few minutes and finally turned to her again, his face composed.

'Agnes, I know I can trust you not to say anything to anyone about me. It is not for myself that I am afraid, but there are many people connected with me and relying on me who would be put in danger. You saw already how suspicious the Germans are and you played your part in getting us out of trouble. You are a clever girl and you will know who you can trust and who you should not, but unless you are absolutely sure, do not confide in anyone. '

Agnes did not know what to say. The praise was wholly unexpected, but she nodded. She remembered the saying she had heard in London.

' "Loose talk costs lives",' she said, in English, without thinking. He smiled.

'You are absolutely right,' he said. It was the first English she had heard him speak and his accent was almost perfect.

When Agnes awoke, the next morning, he was gone. Jean-Loup was nearby, preparing to leave, and Panza was tied by a rope to the tree under which she had slept. His nose lay on his outstretched paws and he was whining softly.

Seeing her sit up Jean-Loup nodded towards the dog, 'He was tied, so he would not follow his master,' he said. 'You had better keep him tied for a couple of days. You can bring him up with the troop if you like or you can stay here and help the women. Whatever you wish, but if you are coming, fetch yourself some bread and cheese to eat on the way.'

Agnes soon settled into the routine of the shepherds' life. On most days, she accompanied Jean-Loup. He was a man of few words, used to solitude and completely at peace whether in his own company or that of others. On the mountain slopes, she wandered for hours, gathering different wild flowers which she pressed between the pages of her poetry book, or paddling in the icy streams or sometimes just sitting quietly beside Jean-Loup as he sat, as still and solid as if he were an old oak tree providing shelter. At times, he asked to look at her flowers and taught her the names of them, pointing out others which grew on the mountain and telling her which plants were good for curing all kinds of illnesses and healing wounds. Some days Agnes went with a group of younger shepherds, enjoying their banter and their songs for a change, and sometimes she stayed in the valley with the women and smallest children, helping them with washing and finding wood for the fire. She was happier than she had been for a long time as she joined in the simple tasks of the day. The evenings were much like the first one she had spent with them, with songs and stories around the fire. She picked up a few words of Provençal. She was surprised by how much she missed the Wolf at first, how much she thought about what he would have said as she listened to the conversation of the shepherds.

Panza was her constant companion. They slept curled up against each other, or raced each other through the meadows and streams, laughing and barking in sheer exhilaration at the space and beauty of the summer mountain world. The women laughed at her and tousled her hair, insisting she washed, from time to time, and treating her as one of their own. Sometimes she looked into the book of poetry. Lying on her stomach in the long grasses and wild flowers, she read the long story poems, 'The Lady of Shalott', and 'The Rime of the Ancient Mariner', to the soft drone of bees and crickets, the tinkling of streams and with the warmth of the sun on her back. Often, she thought of David and the other children and wondered what had happened to them and where they were now. She missed David, especially. How he would have loved it here. How she would have liked to talk to him about the shepherds' stories or the poems she had read. She missed Eleanor and Dilly too, but her life in London seemed so far away that she found it hard to remember in detail. She did not try too hard either, it made her unhappy when she thought how far from home she was. There would be time later perhaps, to grieve.

Weeks passed and the midsummer heat gave way to violent storms, often at night, in which the thunder rolled and bounced off the mountain peaks and lightning floodlit the sky in great sheets of startling brilliance. Agnes had never witnessed storms so loud and violent and terrifying. The shepherd families huddled together in the few erected tents made of huge canvas sheets. Lightning rods were planted away from the tents to attract the lightning. The sheep had to fend for themselves, but packed themselves into dense flocks. In the morning, everything was sodden. The wool on the sheep smelt strongly of lanolin and they steamed gently as the sun warmed their wool. Everything else was hung out to dry.

At length, the storms and the heat faded. The weather began to change. Nights were cold now and talk turned to thoughts of home. One day, it was time to go. A few of the families with younger children left first, anxious to get their children back into school. Agnes bid them a sad farewell, sorry to see them go. Jean-Loup said he would wait a week or two, while the weather was still fine.

October came. The remaining shepherds were to travel together with one vast troop of sheep. All was packed up, the cooking pots, the canvas tents, the odd pieces of spare clothing. The journey down to Provence would take three to four weeks because the sheep moved so slowly. In the few years before the war, Jean-Loup told Agnes, they had begun to travel part of the way by trains or by lorry, but there was no fuel to spare now. It did not matter either way to Agnes. She was going to her grandparents at last. She felt a mixture of apprehension and excitement at the prospect, as well as a touch of sadness that her life among the shepherds was coming to an end, but she was, all the same, eager to be off.

Chapter 12

Prisoner

When icicles hang by the wall
… when blood is nipp'd and ways be foul
Then nightly sings the staring owl,
To-whit.

William Shakespeare

Ten days into the journey, Agnes woke one morning unable to get up. She was cold and shivering and aching all over and she was also running a high temperature. She had influenza. She was too weak to stand, let alone to walk all day. Jean-Loup wrapped her in blankets and tied her onto one of the donkeys for a bumpy ride, but he felt her brow anxiously from time to time. She was clammy and sweating, though still shivering.

When they passed close to a tiny stone cottage, therefore, which was the first sign of human habitation they had seen, he knocked on the door. It was opened in a moment by an elderly man who emerged out of the gloomy interior followed by his wife. The old man wore a greasy hat beneath which tufts of matted hair protruded and his sallow skin hung about his neck in folds.As thin as he was, his wife seemed much better fed, though it was hard to tell under the strange assortment of clothing she wore: a pair of man's trousers over which was a dress, a knitted jumper and a short coat. Her hair was sparse, but also matted and grimy. Her eyes were sharp and small. The old man managed a grunted '*Bonjour*' in response to Jean-Loup's greeting, but the woman said nothing, staring at him and beyond him, at the donkey carrying Agnes. Further off, the huge troop of sheep continued to move down the pathway in a long, straggling line which would take hours to pass. Their bells clanked and the sound of the shepherds' voices calling to their dogs, or whistling, came echoing back among the trees. The old couple's faces were morose and grey, showing suspicion, but no curiosity. Jean-Loup received no encouragement as he tried to explain.

'The child is ill. She cannot go on with the troop at this pace. She will only become more ill. Please, could you keep her here and look after her until she is well?' Neither one of the old people said anything in response, so taking their silence for quiet assent from people who were little used to talking to anyone but one another, he continued, 'I will return within three weeks to fetch her, as soon as I have got my sheep close enough to home for them to be taken care of.' The old couple continued to say nothing, merely looking from Jean-Loup to Agnes, until at length the man said, in a high, whining voice, '*Monsieur*, we are poor, we have nothing to spare.'

'As to that,' Jean-Loup responded, drawing a little leather purse from the bag he wore slung across his shoulder and chest, 'I was intending to give you money for her food and for any other care she requires. Here,' he shook a handful of coins out into his wide palm and held them out to the old man who peered at them as he took them. 'There is the dog too. He will not leave her. He will need some food too, though he will catch rabbits for you, if you can get him to go with you into the forest.'

Jean-Loup turned to untie Agnes and lift her gently from the donkey. The woman had gone back into the cottage and Jean-Loup hesitated at the door, turning to the old man. 'You will take care of her, won't you?' he asked, as if, for the first time in doubt that he was doing the right thing.

'Yes,' the old man assented, 'but only for three weeks.'

'Of course,' Jean-Loup agreed. 'I will be back even sooner than that, all being well.'

He carried Agnes across the threshold into the dark and smoky interior of the tiny cottage.

It took a moment for his eyes to adjust to the gloom and see that the entire cottage consisted of one windowless room roughly furnished with a table and a truckle-bed. There was a hearth with a cooking pot hanging over it and above it an open chimney which allowed the only light other than that from the door to penetrate. The walls and everything else in the cottage were covered with a thick layer of grime from years of accumulated smoke and dust. Jean-Loup laid Agnes down reluctantly on the bed, still wrapped in her blanket, her bag, containing her book and her statue were tucked up inside it with her.

'You do not have a lot of space, I see. How far is the nearest village? I could take her on there.'

'No, No!' the man objected swiftly, his fist tightening over the coins. 'It is too far. I will fix up another mattress for her'

'Well, then, I thank you,' Jean-Loup agreed.

He took a final look around the smoke-blackened room, then placed one of his huge hands over Agnes', small and hot with fever.

'Agnes. I will be back soon. You must rest and get well. These people will look after you and Panza will stay beside you.' He was not sure if she could hear him and hesitated, but she managed a weak smile before drifting again into a fevered sleep. Looking again at the old couple who still stood silently by the door waiting for him to leave, he said, 'Her name is Agnes,' although they had not asked the question.

With that, he stooped to cross the low threshold, momentarily blotting out the light and then he was gone. Not much had been said, but then Jean-Loup was a man of few words, not used to asking for favours and judging the kindness of strangers only by his own simple and unquestioning sense of decency. Had he spent more time in the company of people other than his fellow shepherds and less time on his own with his flock of sheep and his dog, he might have seen something to mistrust in the demeanour of this couple. He thought only that, like himself, they were unused to strangers and conversation.

Agnes was but dimly aware of what was happening and the people around her, but she was conscious, in the period which followed Jean-Loup's departure, of harsh words between the two old people and a short while later, being got up by the old man, a bony hand under her armpit, lifting and pulling her up and away from the bed. She stumbled towards the door where he led her, though she moved awkwardly, wrapped as she was with the blanket around her and holding her bag, tucked inside, with one hand. Her legs felt scarcely able to support her as the old man half carried, half dragged her out to the side of the cottage where there was a lean-to shed. It was a tiny wooden structure added on to the side of the cottage with a door that bolted on the outside. Inside was a large stack of wood and beside it a small space on the earth ground where a shallow layer of straw, no more than dried wild grasses, had been strewn. Panza was tied up in there and Agnes was aware of his presence with a sense of relief that he was close by and that she was out of the smoky, dark room.

The old woman had followed, placing a jug of water beside her. The door to the shed was closed behind them leaving her almost in darkness. After that, when she looked back upon it, she could not recall seeing them for several days. The door of the shed was kept shut and sometimes she was aware of light filtering in through the cracks between the boards, and sometimes she was conscious only of the profound darkness of starless night. She drifted in and out of a fevered sleep and drank from the water jug regularly. It must, from time to time have been refilled for her, but they offered her no food. Sometimes Panza was not there. The old man took him out rabbiting, making use of his speed, and soon he was left untied, when he realised that Panza would not stray from Agnes' side unless led away on a rope. When she woke in the night, shivering, she sensed only that Panza was pressed against her, stretching out his body beside her as if trying to keep her warm.

Days passed and so, eventually did the fever. When Agnes at last felt able to get up she was so hungry that she felt she must go to the door of the cottage. She was very weak and swayed dizzily, then held on to the rough wall which supported the shelter. She felt her way along the wall, to steady and stop herself from falling, to the door of the cottage. She had eaten nothing for many days and finding the door ajar, she leant in.

'Hello,' she said. There was no response, but as her

eyes focussed into the gloomy room she could see the old woman sitting on the bed.

'Do you have anything I could eat please?' she asked. 'I'm very hungry.'

The old woman scowled, but reached down into the ashes of the hearth beside her and held out a potato baked in its jacket. It was almost cold, but it was something. Agnes thanked her and crept back to her bed of straw where, having dusted as much of the ash as possible from the potato, she divided it in half, giving one part to Panza and eating the other hungrily herself.

From day to day, Agnes grew a little stronger, though her progress was slowed by the very poor and meagre food she was given. Nonetheless, the old couple sent her out on jobs as soon as she could stand steadily. There was no water in the cottage, and certainly no electricity. Water had to be fetched from a spring which bubbled up into a stone pool that had some time in the past had been dug out of rock, before seeping away into the hillside. It was Agnes' job now daily to fill the iron pot and drag it back to the cottage. They told her that she must gather wood too, despite the large stack of wood against the cottage, where Agnes slept. She was ordered to go on adding to this, but it meant at least, that she could wander further from the cottage, with Panza for company. Panza had not left her side while she had been ill, growling when the man tried to fetch him away to go hunting. Now, Agnes encouraged him to go when the old man wanted to go out with his gun. He left her reluctantly and came bounding back far ahead of the grumbling old man, but the rabbits or birds he helped to catch or flush out, provided an important addition to their meagre diet, the only other source of which seemed to be a poor vegetable patch behind the cottage, which yielded nothing but potatoes and turnips.

Without any comment, the old woman had stolen her boots while she was ill and was wearing them. Agnes protested when she first looked for them and saw them on the old woman's feet, but this called forth such a tirade of abuse and invective from the woman, none of which Agnes understood, though the tone of it was clear, that she said no more. She was forced to go barefoot and her feet were soon covered in cuts and sores and became inflamed and reddened. At least, however, she still had her bag of precious things. She had kept it close to her while she was ill and they had not found it. From now on, she kept it well hidden.

She had no idea how much time had elapsed since Jean-Loup had left, nor how long she had lain ill, but it seemed as if three weeks must have passed. The old woman began to make jibes.

'Where is he now, your shepherd, eh? Left you here, to eat us out of house and home.' This was plainly untrue, as Agnes was given only one meal a day and that so sparse that she felt permanently weak. In the forest she hunted for berries and nuts to add to her diet, but these finds were few and far between. She could feel her ribs and those of Panza as they lay side by side at night, locked into the lean-to. She watched the path daily, for where Jean-Loup might come, but day after day passed with no sign of him. Eventually one morning, Agnes tried to speak to them.

'I do not know why Jean-Loup has not come back, but I am well enough now to set out to meet him. I will keep to the path and leave word in the villages I pass through. If you would be so kind as to give me a little food for the journey, for the dog and myself ... and thank you for taking care of me.'

This was more than they deserved, but she could not have predicted their reaction for a moment. In fury the old woman rounded on her.

'So, you would leave us now, would you? You have eaten us out of house and home. You think you could just go and leave us out of pocket? No, you will not go until he gets here and pays us what we deserve.'

'But,' Agnes protested, 'he left you money, I'm sure of it.' She had some dim recollection of money changing hands, though at the time she had been almost delirious with fever. She was sure Jean-Loup would not have failed to give them money anyway.

'Ha!' countered the old woman again. 'You think that was enough? Lock her up,' she ordered her husband.

Agnes was once again bundled into the lean-to shelter, the old man gripping her upper arm with his bony vice like grip and the door was locked. Now, in the days which followed, whenever they sent her out, they locked up Panza or whenever Panza was taken out, she was left locked inside. They knew she would not leave without the dog and this was the only way they could make sure they did not both go.

For weeks, she waited. The weather grew colder and colder. Agnes shivered at night, pressing herself closer to Panza's bony flank. He grew thinner and thinner too, his coat and his eyes dull. Why did Jean-Loup not return to fetch her? She wondered every day, desperate with a growing certainty that something must have happened to prevent him. Whenever she was out of the lean-to, she kept her eyes closely on the path. Whenever she was locked up she listened for the smallest sound which might suggest his arrival. At night, the cold frequently kept her awake. The rough wooden planks from which the lean-to was made allowed light to filter in, but also the wind and the rain. Furtive movements in the wood pile beside which she slept indicated the presence of mice, or rats, which prompted a low growl from Panza. By daylight she frequently saw huge spiders run across the ground and though she was not really afraid of them, she did not relish the thought of them running across her face and hands at night.

At last, desperation prompted her to make another plea. This time she waited till she could speak to the old man, out of earshot of the woman in the cottage. Perhaps he would be a little more reasonable.

'*Monsieur*,' she began. 'My grandparents live a little further south. They do not know where I am now, but if I could only get to them, they would send you some money, I am sure. They will send you plenty of money, even enough to buy a dog.'

But the old man replied bitterly, echoing the words of his wife. 'You expect me to believe that, do you? You think you can just go and leave us without help and out of pocket, eh? Go then, but you will leave the dog in payment. He at least can be of some use to me.'

'No, *Monsieur*,' Agnes objected vehemently, 'I cannot do that. And why do you keep saying I have cost you so much money? You feed me next to nothing, and what you give me, I share with my dog.'

At this, the old man uttered a strangled cry of rage, raising his stick and bringing it down across Agnes' thin shoulders. She cried out, as he seized her by her arm, dragging her around to the lean-to shed, pushing her inside and locking the door.

Sobbing helplessly, Agnes clung to Panza who had barked at the man as he pushed Agnes in, baring his teeth. Both of them were little more than skin and bone, their ribs sticking out and rubbing against each others'. She could not understand the rage of the old man and what had just happened. To have come this far and then to die of starvation as a prisoner of these two old people, seemed too much to bear.

From this point on, Agnes was kept locked into the shed and Panza tied. It was opened only to give her food enough merely to keep them both alive and this did not happen every day. If the old man took Panza out to hunt with him, he said nothing to Agnes and quickly locked the door again. Once a day, he ordered her to bring wood from the pile into the cottage and then allowed her to go briefly behind a tree to use as a lavatory, all the time, keeping his gun pointing in her direction.

Winter had come and the nights were frosty now and bitterly cold. Agnes' clothes were the ones she had worn since the summer and provided very little protection against the bitter winds and freezing nights. She had only the shawl to keep her warm, but her feet were red and swollen with chilblains and sores. By now, she had given up all hope that Jean-Loup would ever come. The mountain paths would soon in any case, be impassable with snow.

It is unlikely that she or Panza would have survived the winter if things had continued in this way for much longer. One morning however, the old man appeared to unlock the door of the shed much later than usual. His face was a pale green and he coughed, bent over and rasping.

'My wife is very ill,' he said briefly. His thin, high voice rasped in a sickly grating sound. 'You must fetch the doctor. I am not well enough myself to go.'

'Where is he?' Agnes asked.

'The village is a two or three hour walk away. You must bring him back here by nightfall.'

Agnes' heart gave a leap. Here at last was her chance to escape. She bent to untie Panza.

'Leave it. The dog stays here,' the old man growled. 'I know you. You would not come back if you took the dog. You would leave us here to die.' He looked at her bitterly, but this time he was right, she thought. She had leapt at the chance of leaving, but she could not go without Panza. The old man let her out, locking the door again after her, the dog still tied inside the shed.

'Go now!' he ordered, gesturing down the path. He stood for a moment, watching her go, then turned back into the cottage.

Agnes did not go far. Just out of sight, she waited for twenty minutes, then turning round, crept back towards the cottage. All was quiet. The door was shut, but she knew that the key to the shed was kept on a hook just inside the doorway. She opened the door slowly and as quietly as she could. The old couple were both asleep on the bed, just as she had hoped, but as she reached up for the key, the old man woke, sitting up and shouting at her.

She had not a minute to lose. For all his ill health, the old man was spry and had a vice like grip. She ran to unlock the shed. Fumbling, she turned the key, flung open the door and slipped Panza from his rope. Next, she seized her little bag, which she had kept close beside her, hidden under the straw. She turned again to go. The old man was fast behind her though and coming around the side of the cottage, holding the loaded gun which he kept by his bed.

'Panza!' Agnes yelled desperately, diving behind the cottage and praying he would follow.

'Stop!'

He shouted once, then a shot fired as they rounded the far corner of the cottage making back towards the path, and then another which passed whistling over her head.

Whether he meant to shoot her or merely to frighten her, she never knew, but fortunately, he was ill and befuddled and by the time he fired his third shot, they were nearly out of range and moving fast. Agnes could hear his angry shouts for some minutes afterwards and kept running, though she was sure he could not follow.

In three hours they came into the village. Agnes' feet were sore and painful to walk on, particularly on the rough stones of the downward mountain path, in addition to which it was very cold and her feet and hands had soon turned a ghostly white.

The village was little more than a sad straggle of houses, mostly uninhabited and derelict. There was no sign of anyone in the road and the windows were tightly shuttered. Towards one end of the single street however, there were two or three houses whose chimneys were smoking. Approaching them she saw a glimmer of light between the shutters of one and she knocked on the door. It was answered at length by an old woman, who held the door only slightly ajar to peer from it curiously.

'Yes?'

'Is there a doctor here, in the village?' Agnes asked.

'A doctor? No, there's no doctor,' the old woman answered. 'There a pharmacist though. He'll do for most things. Who wants him?'

'It's an old couple. They live up in the mountain.' Agnes waved a hand in the direction she'd come.'

'Oh,' the old woman paused as if considering whether mountain people were worthy of their pharmacist. 'Well, he lives over there, in that house. You can try him.'

Agnes found an elderly man in the house indicated. She asked again for a doctor and was told that yes, he was a retired pharmacist and that people did come to him occasionally instead of going further down into the valley to look for a doctor, but it depended on the illness. What was the problem, he asked. She explained about the two old people up in their tiny cottage in the mountain, saying that they were both very ill.

'Oh, it's those two old monsters,' grumbled the pharmacist. 'So now they're in trouble they want my help, do they? What are they to you, anyway?'

'Nothing,' Agnes answered. 'They are nothing to me. I am just passing on a message that they were ill and asked for your help.' Which was more than they deserved, she thought.

'Well,' the old man considered. 'I may go in the morning.' He looked her up and down again.

'Who are you anyway?'

'I was up there in the summer with the shepherds. I became ill and my father left me up there, but now I'm okay and I need to get home.'

'And where exactly, is home?' asked the pharmacist. Agnes did not like this. He was altogether too curious and she did not want to answer questions. For all she knew this man might be in league with the Germans, or may try to stop her for some other reason. He was eyeing her bare, damaged feet and her thin clothing. Still, perhaps she should try to get some advice from him anyway.

'My home is near Carpentras. Can you tell me how far it to is Carpentras?'

'Carpentras?' the man exclaimed, 'Carpentras? It would take you more than a week to get to Carpentras and how would you get there, anyway? It's not so easy to move around now, you know, with the Germans here…'

'The Germans are here now, too? In the south?'

'Oh yes. Since six weeks ago. They don't bother us up here of course…but down in the towns…well. No, you had better get back to the old people and stay there till the weather is better. Though I feel sorry for you, if you have had to stay with those two. I have come across them before.' He looked her up and down again, uncertain, clearly, as to what advice to give her. 'Go back now and tell them I'll see what I can do for them, but I won't come up there till tomorrow morning.'

'All right, thank you, I will,' Agnes replied. She was anxious to get away from this village now, with its inquisitive old people. She had done what she felt she had to do, but she did not want to linger any longer. Neither did she want to draw attention to the fact that she was intending to travel on alone, especially not with Germans around. She wanted to get as far away as possible. Who knew what story the old people would tell about her, to keep her as a servant? She turned to go.

'Goodbye,' she said.

'Goodbye,' he replied, already closing the door.

Agnes and Panza walked on for as long as they could. Although it grew dark, there was a moon which lit the path ahead of them enough to see by. It was a long time till they came near another village, and this time a more sizeable one. By this stage, she felt very weak, exhausted in all her limbs and scarcely capable of going forward. Panza too, slunk beside her, so different from the racing, vibrant dog she'd known during the summer in the mountains.

A church bell was ringing as she approached although it was late at night. In the centre of the village was a square on one side of which stood a church with steps going up to the entrance. A small door, cut into the huge arched wooden doors, stood open. People were leaving the church, drifting out onto the street and with them came light spilling out into the darkness. They carried lanterns and were well wrapped up in coats and hats against the cold. Agnes was too far away and well beyond the light shining from the church doors and the little islands of light cast around the people by their lanterns for them to be able to see her, but she was close enough to see the puffs of smoke which came from their mouths in the lamplight and hear their voices as they called to each other 'Good night. Happy Christmas!'

'Christmas!' she thought. It must be Christmas Eve! People were going home after midnight mass. It meant she had been in the mountains, a prisoner of the old couple, for more than two months. Why, oh why, she wondered for the hundredth time, had Jean-Loup never come back to fetch her?

She was shivering violently now and though anxious not to be seen she could not resist a powerful longing to go into the church. It would be warm in there after the service. Perhaps she and Panza could creep in and even take shelter there for the night. People had left quickly, drifting away in all directions from the square, some passing quite close to her where she and Panza stood silently in the shadows. The square was quiet and empty all of a sudden. She approached the church, lifting the latch carefully on the small door and breathing a sigh of a relief as she found it still unlocked. She went in closing the door carefully again behind her. A heavy curtain divided the area just inside the door from the rest of the church. Drawing the curtain to one side where there was a gap, she peered cautiously into the church, one hand holding Panza by the fur at the scruff of his neck. There was no one in sight within, but candles still glowed at the front of the church around the altar. The church was beautifully warm and smelled of wax and incense. Huge painted pillars supported the roof and the walls were richly decorated too in deep blues and reds painted with gold fleur-de-lis and other patterns. The deep colours stood out in the candlelight, though further back the series of little chapels on either side of the pews were cast into shadows. As she stood looking, just inside the curtains, the priest came in from the vestry, to one side of the alter. He was dressed up in long coat, hat and scarf over his vestment and he approached the altar, snuffing out the candles.

Agnes, holding Panza's fur behind his neck, crept into one of the pews near the back of the church and crouched down in the shadows. The priest passed by, holding a lantern, going out between the curtains and she heard the door open and close again and a key turn in the lock.

The church was not in total darkness however. One candle burned in a glass jar near the front of the church. Perhaps the priest had forgotten it or perhaps he had left it since the wick had nearly burned through. Agnes approached the light. The candle burned in a lantern which sat on a shelf above a miniature landscape that had been laid out as a special Christmas display. It was a countryside scene with hills made of moss and rivers made of blue paper; it had tiny stone paths and bridges, houses, barns, stables and many figures of colourfully dressed people, all made of pottery and carefully painted. In the centre of the tableau, was a nativity scene; a lean-to shelter, like a stable, with Mary, Joseph, shepherds and cattle looking on to a manger where the infant Jesus lay. Now she saw that all the other figures seemed to be either walking towards the stable or were looking over to it from further hillsides and houses, to where the star burned brightly above it. The candle was the star; it cast a soft light onto the scene below. There were no fixed pews, as in an English church, but rows of chairs and some benches with high backs. She chose the bench closest to the scene to lie down on, clutching her bag of precious things close to her stomach, with Panza settling on the floor beneath. She lay awake for a few moments on the hard bench, comforted by the flickering candle light nearby until it gently died out while she slept.

She had meant to wake early, to be ready in hiding when the priest unlocked the door and came in, so that she could slip out while he wasn't looking, but she was deeply asleep. Exhaustion from her long walk the day before, weak as she was from the months of illness and then near starvation meant that she slept here, in the safety of the church, better than she had slept for a long time. Panza, too, must have slept deeply, for it was his low growl that roused Agnes eventually, looking up to find an astonished young curate looking at them from the end of the row. Agnes sat up quickly, confused and frightened, swinging her feet down to the ground just as Panza too, jumped up. In the confusion of feet and dog, she fell onto the floor. In a moment the young curate was beside her in his long black robes, helping her gently to her feet, with one hand under her arm.

'Don't be frightened. Don't be frightened, my child,' he repeated. 'What are you doing here?' He looked at her feet and her poor clothes where she stood, trembling inside the pew, blocking her path to the aisle. He did not wait for an answer though, but instead said, 'You poor thing. Look, I have some food next door. It isn't far. Don't run away. Let me give you something to eat. The dog too. Come quickly, before the priest arrives.'

Agnes followed. He led her out of the church through the vestry and a side door which led directly into a little house. In a tiny kitchen he sat Agnes at the table and began to heat a large pan of soup which stood on a cooker. It contained vegetables and mutton. Fishing out the mutton bone before the soup was too hot, he put this, with some of the vegetables and liquid into an old metal dish which he placed on the floor for Panza. Next, he ladled soup into a bowl which he placed before Agnes, finding her also a hunk of bread. Agnes wept, tears falling into the soup. No one had been this kind to her for so long. The curate was still moving purposefully about the kitchen, heating water which he poured into a large tin bowl. The moment she had finished her soup, he placed the bowl of water at her feet.

'Put your feet in here,' he told her. 'Soak them well. I will fetch some soap and a towel.' He disappeared into another room and was gone for some minutes. Her feet were painful as the water seeped into the cuts, but the warmth of the water soothed them. When he returned, the curate carried not only a bar of soap and a towel, but also a pair of boots in one hand and a jacket over his arm.

'Look what I have found,' he said, 'some old boots which I have no use for any more and a jacket which is too small for me now. Both will be too big for you, but they will keep you warm. Look, I have to go now. I am late to prepare for mass. The priest will be waiting for me. But when I come back, I will take you to my mother. She lives nearby and she will take care of you. You can tell us then who you are and where you come from.'

He hurried away, back through the door into the vestry. Agnes looked around her. Everything in the kitchen was simple and so clean after the dirt of the old couple's cottage. Like the young curate himself, his unlined, shiny face and dark, smoothed-back hair seemed also simple and clean. His goodness and generosity had, equally been spontaneous and unquestioning. She did not know whether to laugh or to cry again. Just when she had begun to believe that the world was full of wicked people, here was someone whose deeds told quite a different story. She wondered what would have happened if it had been the priest who found her; would he have been so kind?

She bent down, painfully applying soap to her feet with its caked blood and mud. Gradually much of it soaked off and she dried them with the towel, looking critically at them. They were still covered in sores and cuts, but they felt better for being clean. She picked up the boots. They were indeed much too large for her and well worn, but finding some old newspaper in a basket by the hearth, she fitted layers of it into the bottom of each boot, wrapping a few thin layers finally around her feet before she fitted them painfully into the boots and tied the laces. Next, she put on the jacket; a man's jacket and again, much too big for her, but it was warm. She folded back the sleeves and did up the buttons wrapping her shawl around her shoulders again, to cover the gap left on her chest. Despite his kindness, she would not wait for the young curate to come back from mass. She could not risk being taken to his mother, who might see things differently. She would be bound to ask Agnes too many questions and might be afraid of getting into trouble herself if she did not report Agnes to the authorities.

She could hear the singing of Christmas hymns from the church. He would be gone for some time yet. Still, she could not leave without thanking him for his great kindness. She looked about, hoping to find a scrap of paper and a pencil to write a note of thanks. There were neither in the kitchen and she did not want to go into the rest of the house; it seemed wrong to go looking through his house when he had left her there so trustingly. At last, finding nothing to write with, she took down a large glass jar which stood on a shelf over the cooker and was filled with macaroni. Shaking a few pieces onto the table, she shaped them into one word on the table: '*MERCI*'. Then, replacing the jar and pouring the dirty water from the bowl away down the sink, she opened the back door of the kitchen which gave onto a little yard and thence onto a street. Panza was still chewing the large mutton bone, having eaten the soup and vegetables long since. Most of it was gone, but he was very loathe to leave the rest and looked from Agnes to the bone meaningfully. She picked it up, at which he trotted after her, keeping his nose close to the bone in her hand. They slipped away quietly, along the empty street and out onto the country road again.

Chapter 13

South through the Snow

Yonder a maid and her wight
Come whispering by:
War's annals will cloud into night
Ere their story die.
In time of 'The Breaking of Nations'
Thomas Hardy

She walked as far as she could that day. The countryside was covered with snow and puddles of ice filled the runnels in the dirt roads and farm tracks which she tried to keep to. The roads still tended downwards, away from the mountains, but whenever she reached a point in the road where she could see into the distance, there seemed to be nothing but layer upon layer of hills and peaks stretching away from her, white with snow or grey and blue where rock showed through. Pine forest had given way to leafless, deciduous trees, or a mixture of both. There was little sun visible behind grey clouds, but it was just possible to gauge where the light was coming from and to guess at south. Agnes tried to keep travelling southwards wherever possible, though with no notion if she was really headed towards Carpentras. Walking was still just as painful, the newspaper and the unaccustomed hard boots rubbing against her sore places, but her feet were dry at least. Nonetheless, she walked as briskly as she was able. It was the only way to keep warm.

By late afternoon, she was too tired to go further. It was growing dark already though she guessed it was not much past three o' clock. Already she was hungry again, despite the good bowl of soup she had eaten that morning. The cold and the walking added to her need for food. She began to shiver uncontrollably. Panza walked dejected and quiet beside her, adjusting his pace, as he always did, to stay close to her while she kept her hand on his back as had become her habit, holding lightly to the fur at his neck. They had walked for hours without passing through a village, although sometimes high on the hill Agnes would see a little cluster of houses with a church spire. At length however, they came to another silent village and not far beyond it found a short track which led to a farm and what appeared to be several large barns and outbuildings. They approached carefully, hoping that no dogs would bark, but all was quiet. Soon, Agnes found what she was looking for, a barn full of hay bales, which stood open to one side. She climbed up towards the back of the haystack, calling Panza softly after her. He tried to follow, floundering in the hay, till she came back down and pulled him up. Soon they were snuggled down together, far out of sight. Close together, their shivering soon abated and despite their hunger, they slept.

In the night it snowed heavily again and setting out at first light, they found the path and the road covered with an even whiteness which made it hard to see where their borders lay. Looking back Agnes saw their tell-tale prints in freshly fallen snow, big boots and paw prints. They looked like the tracks of a man and his dog. The next two days followed a similar pattern and Agnes made sure they were as little visible as possible. She did not want to get picked up by the Germans, or the police, at this stage.

Nonetheless, by the third evening when neither she nor Panza had had anything to eat for three days, nor any water other than mouthfuls of snow, she knew she would have to seek help. Both of them were in such a poor condition that they could hardly walk and were making very slow progress. It was thus that she prepared to knock on the door of the next isolated farmhouse she saw, though ready to get away as fast as she was able if necessary.

It was a stone building set only a little way off the road with a house of some two or three rooms and a barn door to one end of it. There was a light visible through the window and smoke coming from the chimney. Presently it was opened by an old man who looked at her and the dog in some astonishment, then beckoned her inside.

'Come in, come in. It's too cold to stand out there. What can I do for you?'

'Please sir, I was wondering if you could spare any food, for myself and my dog? We're very hungry,' Agnes asked.

The old man looked at her again, saying nothing for a moment. This was the moment, Agnes thought when she must either be prepared to turn and run, or he would be willing to help her. The old man's faced creased into a gap-toothed smile.

'You're hungry? Yes, yes, of course. Come on, sit down. I'll get you something.'

Agnes breathed a sigh of relief and managed a weak smile too. She looked around for the first time now, for somewhere to sit. The room was small, but made even smaller by the quantity of stacks of old newspapers and magazines which reached almost to the ceiling in a double layer along two of the walls. There was only a small space left between the door and the hearth, a stove with a wood fire burning in it, beside which was one chair. She gazed at the piles of papers, all neatly tied in bundles. There was a shuffling, snorting movement from the far side of the room and Panza's ears went forward. To her surprise, Agnes saw that in the gloom beyond the hearth there was just a low wall which separated this room from the barn or stable next door. A ladder rose to a space above the stable and beside this, a long face with large ears now appeared over the wall.

'Ha!' The old man cackled. 'He wants to say hello, the donkey.'

He motioned Agnes to sit again, in the one chair by the hearth, busying himself beside her with a pot which he placed on the hot plate on top of the oven. From a sideboard which was the only other piece of furniture in the room, he found a tin plate, similar to the one which already sat on the side of the stove and an old crockery dish.Next, he opened a drawer of the sideboard and took out half of what would have been a large round loaf. From the other drawer he took two spoons and a knife. He cut chunks of bread from the loaf and handed one to Agnes. Then he ladled a thin but meaty stew into the two metal dishes, handing one, with a spoon, to Agnes. Finally he ladled more of the stew into the crockery dish which he set down on the floor for Panza. Agnes moved to sit on one of the smaller bundles of newspaper which was near the old man's chair and he chuckled again, sitting down and beginning to ladle spoonfuls of stew into his mouth, chewing carefully with his few teeth. Beside her, Panza was struggling to eat the hot stew. Hunger drew him to the dish again and again, wanting to wolf it quickly down, but every time he picked up a piece of meat, he was forced to drop in on the floor again and play with it, nosing it, until he could swallow it comfortably. Agnes tried to help, by blowing on the dog's dish. Panza nosed her impatiently aside. The old man found all this highly entertaining. He cackled happily.

'Ha, he's greedy that one. He can't wait till it cools!' he said.

'I think he's very hungry, *Monsieur*,' Agnes replied politely. 'Thank you so much. This food is delicious. You are very kind to share it with us.'

'Oh well,' said the old man, spooning his stew in and chewing on the bread. 'You have to share it, if you have it,' he added, picking up on her words.

Agnes considered him as she ate. He was a simple man, but kindly, clearly fond of animals. Apart from the donkey there was a black cat which had retreated to the top of the dresser and was eyeing Panza with suspicion. He too had been given a small dish of meat set up on the dresser for him. But he was in no special hurry to come down and eat it. He was fat and clearly well fed. The man had not asked her any questions yet and seemed strangely lacking in curiosity about her. It was Agnes who felt inquisitive.

'Why do you have so many newspapers?' she asked, at length, as much to make conversation as for any other reason.

'Well, I like to read them, you know and I don't like to throw them away.' He chuckled. Agnes waited but there was no further information forthcoming, so she said

'You must have been collecting them for years.'

'Oh yes,' he agreed, 'there are papers here from 1919, just after the Great War.'

'1919? But that's …' she calculated, 'nearly twenty-four years ago.'

'Yes, that's true,' he agreed, unsurprised and then, seeing her looking at the piles of paper in wonder, he added, 'this isn't all of them you know. There are more upstairs.'

They finished their meal and Agnes said, 'I had better go now. Thank you so much.'

The old man looked towards the window. 'You don't want to go now,' he said in surprise, 'it's dark outside. Look. You can stay here tonight if you like. You can sleep in the barn with the donkey, or here by the fire. My bed is upstairs.'

She needed no persuading. Her eyelids were drooping already and Panza was fast asleep at her feet.

A few of the newspaper piles were put to good use. The old man built a mattress from them in a flat layer and spread it with blankets for Agnes to lie on. He riddled up the fire in the stove then, putting on extra logs and shutting the door firmly. Then, wishing her goodnight, he climbed the ladder, taking the oil lamp with him. In a few minutes, that too was extinguished and the cottage was in darkness. The only sounds to be heard were the faint crackle of the burning logs in the oven and the heavy, soft breath of the donkey.

In the morning, still sleepy, Agnes was aware of the old man who, having descended the ladder, once again riddled up the fire. He went out of the door and returned a few minutes later with some wood, then he went out again and Agnes could hear him over the wall in the barn with the donkey, talking gently to it and giving it food. She could hear the breathy munching of the donkey as the old man came back into the room carrying a small metal urn of milk. He stepped around her to reach a saucepan and pouring the milk into it, set it on the hot plate. She sat up, rubbing her eyes and yawning.

'*Bonjour*,' she said.

'*Bonjour, bonjour petite*. You slept well.'

'Yes, very well, thank you.'

He handed her a bowl of steaming milk and another hunk of bread. She followed his example and dipped the dry bread into the hot milk, before she ate it.

Again, the old man said very little and asked her no questions, merely smiling at her from time to time. At length, when she had finished the milk she said, 'You have been very kind, but I should be on my way soon.'

'As you wish, *petite*,' the old man replied. Then, his first question, 'Have you far to go?'

Agnes was grateful that at last he had asked this question.

'Yes,' she replied, 'that is, I don't know. I am going to Carpentras. Can you tell me how far that is?'

'Carpentras? *Eh bien…*'

He got up, working his way towards the wall through the stacks of newspaper and magazines. After a minute or two of quiet shuffling and the odd muttered comment to himself, the old man was back, threading his way carefully to his chair by the hearth and carrying a small bundle of old maps, neatly tied with string. Carefully, he unknotted the string and shuffled the folded maps until he found the one he was looking for. Agnes was once again amazed. How had he known where to look for maps amongst all this? He spread the map out on Agnes' bed of newspaper, peering at it and at length, pointing a wrinkled finger as he found it, 'There is Carpentras,' he said, triumphantly, and pointing again, 'here we are.'

Agnes looked where he was pointing. The two places looked some considerable distance apart.

'Oh, it is still a very long way,' she said, remembering the map in the railway station.

'No, no. It is not so far as all that,' the old man protested. This map only covers a small area. It will take you, perhaps five days walking.'

Five days! It never seemed to get any closer. Agnes bent to look again. Jean-Loup had mentioned the name of the village which was nearest to where her grandparents lived. He had said that some other shepherds he knew had heard of them. She struggled to remember the name. It began with G. Yes, there it was! That must be it, a little way to the south and the west of Carpentras. Perhaps another day or half a day's walk, by the scale of distance the old man had told her.

'Would you like to take the map?' the old man asked, suddenly thinking of it and folding it up.

'Oh yes, please. You are very kind,' she said, 'if you are sure you don't need it.'

'No, no. I have others,' he replied, gesturing at the rest of the pile of maps. She smiled at him. He was so strange. The maps were all different, yet it didn't seem to matter to him which ones he kept.

She began to wrap up her feet again in the newspaper she had removed the night before. She didn't like to ask him for fresh newspaper despite the fact that it was the one thing he had an abundant supply of and he didn't offer it, as he watched her pulling on the boots again, tucking the paper in and lacing them up. A final thought did occur to him though. He took the rest of the bread and put it in an old flour sack along with a hardened but substantial hunk of yellow cheese and handed it to her.

Thanking him profusely again and turning back from the road to see his last gap-toothed grin, she waved and set out southwards once more. In one hand she carried the sack, its long neck allowing her to hold it while keeping her hand in her pocket against the cold. Her own little bag was safely stowed in a large inside pocket of the jacket that the curate had given her.

As they walked that day they passed through the

point where the snow ended, or had melted and although it was still very cold, the sun was shining and in the middle of the day, for a brief spell, Agnes felt warm. With the help of the map she saw that she should be heading to the west as well as south and so she began to use larger roads where there were signposts to be found. That night again, she found a barn and had soon eaten the supply of bread and cheese which the old man had given her, sharing it with Panza. Panza was, in truth, too tired to go hunting for rabbits, or he lacked the will and would not leave her side for a moment.

Agnes' concern at being picked up by Germans had begun to abate. The following day a convoy of army vehicles and soldiers passed her, but they took no notice of a tramp of a girl and her dog walking along the verge of the main road. There was little traffic even on the bigger roads and the few cars or vans which passed showed no curiosity towards her. Towards mid-morning she passed a lorry which was parked up on the verge, the driver having stopped to adjust a flapping tarpaulin on the back. Seizing her courage, Agnes stopped to speak to him.

'*Bonjour, Monsieur*,' she said. 'Might you be going anywhere near Carpentras, please?'

'*Bonjour*,' the man responded politely. 'Carpentras? No, I'm on my way to Orange actually, but I could take you as far as the turn-off to Carpentras.' He was looking at her curiously, in her ragged clothes and enormous boots from which scraps of newspaper were visible, both she and the dog so thin and sickly looking. Her educated accent and polite French did not seem to fit her appearance at all. He helped Agnes and the dog up into the high cabin of the lorry, Agnes sitting beside him in the middle of the single bench and Panza beside her, next to the window, then getting in himself he leant across her and opened the window a little, doing the same on his own side. Agnes blushed. They must smell quite bad, she and Panza. It was a very long time since either of them had washed.

The lorry driver asked no further questions than her reason for going to Carpentras which she answered by telling him that her grandparents lived nearby, then he drove on in contented silence, making only occasional remarks about the weather or the roads or traffic. Agnes' spirits lifted, the longer they drove. This ride had saved her days of walking, which she would have struggled to achieve, with no food and making such slow progress. Road signs appeared for Orange and eventually, for Carpentras too. The landscape had changed to blue-green scrub oaks which had not lost their leaves and cypress trees on rolling slopes. Pale ochre stone showed bare in places on the hillsides where last summer's yellow grasses and pale green wild thyme still grew. The colours were all muted with a winter's frost, but spoke of hot summers past.

At last, in the middle of the afternoon, the lorry pulled over by a crossroads.

'Here you are,' the driver said. Agnes had been

dozing, her head against the window, her body and arm lying at an angle across Panza who had curled up beside her and had dozed too, his nose pointing over the edge of the seat towards the floor. The man's voice and the sudden stillness of the lorry woke her and she looked up sleepily.

'You are nearly there now,' the man said, pointing along the road to the left. 'It is only a couple of kilometres to Carpentras. I have driven out of my way to get you closer, but I must turn to the right now to get to Orange.'

'Oh, thank you, *Monsieur*. Thank you so much.' Agnes' gratitude was heartfelt. A flutter of excitement, and nerves, was in her stomach as she descended from the cabin with Panza and waved the lorry goodbye. They were close now. As she walked the last short distance into the town she began to feel nervous. Would they still be there, her grandparents? She had had no news of them since the start of the war. And would they want her? For the moment though, she had to deal with the practical problem of finding them.

The town of Carpentras was quiet and empty as she entered it. The light was already beginning to fade. Nobody was on the streets. In the centre, however, near the railway station and the Mairie, was a bar. The windows were steamed up, but a light shone from within. Hesitating for a moment, Agnes pushed open the door. The room was full of men; some at the bar, drinking some substitute of coffee, with cognac; some were at tables, reading papers, or talking. The air was thick with cigarette and pipe smoke. The men nearest the door stopped talking and stared at her. Gradually their silence spread back to the bar and all eyes were turned upon her. She did not know what to do; she was conscious once again of her beggarly and dirty appearance. Confronting all these staring and unfriendly faces, her instinct was to turn and run. Panza whined beside her, evidently feeling her discomfort, but in the moment that she stood, hesitating on the step, she was saved from making the decision by the barman who came out from behind the bar, wiping a glass.

'Yes,' he said, approaching her, 'what do you want?' He evidently thought she was begging.

'Please,' she started, and her weak voice croaked. She named the village. 'I want to know how to get there, I cannot see any signposts to tell me.'

'Oh, you want directions. It's a long way if you are on foot.' He looked her up and down in a gesture that Agnes had become familiar with, his eyes dwelling on her boots. 'That road out there. Follow that road,' he said. He was by the door now and gestured to a road out of the main square on the opposite side to where she had come in. He held the door waiting to close it, to shut her and the cold out and she moved out again into the street.

'Thank you,' she said. But the door was already closed.

She found the road which he had seemed to indicate and had not gone far when she was aware of footsteps approaching behind her. She turned to see a man hurrying towards her.

'Wait,' he said. 'I know you.' He peered at her closely. 'You're the little girl from Champagne, aren't you?' He stood in front of her. He was young, with a blue cotton jacket and soft peaked cap on his head. 'I recognised the dog. It is the Wolf's dog, isn't it? You've changed a bit, you both have. But I recognised your voice as much as anything. Looks like you've been through a hard time.'

'Yes, but who are you?' Agnes answered in astonishment.

'My name is Louis. I was one of the men in the cellars, that night you came in with the American pilot. But I am from this area originally. I remember you asking about Carpentras.' He spoke in a low voice and looked around in case anyone was watching them. 'I can't believe you have really got this far on your own. Listen,' he went on, 'there's a boulangerie round the corner that's open today. I'll buy you something there. The dog looks starved as well.'

He bought buns for her and the dog and then as she and Panza ate ravenously, he said, 'Listen, it will still take you some hours to walk to the village you want. I have someone to meet in a few minutes, but if you can wait half an hour, I will take you. Otherwise it will be dark before you get there. Besides,' he smiled kindly, 'you have got this far, I would be glad to make sure you reach your destination.'

She thanked him profusely and agreed, at this suggestion, to start walking along the road indicated and wait for him to catch up with her once his meeting was over.

It was thus that some forty minutes later, Agnes having watched anxiously as each of the few vehicles on the road approached her from the direction of Carpentras, that Louis caught up with her. To her surprise, he was not in a car or van at all, but on a motorbike, with a sidecar. He lifted the dome-shaped lid on this and helped her and Panza into the seat, closing the lid on them again. The road followed the contours of the hillsides and was full of hairpin bends. It was noisy and strange to be travelling so close to the ground after the high lorry cabin. Still, Agnes could not believe her good fortune.

After half an hour or so of driving, they drew into a picturesque village at the centre of which was a large, round fountain, though no water ran in it on this wintry evening. He opened the lid of the sidecar.

'Wait here,' he said, 'I will make enquiries. Tell me your grandparents' name.' She told him and he disappeared in the direction of a bar on the crossroads where they had stopped, coming back a few minutes later and starting up the engine.

'It is just a little way out of the village,' he shouted above the noise of the engine, closing the lid on her again.

They passed no houses or any other building that Agnes could see, but followed a road out among the hills, the slopes on either side being covered in rough, scrub oak or fields of vines. A few minutes later he pulled over and stopped the engine again, opening the sidecar.

'This is it,' he said, pointing to a track which led away from the road. A stone marked the edge of the drive with a name engraved on it, '*Domaine des Chataigniers*'. Of course, it was the name of the house that she had seen written on envelopes whenever Eleanor had written to her French grandparents in the past. She had forgotten it until now.

'Would you like me to come with you, to make sure everything is okay?' Louis asked.

'No, thank you. I will be fine, and I would rather go in alone, if you don't mind,' Agnes answered, suddenly feeling shy, both of this young man and of what lay ahead.

'Of course, I understand, and I must get back to Carpentras before dark.' He turned the bike, switching on his headlight in the gloom of twilight, then called to her, 'Hey, if you need anything. You will find me in Carpentras again. Ask for me in the bar where you came in.' He waved and was gone.

Agnes turned to the driveway. In the years to come this journey of a few hundred metres would be so imprinted on her imagination that she would relive every detail of it in her dreams. Never mind that she was to become so familiar with it that she hardly noticed it in every day life. In her dreams, it was always the first time she had walked down this drive. It was as if the path led from one life, her old life, to another.

On either side of the driveway grew plane trees, bare of leaves in this season and with large variegated patches on their pale trunks. Tufts of equally pale grasses grew along the centre of the rough track. To each side of it lay rows of vines, mere gnarled stumps in this season, with none of the green foliage of summer, and then olive trees whose trunks and branches formed twisted, ancient looking shapes, topped by silver evergreen leaves. Beyond these the hillsides rose or undulated away into the distance, a silvery grey in this light. At length the house came into view. It was a large, pale stone farmhouse, with terracotta tiles on the roofs of the outbuildings and barns behind. A terrace, shaded by the four large chestnut trees which gave the house its name, extended in front of the house and beyond that, the land dipped towards more rows of vines, stretching out towards the hills. Here, the silver was touched with pink as the last rays of the setting sun fell upon them.

As Agnes drew closer, she saw that a set of wide stone steps rose to two imposing front doors made of wood, but to the side, at ground level, there was another, simpler door and a window beside that, from which light shone. She approached carefully and for a moment stood looking in through misted glass.

Two figures sat in chairs on either side of a fire which burned brightly. The man had his back to her, the woman she could see more clearly. Her hair was dark, but peppered with white and pulled back into a soft bun and she wore a patterned shawl around her shoulders. She was bent over some sewing. Behind her on the far wall, stood a dark dresser covered in crockery of white and blue. Everything through the misted glass was cloudy and vague, as if in a dream. Agnes stood there for a few minutes, afraid to disturb them; afraid that if she knocked this dream would be shattered forever. The path lay behind her. She could walk away now and they would never know she had been there.

Beside Agnes, Panza whined quietly. She raised a hand and knocked timidly on the door. There was no answer. She hesitated, then knocked again, a little louder this time. There was a sound within, as of a chair being scraped upon a stone floor. Agnes was aware that her heart was beating very fast. The door at once opened to reveal an elderly, but spry and upright man. He stared at her for a moment, until the small, motherly woman with a soft face came to stand beside him. 'Who is it?' she said, as she came.

Chapter 14

Home

I hold it true whate'er befall;
I feel it when I sorrow most;
'Tis better to have loved and lost
Than never to have loved at all.
  In Memoriam *Alfred, Lord Tennyson*

Edouard and Marie-Louise were sitting by the fire in
the kitchen as they did on every winter evening. In
the summer, they could sit out on the terrace under
the chestnut trees as the light faded across the hills
much later in the evening than it set now, and besides,
Edouard was often out in the vines, tidying and
trimming, till dinner time. But on winter evenings it
was too cold even for him to be out in his workshop;
a place where he was happy to while away the idle
hours of an undemanding season. Marie-Louise used
the winter evenings to catch up with mending or
embroidery, whereas in summer she would be busy

bottling fruit or making jam till late in the afternoon.

In the past few years, her hair had begun to turn grey and the lines on her face had fixed themselves in sadness. The death of her only son was a sorrow which sat upon her like a heavy cloak, for all that she tried to stay cheerful for her husband's sake. It hung between them on quiet evenings like this, the knowledge of his absence which could not be filled, however used they were to it. Their daughter-in-law too, who might have offered them some comfort in their old age and a grandchild, far away in London, whom they had not seen since she was a baby and of whom they had had no news for years now, since the start of the war. Marie-Louise thought of her often, but thought that she was lost to her too. A child raised in England, who would speak little or no French. It would be hard to ever know this child, growing up so far away. Edouard grieved for his wife as much as for himself, for he could see how her fine, gentle spirit had been crushed by all that had happened, but there was no comfort he could offer her and both were good at keeping themselves busy. It was just a little harder on the long winter evenings.

Sometimes he read to her, as he was doing now, while she sewed. It was an hour yet till she would rise and serve their evening meal. It had been a fine day, starting with a sparkling frost that lay across the vines and hillsides, till the warmth of the mid morning sun had melted it, the light crystal clear and bright. Then as the shadows lengthened it had grown chill again and they had lit the fire and settled down.

A knock came at the door. A timid knock. There had been no sound of a vehicle approaching. Edouard set down his book, puzzled and rose from his chair.

'Who can that be at this hour?' asked Marie-Louise. She looked up towards the window, but could see nothing but darkness outside, the light from the room reflecting back from the glass.

Edouard opened the door. A child was there and a mangy dog. A beggarly looking child, thin and pale, her dark hair now shoulder length, dressed in a man's jacket and man's boots from which scraps of newspaper protruded. He looked again, more closely. And yet, there was something familiar about the huge, dark eyes that looked at him from the thin face. Marie-Louise was beside him.

'Who is it?' then seeing the child, 'dear God,' she breathed.

'I am Agnes,' the child said. Her knees gave way and Edouard caught her just before she reached the floor.

The first room in the house which grew familiar to Agnes was her father's childhood bedroom, which now became her own, for she spent several days there before she had the strength to come downstairs and discover the warm, homely kitchen she had glimpsed through the window. Her grandmother bathed her, on that first evening, removing the layers of clothes which she burned, having placed the bag she found in the jacket pocket beside Agnes' bed. She sponged her carefully with warm water on a soft towel, brushed through her matted hair and dressed her in one of her own warm flannel nightdresses, tucking her into bed under a thick feathered quilt. She brought her soup which she spooned carefully into her mouth and dressed the wounds on her feet. Agnes slept, so profoundly that she was not aware that her grandmother sat beside her in a chair all night, keeping watch by the light of a little lamp, or that her grandfather came in frequently and gazed down at her, wondering.

In the following days she slept a great deal, but was aware of her grandmother's almost constant presence and her grandfather's quiet concern. On the first day, he inspected her carefully, looking into her eyes and mouth and listening to her chest with his stethoscope, unpacking it from the drawer where it had lain since his retirement. He pronounced that there was nothing that good food, rest and care would not cure and those things, he assured her, would be supplied in ample quantities by her grandmother, if not by him.

They did not trouble her with too many questions in these early days, although she told them of Eleanor's death and her own flight to France, explaining that she had been travelling towards them for eight months now.

'Her story will come out in its own good time,'

Edouard advised his wife. 'Do not press her now. She needs rest and comfort, not to relive what she has suffered these last eight months, by telling it.'

Panza was cared for too. Agnes had spoken of him as soon as she could, anxious that his loyalty to her would be recognised. He had been given a place by the fire, unlike the two farm dogs which slept out in a barn. He was brushed and sponged and his sores, particularly those on his paws, tended. He ate well and slept for long hours and soon grew sleek and healthy on good food and was ready once again to chase rabbits through the vines in the company of the other dogs. Sometimes he stood at the foot of the stairs and whined, until he was allowed to come upstairs for a few minutes to see Agnes, standing by her bed, his tail wagging and his eyes shining with a new brightness.

Despite her grandfather's pronouncement, Agnes was weak and frequently ill, throughout the remaining months of winter, spending much time in bed. Her grandparents came and sat with her and talked gently of daily matters and gradually they grew to know one another. As spring came and her strength slowly increased, she began to tell them parts of her story, though skirting around the disappearance of David and the other children and being careful not to speak too much of anything she had seen in the tunnels of Champagne or about the men of the Resistance movement she had met, in particular the Wolf. She spoke of him only as a man who had taken her up to the shepherds and who had given her his dog. It was, in any case, easier not to talk. There was too much to think about in all that had happened to her over the past year and she was tired, with the kind of tiredness that weighed down her limbs and made her want to do little other than curl up by the fire by day with a book, and sleep for long hours.

Sometimes, Agnes had nightmares and would wake, sweating and lie in the darkness asking herself questions. Her nightmares were sometimes about David and the other children. Always, they were being taken somewhere and she was helpless to prevent it from happening, whatever she tried to do. Often she dreamed about the old couple who had kept her prisoner too. In her dreams, they were always locking her up and taunting her and she was unable to escape. Not least amongst the questions that ran through her head when she lay awake afterwards was the puzzle of what had happened to Jean-Loup and why she had been left for so long with them. She reflected on their cruelty. So many other people she had met had been kind and had helped her, even putting themselves at enormous risk to do so. Agnes remembered what her grandmother Eleanor had said about how people in wartime pulled together and helped each other in a way they might never have done in peacetime. People got involved in each other's lives, facing a common enemy and problems they shared. It was odd, she thought, how even something as terrible as war could bring out good qualities in people.

David was never too far from her waking thoughts as well; somehow she doubted in her heart that he could have been as lucky as her and found his family again. She wondered too what had happened to Frank, the American pilot. Had he got back to England safely and given her message to Dilly and was he still flying planes, or even still alive? Perhaps she would never know.

Some four weeks after Agnes had arrived at her grandparents, her questions about Jean-Loup, at least, were answered. She had gone to rest in bed after lunch and had fallen asleep, but was woken by an excited bark from Panza and the opening of the kitchen door. Her room was right above the kitchen. It was the hub of the house and always warm from the fire which burned in the chimney and she felt never far from her grandparents' movements. She heard the voice of Grandpère and another man's voice which seemed vaguely familiar. She drifted away into sleep again and when she woke once more it was growing dark, late in the afternoon, but still she heard the men's voices below.

The smell of cooking also wafted up from the kitchen. The sweet, rich smell of apples cooking with honey and butter. Grandpère kept beehives and the honey which they ate for breakfast and which Grandmère cooked with (for sugar was in short supply here as it had been in London), was dark and rich and smelled of the wild herbs on the hillsides from which the bees took their pollen. Grandmère was cooking a *tarte tatin* and Agnes' mouth began to water, for she had already sampled Grandmère's rich buttery pastry and honeyed apples. There must be company for dinner that night. She came downstairs slowly, still feeling a little shy of strangers in her grandparents' house and as she reached the bottom of the stairs, still out of sight in the kitchen, she heard her grandpère ask,

'But who is this man, who gave Agnes his dog and brought her up to the mountains? I am curious about someone who would go to so much trouble for an unknown child, and deeply grateful to him of course. We would like to find some way of thanking him.'

In his response, Agnes suddenly recognised the voice of the other man. It was Jean-Loup!

'Ah, who knows exactly who he is? He is a man of importance in the Maquis and is reputed to have done many brave deeds and many unexpected kindnesses, for all that he seems a hard man. Why did he bring Agnes to the mountains? I cannot tell you, but he dismissed it himself, saying he had people to meet up there and messages or instructions to give. I am not the only shepherd, you know, whom the Maquis has enlisted to help. Nor is Agnes the only child to help them, though her circumstances are different to most. And yet, I felt ...' he seemed to search for words here '... as if his interest in your granddaughter was more

283

personal in some way. Perhaps he himself had lost a child, who knows? As to his dog, well, it is true that the dog is an easily recognisable one and may have made his movements more difficult and I think he judged Agnes well as a child who would form a bond with a dog and that they would take care of each other.' Here he paused again and Agnes remembered his long silences, then he added, 'I am only glad the old people did not harm either of them. At last, my mind is set at rest.'

At this point, Agnes slipped into the kitchen and Grandpère, seeing her, beckoned her over towards the fire.

'Agnes, my dear. An old friend is here to visit you.'

Jean-Loup rose from his chair to greet her. She remembered him from just a few months ago, as strong and upright, but now he rose with difficulty helping himself with a stick and seemed to be stiff and in some pain.

'I knew you would come, Jean-Loup,' Agnes exclaimed, smiling at him.

'My child,' he kissed her simply on both cheeks, 'Yes, I came as soon as I could. How glad I am to see you here and well.'

'Agnes,' Grandpère began, drawing her towards him and putting an arm around her so that she leant against his chair, 'Jean-Loup has made the journey to make sure you are safe, although as you can see he is not quite well himself. I think you understand enough for us to tell you that he has been in prison these last months, taken by the Nazis for questioning. Evidently they treated you very badly, my poor man.' This last remark he addressed to Jean-Loup, who merely assented with a slight shrug and a gesture of his two large hands, as if to say, 'Well, you see the way I am'.

Grandpère continued, turning to Agnes again, 'It was only this that prevented him from returning to find you in the mountains and it has been much on his conscience.'

'I knew it was something important that must have prevented you,' Agnes said. He smiled sadly at her and nodded assent. Jean-Loup's dog lay watching her with her head on her paws, close beside Panza. She bent to stroke the dog's head.

'You have not told me how you managed to escape,' Grandpère continued, addressing Jean-Loup.

'Ah, I did not escape. Eventually they let me go. They had no information from me in all the weeks I was there and no matter what they did to me. In the end they decided that I was just an old fool who knew nothing, and perhaps that is the truth of it.'

'Ah,' Grandpère nodded. Then, after a pause, he remarked, 'I can assure you that Agnes says very little of her time amongst the people of the Maquis. No names. You seem to understand the need to be discreet my dear, do you not?'

Agnes nodded briefly, looking from one man to the other.

'She has wisdom beyond her years,' Jean-Loup commented addressing Edouard, then to Agnes, 'bless you child. I cannot tell you how sorry I am for all that you went through at the hands of that miserable old couple. I could not have believed they would treat a child so badly. I went back to them you know, and they told me that you had run away and stolen money from them, which they asked me to reimburse. No, don't worry,' he went on, raising a hand to calm her as Agnes was about to protest in indignation, 'I saw through them straight away. If I had only seen what kind of people they were before, I would never have left you with them. I was concerned, but I could not have believed it. I spoke to a pharmacist in the village below too and he was able to supply a few more details of your state when you left them. She had stolen your boots too, the old woman. I recognised them on her feet and the pharmacist told me you were barefoot!'

'Yes, they were horrible. But they were very poor and had a miserable life,' Agnes replied, 'and you mustn't worry,' Agnes wanted to reassure him. She did not want him to feel any guilt about her, after all that he had since been through too. 'I got here eventually. That's the important thing. Did you know I was here before you came today?'

'No, not for certain, but I had some news which gave me hope that you had made it. After I had been back to the mountains for you, I made enquiries and heard back from a man who had given you directions, or some help in Carpentras. Happily, there is a good network of communication between shepherds and other country people, like a telegraph, you might say.' He relit his pipe, which had gone out and sat peacefully puffing on it, one hand on Panza's head which the dog had laid on the knee of the old shepherd.

'And now, Agnes,' said Grandpère, changing the subject and getting up as he spoke, 'we are privileged to have the company of Jean-Loup to eat with us this evening and tonight he will stay. He has a friend who has brought him here today and will collect him again tomorrow, having business in the town. So your grandmère is cooking something special. It smells good, doesn't it? See if you can help her, while I find a glass of something warming for our guest.'

A happy evening was passed between the three adults and Agnes who listened as they talked of country matters and of news from a little further afield, near Jean-Loup's home. Inevitably talk touched on the progress of the war too. News had got through that the Americans were bombing Germany in earnest. Agnes wondered if Frank was amongst the pilots.

Grandmère had indeed prepared a delicious meal of a rich lamb stew with plenty of herbs and garlic, soft and creamy mashed potatoes and her delicious apple tart. Agnes slept well that night, her tummy full and her heart much comforted by Jean-Loup's visit.

After this, her mind was more at ease on a number of matters. Somehow to have had another adult come and share part of her story with her grandparents made it easier for her to talk to them, and to know that Jean-Loup had really not forgotten her, and that he was safe, was greatly reassuring. She had believed absolutely in his goodness and had been more concerned than she realised for his safety.

Spring came and with it Agnes' strength began to return and she was once again eager to be outside in the wakening world and soft winds. The wild almond trees were the first to blossom. They lined the edge of the woodland around the vineyard. White petals blew off in the winds resembling sudden late flurries of snow in the spring sunshine or confetti thrown over the bride at a wedding.

Grandmère was gentle and kindly. She took Agnes with her whenever she walked out into the surrounding hills to forage for food in the season; wild asparagus and wild garlic. Her knowledge of the countryside was rich and detailed. She knew where to find any kind of plant, what could be cooked, or used to flavour foods, or as medicine. She was delighted to find that Agnes knew some of this too from the shepherds and had memorised the names of plants which Jean-Loup had taught her in the mountains. Together they took the wild flowers which Agnes had pressed in her poetry book and made a new notebook, taping and labelling each flower on a page. She showed Agnes how to feed the chickens and bring them in at night; she cooked with her and sewed and her peaceful spirit soothed and nurtured Agnes till she began to blossom. For Marie-Louise too, the lines on her face began to soften and she found a new fullness in her heart. From time to time she took Agnes to church. Agnes sat dreaming through the chanting rhythms of mass with the candlelight and incense smells, remembering her night in the church on Christmas eve. Her hand crept into that of her grandmother seated quietly on the bench beside her who smiled at her wondering what memory had prompted it. Afterwards, while Marie-Louise chatted outside the church door to friends and acquaintances, she introduced her granddaughter to children with whom she might one day make friends. But Agnes did not miss the society of other children and was reluctant for now to stray from home.

Panza was allowed to remain sleeping in the house and was still Agnes' loyal and constant companion, though equally he grew devoted to Grandpère in particular and would participate in rabbiting expeditions with him and the other dogs with great joy and excitement. Sometimes, in the night, if she woke, she would creep downstairs and join Panza on his rug by the dying embers of the fire. Once or twice, Grandpère had got up and found her there in the early morning and had carried her sleeping back to her bed.

She watched the seasons change with wonder. After so long in war-torn London, the green haze which spread across the budding trees and vines was like a miracle to be treasured and she sat in the sunshine on the terrace outside the kitchen, wrapped in a blanket and with a book laid open on her knees. One day, she saw great puffs of pollen rise from a group of pine trees on a slope nearby and drift away in golden clouds on the breeze.

When she had grown stronger, she went for longer rambles with grandpère, sometimes staying out for half the day, the three dogs bounding beside them, racing off excitedly into the undergrowth to put up rabbits ahead of them. In the spring, there were miniature irises and tiny daffodils growing wild by the hillside paths and around the terrace in front of the house, big purple and yellow flag irises grew. One morning Agnes woke to find all the fruit trees in the orchard were newly dressed in pink and white, like shy brides with their bridesmaids in attendance.

Grandpère made Agnes a proper flower press. He was a skilled carpenter and sometimes she sat and watched him in his workshop as he made or mended things that people brought him. In the evenings, he often read to Agnes and Grandmère, and in this way she grew to know the stories her father had grown up with.

In Agnes' bedroom there was still a shelf containing the books her father had read as a boy, including a translation and shortened version of the story of Don Quixote. Grandpère gasped over the little statuette of Don Quixote when Agnes showed it to them. It was he who had made it, forty years before.

'Why did my father like Don Quixote so much?' she asked. 'David said he was a crazy dreamer who went around attacking windmills, though he wasn't just crazy, was he?' Agnes struggled to remember exactly what David had told her of the story.

'Well, you will have to read the book yourself Agnes,' Grandpère replied, 'but I think what your father liked about him was that he was a man of honour, who continued to believe that an individual can strive to do right even when the society around him is wrong.'

'I see,' Agnes said thoughtfully, 'it's a bit like the people fighting secretly against the Germans here, whereas some people have just accepted them and aren't fighting at all.'

'Perhaps,' Grandpère agreed.

Where Grandmère expressed little curiosity, and seemed to wish simply to involve Agnes in her present life and let her move forward, leaving her painful memories behind, Grandpère was still intrigued by all that had happened to her and as time passed she felt more able to talk to him of these matters. Sometimes on walks, he would ask her questions about the people she had met and the things that had happened as if he had been mulling over each aspect of her story in his mind and wanted to get the details clear. Agnes knew that she could trust Grandpère absolutely. She remembered the Wolf telling her in their last conversation, that she would know who to trust. Grandpère was, she felt, somehow like an old English oak tree, or perhaps, being

French he was more like the plane trees which stood like sentinels along the track to the house, but in either case steady and absolutely solid. Like Jean-Loup, no word that might endanger another, would ever pass his lips. He was intrigued by the secret passages and caves of Champagne, although, as she told him and he instantly agreed, these were things not to be spoken of in front of anyone else, at least till the war was over.

Agnes often thought about the Wolf and could tell that Grandpère was particularly curious about him too, the man who had helped her most. He asked many questions about him, a puzzled frown on his face, but Agnes was reticent. She had promised the Wolf she would not talk about him and even to discuss him with Grandpère, at first seemed like a betrayal. One day, however, in early summer, while Agnes was watching him mending a chair, sitting quietly on an adjacent workbench, she heard him singing a tune which sounded familiar to her. She racked her memory to think where she had heard it before.

'I know that tune,' she said suddenly, 'it was one of the songs the shepherds used to sing around the fire. No, wait, it wasn't,' she reflected. She had got to know all the shepherds' songs quite well over the weeks she spent with them. 'No, it was the one the Wolf used to sing, or whistle, when we were walking in the mountains. I'm sure it's the same.'

Grandpère was carefully filing a piece of wood into shape and did not look up.

'The Wolf? Oh, the fellow in the mountains,' he asked, his voice casual, as if he wasn't really listening.

'Yes, the man who took me up to the mountains.'

'Was it,' he said, 'was it.' But it did not really sound like a question.

Throughout the long, hot summer, Agnes helped her grandparents out in the garden where they grew vegetables and fruit, or in the vineyard where Grandpère taught her how to trim the vines and remove the smallest bunches of grapes to allow the others to grow all the bigger and juicier. In the afternoon, when it was too hot to work, Agnes lay out on a blanket under the leafy shade of the chestnut trees, reading a book and listening to the incessant rhythm of the cicadas. She loved the long summer evenings when they sat out on the terrace to eat and sometimes friends would come to share the meal and she grew to know other children.

One strange thing to remind her of London came to Agnes' attention at about this time. Sometimes, when the three of them were alone in an evening on the terrace, she would ask them to tell her about her father and what he had been like as a little boy; what had he got up to in his childhood. She wanted to know him better. These conversations too reminded her of how she used to talk with Eleanor about her mother. One such evening, she asked if there were any photographs of him as a boy. She had seen none about the house.

'Ah no, we never had a camera, you see,' Grandpère explained regretfully.

'But yes, there is one,' Grandmère remembered, 'when he took his first communion, remember? Someone who had a camera took it and gave it to us. All the children were given a photograph that day I think. It doesn't really look like him; it was much too angelic looking. I will go and find it.'

'I'll go if you like, Grandmère,' Agnes said, wishing to save her grandmother from putting down her needlework.

'Yes, let her go,' agreed Grandpère. 'It's in the bottom drawer of my desk, in the dining room. I'm sure it's there.'

Agnes went into the seldom used dining room and pulled open the bottom drawer of Grandpère's desk. It was full of papers and old letters. She rummaged briefly, finding the photograph easily. Her father was a boy of ten or so, he was dressed up in white with a large lace collar , like a choir boy and did indeed look very angelic. She pushed the drawer to shut it, but as she did so, a cream coloured envelope caught her eye. It bore her Grandmother Eleanor's handwriting, she was sure of it, and addressed to Grandpère. Another envelope was protruding from it, folded. Agnes drew it out, curious. At once she recognised, by its African stamps, the letter which had come for her father some years before in London and which she had afterwards wondered about. She pulled everything out of the envelope and read her grandmother's letter quickly, taking in only odd sentences.

'I have checked with the shipping line and they were both on the passenger list…almost certainly this can mean nothing, but it is curious that it came from Africa so long afterwards … I am forwarding the letter to you since it was written to Pierre … forgive me for having opened it.'

Agnes unfolded the letter in the other envelope which was addressed to her father.

'I hope that you are safely returned to London and have found your daughter and mother well,' she read in the first sentence.

'Agnes,' Grandmère was calling, 'have you found it my dear?'

Her heart thumped. She had no right to read other peoples' letters. She folded them hastily back into their envelopes and replaced them in the drawer, under some other papers, then shut the drawer, just as Grandmère came in.

'Yes, I found it,' she said.

'Oh good. We wondered what was taking you so long. Bring it out into the light.'

Later, when she had time to think, Agnes pondered for a long time on what the letter had meant. Had Eleanor thought for a time that her father had not been on the ship which sunk? If he had been on the passenger list, she must have confirmed that he had been on it. Perhaps that's why she never spoke to her of it. She did not want to raise her hopes. But then why had she sent the letter on to Grandpère? It must have meant nothing after all. She could not ask him about it though, she should not have read something which did not belong to her, and soon, she put it out of her mind and forgot it.

In the Autumn, Agnes started school in the village. She had not been to school for several years now, and though her French was fluent, she was behind the others in her writing. She read easily however, having read a great deal and exclusively in French, over the last year, with the exception of David's book of poetry. She was older than the other children and should by now have been at the senior school. But that was a long bus ride away and her grandparents decided to keep her close by in the village school for a year. Besides, like many of the children in the village, she was anxious to take the time off school to help with the grape harvest when the moment came.

The leaves on the vines were beginning to turn red and orange when Grandpère announced that the big, juicy purple bunches were ready for picking. He had tasted them every day, saying 'No, not yet,' then, one day, 'yes, that's it. We will start on Monday.' On Monday, magically as it seemed to Agnes, men appeared in the vines with baskets and clippers and snipped at the bunches dropping them into the baskets all day long, with a break for lunch and a quick rest. Grandmère served all the men a big meal and plenty of wine every day at lunch time on long tables set up on the terrace and it was Agnes' job to help her. Grandpère drove the tractor all day long, collecting full baskets and replacing them with empty ones all along the rows, taking the grapes away to a waiting lorry. He no longer made his own wine, he had explained to Agnes. He was too old for that and preferred to give his grapes to the village winery, receiving a share of the bottles produced in return.

Agnes loved the activity in the vines, the occasional shouts and jokes between the men, the quiet snipping. At lunchtime, they came to the outdoor pump and washed sticky grape juice from their hands, before settling down with great appetites to Grandmère's splendid meals. School seemed a tremendous anticlimax when finally she went back, but it was an experience she shared with many of the other children as almost all came from farming families and were required to help with one harvest or another.

The year faded and there were olives to pick in November. This was a quiet affair with just the three of them. They shook the olives from their branches onto big nets laid out below the trees, climbing on ladders to pick the last tenacious green berries, then laid them on racks in the sunshine. Though nearly winter, the sun was warm at midday and they could work in shirt sleeves. In a few days, Grandpère took the olives away to the mill.

Agnes was very conscious that nearly a year had passed since she had come to her grandparents' home. It was a big milestone for her. This was her home now. She could not imagine being, nor did she ever wish to be, anywhere else. She felt a great peace, though there were still times of deep unhappiness.

Often, in the last few minutes before she slept, Agnes would take up David's book and find a poem to read and think about. The book was a little more battered than when David had given it to her, and some of the pages had been stained by the wild flowers she had gathered in the mountains. But the title page, which she looked at often, would always bear the inscription in beautiful, scrolled handwriting. 'To our beloved son, David, on his fifteenth birthday, January 10th 1942, from his loving Mother and Father'. She thought of him often, the wise and kind boy, who would now have been nearly seventeen, on the verge of becoming a young man, who had so much to offer to other people and who had so much before him in his life.

It was also in reading the poems which were sometimes difficult and obscure, that she missed her grandmother Eleanor most. Somehow, over the last year and a half, while Agnes had been making her long and adventurous journey down to her grandparents in France, and then, while she was recovering her strength and health in the early months of the year, she had not really had time to grieve for Eleanor. Now, at night, sometimes, memories flooded back in her dreams and she would wake with tears on her cheeks. Although she missed her parents too, she had grown used to their absence after so many years. It was Eleanor who had raised her, loved her and cared for her and taught her almost everything she knew; it would have been Eleanor who would have read the poems with her and explained the things which she did not understand. Now, much as she had grown to love Grandmère and Grandpère, she had no-one who could read or speak with her in English. She missed Dilly too, but knew that she would see her one day again. Eleanor was gone and David too, for as time passed, the certainty had grown within her that she would never see him again.

The tide of the war had changed and by mid-October, 1943, Italy had changed sides and declared war on Germany. People in France were beginning to admit their belief that with the Americans firmly in the war and fighting for the allies, the German army would soon be beaten and that France would not be occupied for very much longer. At the same time, people began to talk openly about the disappearance of Jews from cities all across Europe, and vast prison camps that had been set up in Germany and Poland, from which no-one came home. It was also told, though in deeply hushed tones, that thousands of children and their families had disappeared from France.

It was a poem that she found one day in David's book, which began the slow mending of her heart. The poem was called 'Remember'.

> *Remember me when I am gone away,*
> *Gone far into the silent land;*
> *When you can no more hold me by the hand,*
> *Nor I half turn to go, yet turning, stay.*
> *Remember me when no more day by day*
> *You tell me of our future that you plann'd:*
> *Only remember me; you understand*
> *It will be late to counsel then or pray.*
> *Yet if you should forget me for a while*
> *And afterwards remember, do not grieve:*
> *For if the darkness and corruption leave*
> *A vestige of the thoughts that once I had,*
> *Better by far you should forget and smile*
> *Than that you should remember and be sad.*

Agnes read this poem many times over the coming weeks until she was quite sure of the message it had for her; that she was not to grieve, that Eleanor and David had both taught her, and the example that they had set for her, to lead a good and useful life; that they would both want her to remember them with joy, not with sadness.

For David, his life had been changed and perhaps taken away before he had had time to do all the wonderful things that he no doubt would have done. It was up to Agnes now, not to waste her time; to make the most of her life, for his sake, for Eleanor's, for her parents and grandparents, for all the people who loved her. David's book would stay, she decided, on her bedside table for as long as she lived, so that she would never forget him.

Chapter 15

Saint Sylvester's Day

So we'll no more go a-roving,
So late into the night,
Though the heart be still as loving,
And the moon be still as bright.
We'll no more go a-roving
Lord Byron

It was Christmas eve, 1943. Nearly a year had passed since Agnes had arrived at her grandparents' house. Grandmère and Agnes had gone to an early evening service in the little chapel on the hill. It was only opened twice a year, on Christmas Eve and on the feast day of St Christophe for whom it was named. Agnes had joined the other children in a candle-lit procession around the outside and into the church and some of their neighbours had come home to their house for a glass of walnut wine and some crescent-shaped biscuits, made with almonds, before they had all gone home in the dark with lanterns. Grandmère and Grandpère and Agnes had watched the procession of lamps wind their way down the rutted drive until they were out of sight. It was a dark night, starless and with no moon visible. The gathering frost made them glad to get back into the warmth of the kitchen fire.

Grandmère prepared soup for the three of them. Earlier that day Agnes had helped her grandmother to make a little scene with pottery figures to represent the birthplace of Jesus in Bethlehem on a large wooden board which she placed on the kitchen sideboard. It was just like the one she had seen in the church where she had sheltered exactly a year ago, with a gentle landscape of moss which they had gathered earlier and a blue painted river, but a smaller version. Grandmère was very touched by Agnes' account of the candlelit scene on that desolate night.

'I thank the good Lord that you had that brief comfort, my poor child. There will be no more lonely Christmases like that for you.' Now they unwrapped from their newspaper covering the little pottery houses and the stable for the holy family and a bridge to cross the river. The figures were all dressed in Provençal costumes. There were shepherds and sheep, just like the ones Agnes had known in the mountains; women with baskets in brightly coloured dresses with black shawls; old men and children.

Finding a place for each figure in turn and setting them down, Grandmère told her, 'When your father was a boy, we collected all these characters, year by year. He painted them himself. They have been shut away in the attic for a long time now. It is good to see them again. Tonight, while you are asleep, the baby Jesus will come. You will see, in the morning, he will be in this little manger beside his father and mother.' Agnes smiled at her.

Panza could not settle that evening. He whined at the door, or lay by it with his head on his paws, but would go out and then come straight back in when they opened it for him, wagging his tail feebly at them. Perhaps, they surmised, there was a wild boar nearby, or he did not feel well. In addition to their soup, Grandmère had prepared the traditional 'thirteen desserts', a large round plate on which thirteen different delicious treats were laid out, there were large dried raisins and dates, walnuts and sugared almonds, more of the little crescent shaped biscuits and some goat cheese to keep Grandpère happy. They admired the colourful array as Grandmère laid it on the table, Agnes counting the thirteen different types of food carefully. They had just begun their soup when the dog suddenly let out a desperate howl, then barked a high bark at the door. Grandpère got up quickly,

'What is it boy?' he opened the door and the dog raced out. Grandpère followed shutting the door against the cold, behind him. Moments passed and he did not come back. Finally, Grandmère stood up, removing her apron.

'What can it be?' she asked. Agnes followed her to the door.

Outside and just beyond the circle of light cast from the kitchen door, Grandpère and a tall, dark bearded man stood locked in a bear hug while Panza danced yelping with joy around them both.

'Pierre!' Grandmère exclaimed, her voice full of shock, her eyes wide and her hands at her mouth.

From his father, the man turned to his mother and as she ran into his arms he caught sight of Agnes over his mother's head. Her face was one of bewilderment, astonishment and eventually that firm set to her chin which she had had so often as a young stubborn little girl.

The Wolf, her father!

Pierre released his mother.

'Agnes,' he said.

'How could you!' she said, tears of anger springing to her eyes, 'how could you not tell me? How could you be so unkind!'

He took two quick steps towards her and held her in his arms, pressing her head against his rough coat. 'Agnes,' he held her to him and stroked her head. 'Forgive me,' he said. 'Forgive me, Agnes.'

Through her tears, a sudden image came to Agnes' mind. She remembered, in a split second, the moment in which the Wolf had thrown the little boy, child of one of the shepherds, up above his head into the sunlight and in that instant she'd seen the expression in his eyes and his large hands and had such a vivid recollection of her father doing the same thing to her years before. Suddenly, all kinds of tiny memories began to slot into place.

Pierre gently released her, but kept his arm around her shoulder.

'Come, you three, you must let me in. I haven't got long.'

However little time he had, there were urgent explanations to be made. The first part of this was very sad. Pierre told of how, four years earlier, he and his wife, Agnes' mother, were on the point of leaving Africa where they had successfully set up a hospital which had been vital to a large and far flung community of poor people, to return home to London and Agnes. As they made ready to board the ship which would take them back to England, they had news that a fire had devastated part of the hospital. Pierre made the hard decision to return there alone, to help the African people to repair the damage and get the hospital running again. He would follow on the next boat. Agnes' mother boarded the fated boat alone and was lost at sea. In England and in France people assumed that Pierre too, had been on the boat as planned. War had reached Africa and communication was very limited. The subject of the letter which came from Africa was raised by Grandpère.

'I said nothing of it to your mother,' he told Pierre. 'I did not want to raise her hopes. It seemed to be a mistake. You were still on the passenger list. Eleanor had checked this, as she told me in her letter.'

'Yes, that is strange,' Pierre agreed, 'but then, things were very confused in Africa at that time, with the war just started. It must have been an oversight that I was not removed from the list, when I did not board the ship. Still, that oversight was useful to me, for I came to France with perfect anonymity, since everyone believed me dead. It was cruel to you – to the three of you, but I have been able to do good work for France, without ever knowing if I would survive this far.'

Somehow, as Pierre explained, he found his way back to occupied France by another boat and decided that he must use his anonymity to help the Resistance. Soon he became an indispensable leader among the men; his skills of organisation were already established and he was fluent in English and could speak some German, so was vital in communications. He did not dwell on his own unhappiness. He had lost his darling wife and could not get back to his daughter, but he said that it made him hard and determined to rid France of the cruel and arrogant treatment being meted out by the Nazi-led army.

'You must believe me, all of you, how hard it was not to let you know that I was alive, and not to come and see you. But I feared to put all of you in danger and to cause you only more sadness should something have happened to me.'

Then he met Agnes.

'When did you know it was me?' she asked.

'Almost as soon as I looked at you. Although I could not believe it at first. You look so much like your mother you see,' he said, sadly.

He looked at her for a long moment. She had grown in the last year, though she was still petite, small of stature and with a pale, olive face which was a perfect oval; her large eyes were framed by dark hair which had grown again to shoulder length now. As she grew older she was becoming very pretty, losing that fierce setting of the jaw when crossed, but there was still enough determination in her face to remind Pierre again of the slightly chubby little daughter he had left in London all those years ago. 'And then,' he went on, lightening the mood, 'you were so stubborn and determined, I thought you had to be my daughter!' he smiled. 'Seeing my little statue of Don Quixote again, after so many years, was the hardest moment. I wanted so much to tell you then. You must believe me, Agnes.'

'Why didn't you?' she asked, bluntly.

'I couldn't.' He repeated what he had tried to explain before. 'It would have put you and Grandmère and Grandpère in danger, as well as other people. And then, the work I have been doing has been very dangerous. You all thought I was dead. You had grieved already. If I had died in the last year, you would have had to go through that unhappiness all over again. No, it was better you didn't have that burden.'

'And now?' Grandpère asked quietly. 'The Germans are everywhere. It is not safe here now.'

'I am leaving tonight. I am going to England. I have become too well known to the Germans here in France to be useful to the Maquis anymore. De Gaulle has moved his headquarters to North Africa now, but he has left behind an organisation to run from England. I have been given an appointment if I can get there.'

'Oh, you are leaving so soon,' his mother exclaimed sadly.

'Yes, Maman. I am sorry, truly, not to be able to stay longer, but it is best this way. I should not really have come to you this evening, but I could not leave without saying goodbye and making sure Agnes was all right.' He looked at her, almost shyly, then went on, 'They are sending a small plane to land on the airstrip up in the hills, you remember it, Papa? God willing, a light aircraft will easily land there and it is a dark night, which is good. The time and date were settled only this morning. They had to wait for the right weather conditions. I can stay perhaps a couple of hours.'

'I will warm you some soup,' Grandmère stood up, wiping her eyes with the corner of her apron and bustling about.

'A bowl of your good soup would be wonderful, Maman, but first, some hot water please and a change of clothes if you still have anything that fits me. I am going to wash and to shave my beard off!'

'I should think so too, you look a mess my boy,' said

his mother fondly. Pierre and Grandpère and Agnes all laughed at her, treating her rugged grown man of a boy as a child again. He stood up and gave her a hug.

Pierre emerged a short while later, newly shaven and refreshed. Agnes stared at him. For the first time she could see clearly the father she knew from the photograph on the piano at home in London and its copy here, on the dining room dresser, though older now, with new lines on his face and touches of grey in his dark hair.

Grandmère was busy in the next room, preparing his soup and Grandpère offered to fetch him a bottle of wine from the cellar.

'A glass would be nice, with my meal, Father, but no more. I must stay awake!'

As soon as he was alone with Agnes, he said hesitantly, 'Agnes, I am glad to have a minute to talk alone with you. I wish to say how sorry I am that I had to deceive you. Do you understand the reasons why I could not tell you who I was?'

She nodded, 'Yes. Yes, I do,' she said thoughtfully and sadly. 'It was too dangerous. But I wish I had known you were alive, all the same.'

'I understand,' he said quietly. 'But also,' he went on, 'I want to apologise for being so hard on you. We were in terrible danger at every moment on that trip. At least, until we were right up in the mountains. For the first time since I had been working with the Maquis, I was very afraid. Not for myself. I was afraid I would lose you again.' He paused. 'Agnes, when I come back to Provence, when the war is over, I will be a doctor here. Our home will be here, and I promise you I will be the best father that a girl ever had. I will make up for all the time we have lost. And I will have time to talk to you about your wonderful mother.' Agnes said nothing. Her throat felt tight. 'Agnes?' he prompted, 'you do know that we both always loved you very much, don't you?'

She nodded. Finally she managed to say. 'Yes, I know. I always did.'

While he ate his soup, Agnes asked the question which had been puzzling her for the last hour.

'Grandpère, when did you realise that the Wolf was Papa? Because you did, didn't you?' Grandpère looked at her with a twinkle in his eye.

'I had my suspicions – strong ones, too. There was the name of the dog, of course, Panza. Your father loved the Don Quixote stories as a boy. It was possible that he might have named his dog for a character in the book. I used to read it with him, and then you told me about how interested this "Wolf" was in the little figure you showed him. Of course, there may have been many other boys who had such a fixation with a mad Spaniard, I don't know. But then, why should a man who had such important things to do take the trouble to accompany a little girl into the mountains to help her find her way home? But not even that was conclusive. No, it was the foolish man who lost his donkey which made me certain.' He began to hum the tune that he had sung while he worked at his carpentry.

'Oh, the song. The one you whistle or sing when you are doing your carpentry. I remember now, I told you it was the same as the one the Wolf whistled and sang in the mountains.'

'Did I sing a song?' Pierre asked, surprised. 'I don't remember.'

'You see,' Grandpère continued, talking to Agnes. 'It was a song that Pierre made up when he was a boy. It was like the traditional Provençal songs, but it wasn't one. In fact, the words are a little foolish and concern a man who kept forgetting where he had left his donkey. But no one else could possibly have known that song.'

'Well, well, well. The things that give you away,' Pierre chuckled wryly.

'And why did you never say a word of this to me?' Grandmère asked indignantly.

'For the same reasons that Pierre did not tell us himself that he was alive, of course. There was no point in raising your hopes when I could have no idea what would happen to him.' As often, Grandpère's tone was grumpy, but he was not cross. He patted his wife's hand. 'We still have to get him safely to England tonight, my dear. I will come with you to the airstrip, my son. It is a twenty-minute walk and you may have forgotten the way.'

'No father, it is too dangerous, and I have certainly

not forgotten the way. I have friends who will meet me there in any case. They will be there to help guide the plane in.'

'Ah,' Grandpère nodded. It is well hidden by the surrounding hills, and in any case, I have heard that the Germans are all expected to fill the bars in town tonight. Drinking our wine and eating our sausage!' the old man snorted with indignation and contempt.

It was past midnight when Pierre left to make his rendezvous. Grandpère and Agnes stood outside in the dark for several minutes after Pierre had taken the track up into the hills, Agnes holding Panza tightly so that he did not follow, then they turned back into the warmth of the kitchen, still lit by the fire's glow.

Grandmère had dried her eyes again, and was composed. They sat and talked by the fire, straining sometimes in case they could hear the noise of an aeroplane engine overhead, but they heard nothing. The plane would, in any case have passed at some distance from them. Time passed and at length Grandpère announced that they should all go to bed. It was after two o'clock.

'It's Christmas day,' said Agnes. She did not think she would sleep, she was far too excited. Grandmère held out her hand to Agnes from where she was standing near the bottom of the stairs, by their nativity scene.

'Before you go upstairs Agnes, come and see. The baby Jesus has been born. See, he is in the manger.'

Agnes smiled. They stood looking down at the scene, lit by candles, of a mother and father in a stable, watching over their new-born son.

'Happy Christmas, my dears,' said Grandpère, joining them and putting an arm around each of them.

Twelve days later, a postcard arrived.

It had been snowing for several days, since just after the new year. It had been impossible to go to town for several days as the snow drifts had been so deep and it had taken three days for Grandpère to dig his way to the end of the drive. From the eaves of the house hung a row of thick icicles a metre long. Agnes had rolled an enormous snowman which sat in front of the house on the buried terrace and had played in the snow with Panza who had run about in mad circles in the powdery white stuff, trying to bite it up, or catch the snow balls Agnes threw at him only to find they shattered at his bite. Back in the warmth, Agnes gazed through the windows at the sparkling white landscape. The olive trees stood out, a dark, silvery green, like giant snow laden spiders and the vines had all but vanished beneath the drifted snow.

Towards midday, there was a knock on the door. In the way of country people this was followed instantly by the entrance of a well-muffled man who had not waited for a response. He stood on the mat inside the front door, stamping his feet.

'*Eh, bonjour*, Gaston,' Grandpère greeted him from

the fireside chair where he was mending a stool. Gaston was their postman, though they seldom received letters. 'How did you manage to get out here?'

'Not easy, I tell you my friend, but I thought you would want to have this.' Gaston replied, reaching into his coat and drawing out a rumpled card. He handed it to Grandpère, who looked at it for a moment, then passed it on to Agnes.

'It is for you, child,' he said quietly.

The postmark on the front was French; it had been posted in Marseille, but clearly someone had brought it from England. Agnes read it and passed it back to her grandpère without a word. He read it out loud for the benefit of Grandmère :

'My dearest Agnes,

I am safely arrived and all is well. I have visited Diligence who is very relieved to hear news of you. I have promised her I will bring you to visit her when the war is over so that she may scold you properly!

Things are moving apace and I feel safe enough at last to say that it is only a matter of time till I am with you all again. Kiss Grandmère and Grandpère for me. I am missing you all.

Your loving Papa.'

Grandpère got out a bottle of brandy and poured a small glassful for himself and for Gaston. They drank solemnly to Pierre, and to each other's health. Then they drank another to the end of the war and the sooner the better. Eventually Gaston rose, his cheeks rosy from the fire and the brandy and said he must get back to town before it began to grow dark.

'One moment Gaston, and you, Edouard,' Grandmère said, addressing the two men and rising from her chair, and walking over to their nativity scene. 'You know what today is?' she looked at Agnes and the men. They all looked blank.

'Today is the feast of Saint Sylvester, the twelfth day after Christmas. I think you two had better come and watch while Agnes and I place the three wise men in the stable. It is after all, a day to celebrate for its good news and safe arrivals.'

*